Golgotha

'Cracking good

'Gardner slices
real worth of thi
phetic vision . . .

'A neatly constru

'A thoroughly gripping bit of fiction'

'A sure touch with the suspense and some pithily drawn characters carry the reader . . . to the final literally earth-shaking climax' *Now*

GOLGOTHA

John Gardner

Star

A STAR BOOK

published by
the Paperback Division of
W. H. ALLEN & Co. Ltd

A Star Book
Published in 1980
by the Paperback Division of
W. H. Allen & Co. Ltd
A Howard and Wyndham Company
44 Hill Street, London W1X 8LB

First published in Great Britain by
W. H. Allen Ltd, 1980

Copyright © John Gardner, 1980

Printed in Great Britain by
Hunt Barnard Printing Ltd., Aylesbury, Bucks

ISBN 0 352 30635 1

For
ALIDA
With all my love
and
Because . . .

And they came to a place which was named Gethsemane ... and immediately, while He yet spake, cometh Judas ... and as soon as he was come, he goeth straightway to Him, and sayeth, Master, master; and kissed Him ... And they bring Him unto the place Golgotha, which is, being interpreted, the place of a skull.

The Gospel According to St Mark
Chap. 14 vv 32, 43 & 45; Chap. 15 v 22

We are passing from the sphere of history to the sphere of the present, and partly to the sphere of the future.

V. I. Lenin

All the men were volunteers and readily so. After the tests, they were told, each one of them would be relieved from overseas duty for the remainder of their service – except in the case of dire national emergency.

There were eight teams in all: twenty-five men to a team. All were recruited from the Engineer Battalions of the United States Marine Corps. The medics said that the tests were to do with inducement of sleep. There was no danger, and each team would be called in for the tests and experiments on a rota basis. They all underwent the experience at a United States Army Hospital near Gloucester, England.

The eight teams spent one week each at the hospital – eight weeks in all. They would arrive on a Monday to be greeted by the small special staff of doctors and nurses that had been flown in from the States, go through the experiments and tests – in complete isolation, housed in a wing that had been specially built for the purpose – and leave, happy and contented, on the following Sunday night.

After the eight weeks were over, the doctors and nurses went back to the United States.

'It was great,' said one young Marine, after returning home to his parents in Maine. 'They gave us a couple of lectures and told us that we'd experience very long periods of sleep. No dreams. You get all my letters from that place?'

'All here, son,' his father said.

'We liked your descriptions. You should have been a writer,' his mother added proudly.

'Yeah, we had these two-day periods of relaxation all the way through,' the boy continued. They were at lunch on the first Sunday of his leave. 'That was when we were able to write home, see movies and all that stuff. No outside contacts, though. They wouldn't take married men, or men who had girlfriends in Europe. We sure didn't expect it to last as long as it did, though. They said a few months, but a year! Geez, I slept for nearly a whole year. Injections. I guess there was some hypnosis as well. Sleep. So much sleep, but we always seemed to be tired, like we were doing really hard physical work: you know how you feel when your body's been on the go for hours at a stretch? Except at the end, when we all felt great.'

Somehow, the week at the hospital near Gloucester, England, had turned – for all eight teams – into a year.

The year was 1975. By January 1976 there was a bulky file locked away in the fireproof vaults of the CIA Headquarters at Langley, Virginia. The contents of this file were not transferred on to the computer tapes, and it was one of the very few that could only be retrieved by the President himself. No single person had ever read the entire file, which stayed locked away and unused for over a decade.

Incoming Presidents learned the gist of it from outgoing Presidents, like a father passing down some family treasure to a son. But the seals were not broken for all that time.

The file was stamped, GOLGOTHA: FOR THE PRESIDENT'S EYES ONLY.

★ 1 ★

Europe was again in flames. The many crises, through which countries had staggered during the last half of the twentieth century, festered and finally erupted.

The first sparks which ignited the fire came from Yugoslavia: just as countless analysts had predicted.

Certainly there had been unrest, mainly in Belgrade itself, since President Tito's death, and a gradual erosion of that country's particular type of 'acceptable' communism. The leaders were now tied more tightly to the Kremlin, and the unrest eventually welled up, breaking into violence.

The Soviet action was fast and predictable. Two battalions of tanks, and Motor Rifle Companies, swept in from Hungary and Bulgaria. The battalions were already known to be there – they had been on 'routine exercises' for the past six months.

Armour poured across the frontiers of Europe, supported by the Soviet Air Force and ground troops. The guns roared once more, but this time the guns were joined by rockets and all the latest weapons at the disposal of the Soviet and European armies.

The Soviet plan had been in readiness for a long time, awaiting the right moment. America was neutralised, through political and military treachery, and, when the circumstances arrived – with the trouble in Yugoslavia – action developed with terrifying speed. Battalions, divisions, and whole armies moved with such fastness that, in comparison, Hitler's *Blitzkrieg* tactics, in the long ago Europe of the 1940s, seemed like a slow-motion action replay.

Support troops, many dropped by air or lifted in by the

9

huge *Harke* helicopters, swarmed into all the satellite states of the Eastern Bloc.

There were pockets of violent resistance; all the aspects of sudden and horrific war, courage and cowardice, went hand in hand; death hung over the great cities and small villages of the continent like a plague.

For instance, it took only four hours of intense action to breach the infamous Berlin Wall. Vienna fell quickly. In all it took only three days to overrun Austria, and the entire Federal Republic of Germany.

Italy crumbled in hours; Spain, Portugal and Greece began by fighting bravely but disintegrated into only a token resistance under heavy air and sea bombardment, coupled with massive parachute drops; while the, now reinforced, Soviet armies in Germany turned towards the Netherlands and Belgium, then started to pour into France.

And America had been neutralised.

In England the old class hatreds – still kept alive over the years by the infiltrated unions and Labour Party – exploded. Barricades went up in the streets; the police and military forces became confused, and it was at this point – with the Soviet tanks grumbling and destroying their way along the French coast and turning towards Paris – that the British Prime Minister took, so the information claimed, an unprecedented, almost unbelievable, action. He appealed to the Soviet Union for military assistance.

Within twenty-four hours, Britain was virtually occupied by a Russian 'peace-keeping' force. There were no reports of resistance, armed or otherwise.

In Washington there was undisguised fury at the way in which America had been neutralised. Britain's duplicity was attacked daily by politicians, the military and the Press. Tension grew, and the President announced he would make a statement to the nation on television. The manner in which the United States had been cut away was not fully made known to the public, though most people could see exactly what had happened on the political front.

There had been limited fighting in the Middle East, which

was almost entirely Communist-dominated in any case. Japan announced neutrality, as did Canada, Australia and New Zealand. In Europe, only Switzerland and the United Republic of Ireland (the North having merged with the Southern Republic in the mid-eighties, with help from the, then, European Monetary Fund), remained neutral – free zones, right for negotiating territory.

On the day of the President's historic statement to the United States, China announced the signing of a non-aggression pact with the Soviets. Europe, together with great tracts of the Mediterranean, was virtually sealed off from the rest of the world. What little information there was now came in through Switzerland and Ireland.

The Vatican remained sacrosanct, and His Holiness, Pope John Paul IV, made one small plea for sanity among the great nations.

But America had been neutralised.

*   *   *

The President of the United States of America was watched by at least ninety-eight per cent of the country's citizens.

'My fellow Americans,' he began. 'In the past two short weeks, Europe has been plunged into a new dark age. The Third World made its political choice long ago. Now, with today's news that the People's Republic of China has signed a pact with the Soviets – both old and new – America appears to stand alone, some say impotent, in the world.'

As always, on telecasts like this, the President sat in the Oval Office of the White House. He was not a young man any more, but, in spite of spirited efforts by the television make-up girls, he looked even older than his true age, the face ragged and lined, dark bruises under his eyes denoting lack of sleep. The President's hair was thinner and greyer than anyone could remember. His first term of office had been back in the eighties. This, his second term, had begun only a year before – an old man returned, some said, by public sentiment.

11

Yet, when he spoke, the famous resonance, even arrogance, was strong in his voice, reminding aged viewers of the cadences of the President's long dead brother.

He paused for a moment, as if to allow the first chilling words to sink in, before continuing.

'As many senior citizens, and those who study their history, know well, it is now half a century since our former ally, Britain, seemed to stand alone in Europe. At that time, in 1940, a great statesman, Winston Churchill, spoke to the beleaguered British people – much as I am speaking to you this evening. He did not have the dubious benefit of television, and, at that moment, the enemy hordes – the Nazi, Fascist hordes under Adolf Hitler – were at his gates. He told the British people that they would fight on. His words then have always been a source of courage, comfort and inspiration to those of us who love and stand for freedom. He said, "We shall fight on the beaches, we shall fight on the landing grounds, we shall fight in the fields and in the streets, we shall fight in the hills; we shall never surrender."

'Some of you listening to me tonight must dread that I am about to follow the example of Sir Winston Churchill, and – even though we have not been directly involved in the recent conflict – speak to you in the same vein, and with the same kind of rhetoric. To do so, we all know, would be likely to bring Armageddon down upon us. Let me, therefore, put your minds at rest. That is *not* the message of cold comfort I bring to you.

'Some of the things which have happened, with such speed, violence and unexpected treachery, in these last years and weeks, have come as a direct result of our own errors – not simply in this administration, but in those of my predecessors. Our handling of world crises in the past two decades could have been more efficient: and I speak, of course, of the energy crisis which raised its head as long ago as the nineteen-seventies; the crisis of the world supply of food; the more recent series of economic recessions, which we had all hoped were behind us in the eighties. We have also failed in long-term planning, in policy, in our insularity and apathy.

'Since our last active war, the horror of Vietnam, we have avoided direct national conflict, taking the policy of looking inwards at our own domestic problems, and putting them before anything else. We have been content to do business with Europe through our own multi-national companies. We have kept out of other people's politics, except with regard to NATO.

'As you all know, it was only until very recently that we supplied arms, materials and manpower to the North Atlantic Treaty Organisation. It was only a few months ago that Britain – betrayed, we believe, by her own government, and undermined by years of financial instability – denied us our essential bases in England and Scotland. When the ultimate treachery struck, as you all know, we were withdrawing, on a purely temporary basis, from the NATO Pact, until a new alignment could be attained.

'Yet, when we withdrew the bulk of our forces from Europe, there were many of you who showed great pleasure. We all remember the demonstrations and placards outside the very building from which I am speaking to you: "Let Europe get on with being Europe. Yanks come home."

'Well, they came home – your sons, husbands and brothers. Because they came home, we are alone now, and threatened. Only history – time – will show if things would have been different had our forces been on the spot in Europe and the Middle East. What we can be certain of is that, had our armed might been there, we would *not* be standing alone as a nation now. It is also true that, had that been so, we might *not* be standing *intact* as a nation at this moment in time. We can only conclude that, for some reason, we have been preserved by Almighty God for a purpose.

'No, my good friends, tonight I am not going to tell you that the United States of America is going to fight on the beaches and landing-fields, or in its streets and hills: for that could only bring down upon us the final Holocaust; Arma-

13

geddon; the Apocalypse; Götterdämmerung.

'It would be suicide for our future, and the futures of our children and grandchildren, to embark upon a conflict of this magnitude.

'I have personally sent a note to this effect to the Soviet leaders, and within a week or so we shall be setting up a summit meeting with the Heads of State – both Soviet and Chinese. There is no point in my hiding from you the fact that they have declined my offer of a summit meeting here in Washington. We are to seek humility and go to them. Our aim now is to pursue a conciliatory path; to agree to disagree with the ideology of Communism, which now holds the bulk of Europe in its grasp; to try and work out some kind of formula for peaceful and lasting co-existence with the new Europe; to carry the ideals and hopes, set out in the American Constitution, on into the twenty-first century without bowing to ideals we cannot accept, or taking up arms in the sea of troubles which seem to surround us.

'I ask you to remain calm and patient; to pray for those of us who will be making huge efforts of diplomacy. It is a testing time for our politics, our national pride, our ingrained beliefs, and I shall close tonight with words from that Book which means more to me, personally, than any other – "Thou shalt not be afraid for any terror by night; nor for the arrow that flieth by day. For the pestilence that walketh in darkness: nor for the sickness that destroyeth in the noonday. A thousand shall fall beside thee, and ten thousand at thy right hand: but it shall not come nigh thee."

'Goodnight, and God bless you all.'

* * *

Paul Fadden, in his cell-like room, in the basement of the CIA Headquarters at Langley, Virginia, sighed, rose, walked to the television set and switched off. He returned to his easy chair, sat down and stared into space.

People often said of Fadden that he was built more for speed than comfort – slim, short, wiry with an unmemorable face, except when you looked hard, and saw that it had been altered, forged into a raw toughness of character which did not appear, at first sight, to fit his frame or general personality.

At the moment he was to all intents and purposes, a prisoner. Indeed, all the British members of the intelligence community in Washington, together with British diplomats, their wives and staffs, had been confined to certain areas. Some took up space covering entire floors of hotels. It had been like this since the full impact of the emergency struck.

This kind of house arrest was as much for the British personnel's own safety as for security. The American people were, almost entirely, bitter and resentful of the way the British government had acted in the last year, and in particular the last month. There had been ugly scenes at the Embassy before the last days, and two British citizens had been lynched out at the airport. Fadden really did not know whether to count himself lucky to have been in the United States when the storm broke.

He had, in fact, only gone to Washington in a last-ditch mission to shore up the fast-crumbling relationship between the British and American security services – a relationship which had begun to break down altogether when the last extreme left-wing Socialist government took power in Britain: this in spite of the fact that all democratic intelligence services were apolitical.

As a member of the Secret Intelligence Service, Fadden's allegiance was to his country and against all who threatened it. With regard to Ministers of the Crown – even the Prime Minister himself – Fadden, as an officer of the SIS, was concerned with the posts these politicians held, not their individual politics. It was only within the totalitarian states that intelligence and security organisations were politically committed.

Even so, what eventually happened in Europe came as a severe and traumatic shock. Since the final days, Fadden had often reflected that the events should not have affected or shaken either his colleagues or himself. God knew, the straws had been in the wind since the nineteen-sixties. If anything, they should have been surprised that nothing had happened earlier.

When, as a young man, he first joined the security services, in the late nineteen-sixties, Fadden's own branch had firm evidence of the large and growing number of left-wing Socialist Members of Parliament who were, to use the phrase current in those days, 'agents of sympathy' with the Soviet ideology. More, there were signs even then that the 'agents of sympathy' spread into the most sensitive corridors of power, into the Cabinet itself.

In those early days, Fadden was a natural street man, as the jargon had it: a field operative running sources, and one or two agents who produced raw material for processing into hard intelligence. It was after a long tour in the field – mainly in Europe and the Middle East – that he returned to London at the time of the Conservative Election victory of 1979.

Even then it was too late, he reflected. The rot had set in. It did not really matter which party gained power, or with how many seats or votes. Infiltration by the Soviets had already scythed through the trade unions and the Labour Party. Both were being led almost directly by the nose from within the Kremlin. The country was, to use another of old Winston Churchill's quotes, 'descending incontinently, fecklessly, the stairway which leads to a dark gulf'. There was no doubt that the dark gulf led to what that statesman also spoke of as 'the enchanted quagmire'.

Many other things contributed to Britain's slide: constantly changing policies (which went with its changing governments); the years of economic disasters; high taxation; the lack of business and commercial incentive; the deep wounds inflicted upon a society which had long rested on the laurels of a Welfare State falling apart at the seams.

After the Conservative rule, beginning in 1979, there had followed years of confused indecision on the part of the electorate: the government altering almost yearly, with no party producing clear qualities of leadership, or strength of will to stand firm against the Left Wing inroads. In plain

16

language, there was nothing to halt the monotonous catalogue of failures within what had once been Great Britain.

Then came the final straw. Only last year there had been riots, strikes and disruptions on an unprecedented scale, six debilitating General Elections in a matter of fourteen months, the pendulum swinging from Conservative to Labour and back again, until it finally settled with Labour.

By then, the pressures on Britain – mainly from its NATO allies – were so great that the new Socialist government almost immediately announced a policy bent on setting its own house in order and withdrawing its – by now - token force from NATO. With this withdrawal came the British request for their old friend, America, to quit its well-established bases within British territories.

To the United States and NATO itself, these demands were almost unthinkable. The nuke submarine bases – like the one at Holy Loch – and the many airfields in England were lynchpins within the NATO defence plans.

Even in the nineteen-eighties, the war planners, knowing that any Soviet military aspirations would initially be confined to Europe, relied heavily on the British bases from which in-flight refuelling tankers and ground rearmament bases could operate as a back-up to the incoming bombers and fighters from the United States, which would arrive at an estimated rate of one every four minutes.

But the rug had been pulled out from under the feet of NATO. The United States had no option but to withdraw, and plan for a new alliance and the setting up of new bases on the continent. The men at the Pentagon, and on the ground at NATO Headquarters, started the difficult business of restructuring the entire defence plan from a new strategic, geographical and tactical viewpoint. The troops went home and the American people rejoiced. Wrongly.

At the time, Fadden's job was to monitor intelligence regarding troop movements within the Eastern Bloc. Almost as soon as the last American soldier left Britain, he found his information beginning to dry to a trickle, then cease altogether. It was like someone turning off a tap.

Fadden's colleagues – both within the SIS and among the Americans – began to experience similar difficulties. The first safeguard against any surprise military attack was being denied them.

It was at this point that Fadden sought permission to fly to Washington and confer with his colleagues. There was much dithering on either side of the Atlantic. Fadden did not expect his request to be granted, so was surprised when his immediate chief told him to go quickly. There was tension in the air, the feeling that a night of the long knives was imminent. Fadden was actually on his way to America when the flames first fired in Yugoslavia.

On arrival in Washington he was told the news, and worse. The great, and highly technical, American electronic early warning and communications satellite systems had all begun to show signs of serious malfunction.

Technologically this was considered to be impossible. The boast had always been that there were so many built-in backups, and fail-safes, that the communications and intelligence networks could never completely break down. One section might go, several components could fail, but the complex, dovetailed, electronic links were designed to cope with every conceivable type of failure.

This time, something unexpected and totally impossible seemed to be building up.

First, the screens at the North American Air Defence Command's underground Operations Centre, deep in the Cheyenne Mountains near Colorado Springs, began to snow or black out altogether.

Then the BMEWS screens in Alaska and Greenland started to act up.

Within seconds, there was an escalation of these problems. Like some contagious disease, carried on a wind at the speed of light, breakdowns and faults occurred in the Air Force and Fleet Satellite Communications Systems.

Even the Airborne National Command Post aircraft – which would include the President's own Command Air

Post in time of crisis – lost all their electronic intelligence capabilities.

Operators, senior officers, even command generals became completely bewildered, for this could *not* happen.

Even when sporadic reports began to come in, suggesting that the great intelligence satellites – the DSCA IVs and NATO IVs – were not providing information, nobody really appreciated the extent of the catastrophe.

The need-to-know system of intelligence, which had prevailed for years throughout the United States Services and Intelligence Organisations had, at this moment, activated against itself. Only a very few people knew – and needed to know – that for some time the Soviets had been working on highly superior, orbital jamming devices for use against satellite communications and ELINT (Electronic Intelligence).

The United States was also far advanced with similar equipment, but nobody had realised that the Soviets were so far ahead of them.

Once more, the Chiefs of Staff, the policy-makers, even the President himself, dithered, none of them willing to accept, or believe, the obvious: that, as far as detailed satellite intelligence and communications were concerned, the United States was blind and deaf to what was going on in the most sensitive part of the globe – Europe.

America had been neutralised.

Two of the most recent development types of the old *Blackbird* aircraft – the famous SR-71 high-fly photo-reconnaissance craft – were dispatched immediately on missions over Europe. Contact was lost within two hours, and both aircraft failed to return.

The President went through normal diplomatic channels but, anxious not to precipitate any dangerous situation which might involve his country in armed warfare, ordered all aerial reconnaissance to be immediately discontinued.

Within days of his arrival in Washington, Fadden found himself cut off from the rest of his own herd.

He looked at the blank television screen, wondering what

was going on in the Oval Office now. His room did not look like a cell, but he knew the door was locked from the outside. There was a telephone, video and tape machines; plenty of books and magazines. There were also daily visits from his CIA contact officer, Tim McPherson.

He tried not to think of England, or Europe. All that was going on over there was a great game of the gods. If he thought about it for too long, the desire to be able to take part in events usually soon became swamped by deep depression and a sense of hopelessness.

He got up again and crossed the room to look at the fresh set of video tapes that had been left that morning. They were all harmless: old movies from the seventies mostly – *The Goodbye Girl*, *Close Encounters of the Third Kind*, one or two he had never even heard of. He was trying to make up his mind between *Murder On The Orient Express* or listening to some music – noticing there was a recording of the Bernstein Eighth Symphony (Ruth) among the tapes – when the locks sounded on the door, and Tim McPherson slid into the room.

Fadden turned to greet the small, cherubic and good-natured man who spoke even before the door closed behind him.

'You hear the man?' McPherson had a voice like his face, a timbre which made one think immediately of ripe and juicy apples. There was hardly any nasality. Fadden guessed he came from Boston, though that had little to do with apples; more with beans and cod.

'Yes, I saw him. Mac, when the hell're you going to move me out of here so I can be with the others?'

'Patience, Paul. What'd you think?'

'I'd have preferred it if the President had simply done the whole Churchill speech.'

McPherson smiled, a cleft in the apple. 'Don't be so Dunkirk and Battle of Britain, Paul. You know better'n that. What Presidents say to the nation is not always indicative of what they're thinking, or doing, privately.'

Fadden nodded. He knew that well enough, only the grim,

20

wretched stalemate of the situation, the betrayal of his own country, crept into every thought. Soured him. 'When do I go in with my own kind? If we're all being kept safe, why can't I be with them?'

'Because there may be a job for you.' He said it in such a matter-of-fact way, that first indication, that Fadden could never have guessed at the horrors and hazards to come.

'You pulled me out of the last one.' As soon as the news came through that the British Prime Minister had invited the Soviet army into his country, all members of the British intelligence community had been quietly moved from any sphere of sensitive activity – even the simple job of taking telephone messages between Langley and the Pentagon, a duty Fadden had handled during his first two days of emergency in Washington.

'This may be bigger. Don't know yet. You're to stay here until called.'

Fadden shrugged. 'On whose say-so?'

'The Director himself.'

'You mean the Director of the CIA knows I'm here?' Fadden threw up his hands in mock anxiety, suiting his voice to the action.

'He may want to see you in the flesh. Soon. In the meantime I'm to be your personal companion. I'm to take you out to dinner.'

'Bodyguard, eh?'

'What Don actually said was, "Mac, be his shield and buckler." '

'Which goes to prove that not only the President knows the ninety-first psalm.'

'You know Don. The first soldier-priest to lead the Company since Bill Colby of blessed memory – and I'm not joking. Religion's really in at the White House, and on the Hill, let alone at Langley.'

'Everyone turns to God when they're in a fix.'

'Come on.' McPherson grinned. 'I know a nice little place in Georgetown.'

'Will the KGB be there? Watching every move?'

'I should imagine so, but since when has that bothered you, Paul?'

He held the door open, and as Paul Fadden passed through into the bare corridor he had one of those sudden flashes of memory-montage which come so unaccountably.

He saw his father on the last day: the old man, still ramrod straight from years of military service, standing by a bed of hollyhocks, the colours burning against the grey Cotswold stone, and the sky deep blue above the cottage. The old man had gripped his hand strongly, and there had been no thought that this would be the final parting. Death seemed to be where he was heading, not his father – it was in the army days and Ulster. The message was waiting when he got to the holding unit that evening. His father died almost an hour to the minute after Fadden had left the village. A sudden heart attack, fast as the bullet which should, by all the laws of chance, have killed him sooner.

He also saw Pat, her hair falling in front of her face, almost hiding the tears, in that rather seedy little Bayswater hotel where they had said good-bye for the last time. He even felt the ache and misery he had experienced as he went down into the lobby, knowing it was over and that there was no turning back.

Leaving this quite comfortable cell (it was a spare Duty Officer's room really) deep in the bowels of Langley, suddenly took on a fleeting, new, different dimension, as though it too was a junction in his life: a long farewell.

'I bet it's busy in the White House,' he said, for the sake of hearing his own voice and banishing ghosts.

McPherson grinned again and put on an old-fashioned newsreader's voice. 'Tonight, the lights will burn late in the Oval Office.' He laughed aloud, though there was nothing amusing about it.

★ 2 ★

They had cleared away the television cameras, the lights and the crew: all gone within fifteen minutes of the President finishing his speech.

The Military, Air and Naval advisers had been on call most of the day. Don Marks had received his message to be there just before the President had gone on the air.

Inside the famous room, the President was now cloistered with the Secretary of State – that tall, granite-faced, white-haired man upon whom the President had come to lean most heavily through the last days.

He did not want to hear more from the military people. Their news had been grim enough. No possibility of clearing the giant Soviet anti-communication satellites for at least a month; and then only by placing their own new communications and intelligence satellites into different orbits. The vehicles were on the launch pads – had been for a long time; but nobody had considered they would be needed in a hurry if there was a sudden Red Priority. It would take a month, but, it was explained, these satellites contained the latest in anti-interference screens.

The President had barked at the military men and told them he wanted action within two weeks, even though he knew it was unlikely he would need the new satellites in orbit for around six weeks. The plan he was forming – the last desperate throw – required only a limited period of satellite surveillance.

'So they've bitten,' he said to the Secretary of State.

'Hook, line, sinker. Everything. Just as we thought. When they turned down a summit here, you had to turn down

Switzerland or London. There was only one alternative. Dublin. You'll be going home, Mr President.'

The President gave a wry smile. Near enough, he said before picking up a phone to tell the military advisers that they could return to the Situation Room.

Then he asked the Secretary of State about the Chinese.

'It all stands up, but they're putting the pressure on. We have a month or they'll go it alone, and that means nuclear, and it means the whole of Europe.'

'That's always been the worry. A month?' The President rose, turned and looked out through the big window which was undraped, as though to let people see that he was still working.

It had always been the worry – the private and most secret arrangement which the United States had entered into with China, during the closing years of the seventies and the beginning of this present decade. In the event of the Russians and the Eastern Bloc entering into a conventional colonising war in Europe, China would immediately negotiate a non-aggression pact to gain time. There would follow intensive realignment with America, a combining of forces, and a covert plan for the devastation of Russia. The Chinese said, 'No matter what the cost,' and the then President and Secretary of State had agreed.

'There can be no doubt that they're playing it straight, as arranged?' The President turned and faced the white-haired diplomat.

'I see no reason to doubt them. All the correct signals were in their initial announcement, and we've been in touch. The covert channels are working.'

'And the Soviets believe it all?'

'That doesn't matter at this stage. Unless they decide to escalate quickly, by which I mean a fast strike that would neutralise us completely. It would serve no purpose. They've effectively neutralised us already to some extent, and they'll have their hands full. I think we have a few weeks breathing space. If we don't pull something off – or if you don't pull something off – in Dublin, then the whole of Europe will be in a worse state than it is now. The retaliatory strikes will land here as well as on China.'

The President nodded and seemed about to open his mouth, when one of the six telephones on his desk began to purr and wink. He spoke quietly for a few moments, then replaced the instrument. 'Our boys are back from London, Paris, Berlin and all other embassies.' The lines deepened on his forehead as he said it.

That was one of the multitude of facts which would be kept from the public. While the American embassies in Europe were still intact and, to all intents and purposes, operating, the Soviets had expelled some five hundred individuals. All were intelligence personnel and, as far as London was concerned, the lists had been filched straight from MI5 and SIS, Britain's two main agencies. The last aircraft bringing them home had just landed, and now one word formed in the President's mind. It was the word he did not even dare speak to his friend and chief adviser who was looking sadly at the carpet.

'O.K.' For a second the Secretary of State felt a new spring in the President's manner. 'O.K., set up the Dublin summit. You'll want an advance party cleared for Ireland in what? Four days?'

'Four. Five. Yes.'

'I may wish to give special instructions about that. Just draw things up in your own way, and let me have everything. I'll probably add a name or two.'

The last words were almost dismissive. The Secretary of State rose. 'Ted . . . ' he began, then 'Mr President . . . '

When he had taken office, the President had let it be known that, whatever the precedents set by previous First Executives, there was to be no familiarity: no first names. The Presidential dignity had been undermined so deeply in the previous years that it was a new start.

'Mr President, don't take too many chances. Risks. Please keep me informed. I shall be in Dublin also, and we must co-operate.'

'When haven't we?' There was a tiny edge to the President's voice as he turned and picked up another telephone, asking for the Director of the CIA to come in. The Secretary of State just nodded and left by the side door, avoiding the ante-room.

Don Marks, tall, elusive as a stick insect, came in almost too quietly, and the President gestured him into a chair.

'They're all back.' The President searched Marks' face for signs of emotion, but the Director of the CIA merely nodded. 'You had the names at the briefing last night. Who's left?'

Marks shrugged, 'Where, sir? England?'

'You know well enough. England and Germany.'

'Contact is bad. The ciphers are up the chute. We're using double-talk. I've got two people in Ireland who're getting some stuff to us. I'm told there's only one certain stay-behind agent in London. There are probably another six or seven, but we've no way of knowing. In Germany we can be pretty certain of two. I wouldn't bank on more. Come to that, I'm pessimistic about England. The expulsions have been very accurate and they've left two important names off the list. They can't be raised, and that means they're either dead, defected or being dried out.'

'Have they access to true names, or cryptonyms, of stay-behind operatives?' The President was snapping questions, fast, as though time was of the essence.

'No. The one I'm certain about is mine alone – or at least the Company's alone. Not more than three people have access to that source, and they're all Caesar's wives.'

'Good. Germany?'

'We'll sew it up once I've seen the people who've come back. The whole shooting match've been taken off to Langley, and we're dividing them up into sections. Full and deep interrogation. There'll be a lot of dry information to evaluate and analyse. Last night you mentioned . . . ' He let it hang there.

'Golgotha.' For the first time that evening, the President said the word aloud. He took a deep breath and quickly told the Director of the latest diplomatic moves – the proposed summit in Dublin, the one month's grace they had from the Chinese. 'I have to explore Golgotha,' he ended. 'From what I know already I'm going to need a dedicated innocent to be put into England, and another into Germany. You mentioned a German yesterday. Any luck with the British?'

'We might just have the man. I've got him close mew'd up, as Shakespeare says. The German's agreed, yes?'

'From what you gave me yesterday, I should think so. As for the Englishman . . . Well, we'll have to be certain. I'll have to be certain. I can't even be sure whether Golgotha is of any use to us until I've been through the file. You know the bleached bones; I know the bare bones. Nobody knows the full extent, or what's really needed in England or Germany.'

The Director rose. 'Then, with respect, sir, don't you think you should find out?'

The President nodded and picked up a telephone. He used one word which denoted he wanted a helicopter, and the full cover given to a President of the United States when he left the White House.

'We'll chop along to your place, then.' The President smiled as he put down the telephone. 'You can brief me about the Englishman while we're on the way.'

⋆ 3 ⋆

The giant spotlight beneath the nose of the Presidential Sikorsky helicopter beamed light down on to the helipad and the West Wing as, with a roar, the machine lifted, tilted and then began climbing, turning and settling on its southern heading towards the CIA Headquarters.

In Georgetown, Paul Fadden and Tim McPherson heard the sound of the motors as they stepped from the car, which had just come to a stop outside the restaurant.

'Hurry, hurry, hurry. The President's always in a hurry.' McPherson tried to make light of it.

'He damned well needs to be now.' Unsmiling, Paul Fadden followed his gaoler under the awning and into the small restaurant where, it was said, you got the best French food in the city. As the sound of the motors faded and was overtaken by the soft tinkling of a piano playing a medley from the latest Broadway hit musical, *The Visitation* by that doyen of the musical theatre, Marvin Hamlisch, Fadden never dreamed that up there in the bumpy air over the suburbs of Washington, he was being discussed.

The latest soundproofing of the Presidential helicopter's cabin was eerily effective, the noise reduced to a low whine, like an old air-conditioning unit.

The two men – the President, and the Director of the Central Intelligence Agency – sat side by side, briefcases open on the table in front of them. The steward had withdrawn, as had the two Secret Service men. Glasses, together with a bottle of branchwater, trembled on the table. The President had not touched alcohol since the day he was nominated.

28

'O.K. So you think you have the right Englishman. Let me hear.' The President settled back in his padded chair, closing his eyes so that he could concentrate.

The Director shuffled his papers and began. 'He's here in Washington, as I said. Name, Paul Fadden ... '

'Real name?'

'Yes. Born in Newton Abbot, Devonshire, England, April 1948 ... '

'That makes him pushing fifty now?'

'Correct.'

'Bit old for the field, but ... '

'Father a career army officer. Retired 1956 as a full Colonel. Brigade of Guards, distinguished service in World War II. DSO and a dozen other decorations. He died in 1968.'

The President grunted.

'Educated at Marlborough – that's a ... '

'I know what Marlborough is, and was.'

'Marlborough and Sandhurst. Passed out third in his year. Posted to the Special Air Service where he did all their training. Grade One. Worked for them, undercover, in Germany, with various units, and in Ulster long before the SAS went there in force. He was there in 1968, for instance, when he got a direct approach from MI5. Quite rightly he reported the matter to his Commanding Officer on returning to England. MI5 got pipped at the post. The SIS already had their eyes on him and had requested a transfer. He accepted. Been with them ever since. German and Russian speaker. Initially they went through a cashiering charade from the Special Air Service, for a Dangle Operation in Germany, but the target didn't hit the bait. He was a field officer until 1979. Very highly recommended. From '79 he's been on evaluation and analysis. For the last few years he's been running surveillance on Red Alert sources. He was the first one to bring their vanishing tricks to anyone's notice.'

'Politics?'

'Would suspect an old school Conservative at heart, but completely conformist with apolitical action.'

'Hobbies?' The word meant more than woodwork or building model aeroplanes.

'Heterosexual. Two smashed engagements. Work came first; duty first. They don't mix for him. Girl friends, yes, but always controlled. No entanglements.'

'And in your view?' The President paused to allow the Director to realise that it was him, and not the President, who was making the initial recommendation. 'In your view he's antiseptic?'

'Safe as one can ever judge. I've got his detailed documents.'

'Box him first thing.'

'O.K. And you'll see him?'

'If the file I'm collecting from you now contains the right answers to the questions I'm already asking myself, I shall need some more names from you. First thing tomorrow. Say, six-thirty in the morning. If that comes out right, I'll see the German at nine. Breakfast with him. Then this man, Fadden, for lunch. I may need more time with him.'

The Director nodded.

'You'll be staying on here, I presume?' The President was telling him and not asking.

'I have the de-briefings to organise – our people from the embassies.'

'We'll want to know if we can get them both in – Germany and England – from Ireland. I'd figured, if Golgotha's what I think it is, that they'd both go over with the advance party for the summit, and make their respective hops in from there.'

'I'll try and find out by first thing.'

'Box Fadden at the White House. I gather there's a room in the EOB.'

There were two suitable rooms in the White House Executive Office Building. Marks smiled to himself, for boxing was the old word, only recently back in fashion. Most of his own CIA life they had called it fluttering, but gone were the days of the polygraph, lie-detector, with its electrodes and graphs. Now the subject did not even know it was happening, had not needed to know since the arrival of the Psychological Stress Evaluator in the 1970s: and they had made vast strides since then. Even the President did not know he was boxed quite regularly.

The steward knocked at the cabin door and entered with the request that they fasten their belts and the information that the pilots were bringing them in at the front of the building as there was a lot of activity on the pads in the rear.

'It'll be quicker,' the President said, turning to look down at the floodlit complex blazing from the darkness beneath them.

The Secret Service men were out of the helicopter first. There were half a dozen CIA officers around to greet them, and the President, with the Director at his side, walked briskly towards the main entrance.

They paused only once, by the bronze statue of Nathan Hale, the first American spy, captured and hanged by the British during the War of Independence.

'An amateur and he didn't make it with the British.' The President coughed. 'Let's hope an Englishman can do it for us against his own.'

A few moments later they were in the elevator which took them into the vaults.

The Head Archivist had been alerted, and led them through the corridors, passing them over the electronic eyes and along the passages from which doors took you into the dustless computer rooms.

Finally there was a last hurdle of three sets of metal grilles and bars, before the three men were in the small vault, its walls lined with steel box fronts, like an ordinary safety deposit vault in a bank.

Here the normality ended – by a box marked PRESIDENT ONLY. The Archivist, Director, and the President produced a key each, which they inserted, in rotation, into the locks, each turning the key in correct order. Then the President stepped forward. In his left hand was a small piece of plastic card, like a credit card, which he inserted into a slot above the locks. There was a distant whirr and the locks clicked back.

The Director and the Archivist turned away while the President opened the box, flicked through the files, and withdrew the bulky sealed document marked GOLGOTHA: FOR THE PRESIDENT'S EYES ONLY.

★ 4 ★

He took the file back to the White House in a security briefcase. In the event of an emergency, the Director of the CIA knew the combination. Nobody else. Any unauthorised handling would cause the immediate destruction of the file within.

The briefcase was locked in the President's personal safe in the Oval Office while he took a short break, and dined, quickly and with little relish, as a man will take a necessary snack in order to fuel his body for the next stage of a journey which has to be completed by a certain time.

It was a kind of journey, for the President knew that he was the first Chief Executive who had been forced even to examine the whole long dossier.

He said good-night to the First Lady, and his son, who was staying with them for a few days, then gave orders that he was not to be disturbed.

In the Oval Office, he settled behind his desk, went through the correct combination of the briefcase, and placed the file directly below the shaded strip reading lamp. As he broke the seals, the President glanced up and saw the small plaque which had stood on that desk during his brother's term of office, which seemed so long ago now. The plaque read, *Oh God thy sea is so great, and my boat is so small.*

The first sixty pages of the dossier were maps and graphs, place names and trajectories. The sixty-first page bore the legend 'Golgotha: Unauthorised United States Ballistic and Nuclear Missile Silos, Secreted in Britain and West Germany as Stay-Behind Weapons in the Event of Those Countries Being Overrun. Their Locations. Operating Systems and Labyrinth Method of Detection'. This section ran for one hundred and twenty pages.

The following page carried a new legend. 'Systems Operation Panel. The Jig-Saw Post-Hypnotic Method of Identification.' That took in another hundred pages, and then the final section: 'Use of GOLGOTHA Systems Operational Panel and Suggested Activations'. This last section had a series of amendments dated back to 1976. At the end of the dossier were a further four pages, listing Jig-Saw Post-Hypnotic Method of Identification Updating. All four pages had names running in series, and most of the names had, over the years, been deleted and new ones put in their places. They ran right up to some renewals made only two years previously. The names were cryptonyms and not real, but the President knew they were all as real as death itself.

With the devout concentration of a priest at prayer, the President began to read the dossier. He was still reading when Don Marks arrived just before six-thirty.

* * *

'It's going to take time to get a complete analysis from our prodigals.' The Director wondered if he looked as tired and grey as the President.

'And, if things're going to run to any kind of a schedule, I have to get this file well into my brain very quickly.' The President had rung for coffee – it was his seventh pot since he had started to read.

'Will it work?'

'Depends. In theory it should, though how we're going to use it to prevent the annihilation of Europe, let alone this country, is the problem. It's a classic case of tactics and strategy working on two fronts at once – diplomatic and military. They'll have to be used in conjunction, and if the diplomatic moves fail, or go wrong, then we all have to pray and brace ourselves. A great deal depends on the German, and the Englishman, Fadden. Also who's left over there.'

The Director took the proferred coffee, reached into his breast pocket and pulled out a small stack of three-by-five cards, which he began to examine. 'I've got the German here for you; and Fadden's waiting over in the EOB. From the first quick look at the material coming in from our people, Germany's no problem. We can get him in. England's another matter. They've got that island sealed up tight as hell.'

'That's natural. Britain's strategic importance has never been in doubt. What about our people in Ireland?'

'They indicate they can get Fadden in. There are also strong signs that we still have people active in England. I can't be sure of loyalty however.'

The President turned the pages of the file on his desk, flicking them as though at random. 'I give you some names,' he glanced up. 'You tell me what's known. Ready?'

The Director nodded.

'Nightingale.'

'That's the one I'm sure about. I mentioned that source yesterday. I'd put everything I own on Nightingale.'

'Then we've got the first link. Are we in contact?'

'Yes. Irregular. Through Dublin, but irregular. Nightingale is active.'

'Samson?'

'Probable.'

'Swallow?'

'Uncertain.'

The President went through four more names – Sappho, Vesta, Lark, Stag. As far as the Director could tell, all were there, but whether active or not he could give no firm evidence.

They went through a similar routine with cryptonyms of stay-behind agents in Germany. The results were equally unsure: two definite, the rest uncertain. The President said they were in with a possible chance.

'You've got through a lot, Mr Director. Anything big, really big, from behind the new curtain?'

The Director shuffled his three-by-five cards and nodded.

'One thing about the British situation.' He began to talk, the President listening carefully. When he had finished, the President was sitting bolt upright in his chair.

'That has to be followed up.' He looked happier. 'If there's truth in it, and I can bluff them into having other Heads of State in Dublin, we might pull off the diplomatic side. But only if the German and Fadden can work their way through the maze.'

He said he would see the German, as arranged. In the meantime, the Director should see Fadden himself, and go through the procedures they had spoken about the night before. He would meet Fadden for lunch. If there were any doubts about the Englishman, the Director was to communicate with him straight away.

At eight-thirty, half an hour before the German was due to arrive for the breakfast meeting, the Secretary of State rang through to ask for a short word. The old man was an early riser and could get through a day on a minimum of sleep. He was always in his office by seven-thirty, and was ready now to take the short ride over from State.

'We're up and running, Mr President,' the Secretary of State began, hardly before he was inside the Oval Office. 'They've agreed to the summit in four weeks. That means we start, in Dublin, on 20th June. I've informed our embassy there that your advance party'll be leaving at the end of the week. Five days.'

'Lord help us,' the President made a weary gesture. 'O.K. I'll probably require two people, nominated by myself, to go with the advance party.'

The old man's eyes glittered for a second. 'I presume, Mr President, that they will not be staying in Dublin.'

'You presume right. There'll have to be some cover, but Don will organise that. These two have to go on from there, and I'm not sure, myself, how we manage that trick.'

There were two more most important instructions he had to deliver to the Secretary. First, he wanted to go to Dublin via Rome. The President was anxious to have an audience with the Pope before the summit. Second, it was imperative

36

that the Soviets agree to the British Prime Minister, the West German Chancellor, and the President of the French Republic being present in Dublin.

The wheels began to turn.

The President left the Oval Office and made his way to the East Wing where he bathed, shaved, changed into clean clothes and went to the First Lady's room where he sat and talked, over yet more coffee. His day ahead was busy, for the international crisis had not completely taken over his function of overseeing the running of the country.

During the afternoon he had meetings with Senators, the recently appointed Secretary of the Treasury, and a delegation coming especially from the Mid-West. That night, he and the First Lady were to attend a Commemoration Ball in his honour. Psychologically he had to be there.

After a few words with his valet, the President took the elevator down to the Situation Room; he scanned the incoming reports, spoke for a while with one of his advisers, and was back in the Oval Office in time to meet the German who was brought over from the EOB.

In the meantime, Paul Fadden, bewildered by the suddenness of events, waited quietly in a room in the Executive Office Building. Life had changed drastically for him when he returned, on the previous evening, from the dinner with Tim McPherson.

⋆ 5 ⋆

They had got back to Langley at around eleven, and Fadden felt a different man. The trip out, with good food and a bottle of wine, coupled with boisterous conversation, had banished the disquiet and unrest in his mind.

On their return, however, it was obvious that great activity was taking place in the large complex. Helicopters were ferrying people in and out from the pads at the rear, and there were a lot of cars in the parking lots.

McPherson showed no sign of surprise, and went on behaving as though nothing unusual was going on. Fadden noticed, however, that there was a message waiting for him as he signed them back into the building.

'Don't go to bed just yet,' the CIA man cautioned him when they got to the basement cell. 'I may just have some kind of news for you.'

He was away for a good hour, during which Fadden listened to the dramatic Bernstein Eighth – the operatic theatrical symphony titled Ruth, which had been the supreme work of the composer's later years.

'You're not going to get much sleep,' McPherson told him on returning. 'Rest now, but stand by for a move; you're going to the White House. Early. Around six o'clock. The Director'll see you there, and, if that interview goes well, you could be having lunch with the President himself.'

He hardly slept. They woke him at five with coffee, and Fadden shaved, showered and dressed. From the helicopter he looked down on Washington, beautiful in the early spring morning.

Now, he had waited for a long time in this small, innocuous room in the EOB, knowing that he was not far from America's seat of power.

Don Marks eventually came at around nine-thirty; he introduced himself and shook hands. He was taller than Fadden imagined – tall and very slender with the watchful eyes and movements of a monk; spare and devoid of unnecessary gestures. Behind the eyes, Fadden thought he could detect that dedication and shrewdness which is the hallmark of a good Jesuit. 'The first soldier-priest the CIA's had since Bill Colby,' Tim had said.

'It's good to see you, Fadden. Let's talk a little, over here.' Marks did not gesture, but inclined his head towards the settee near the window.

They sat together, the Director quite close to him. No coffee, not even the offer of a cigarette. The table was out of reach. There were no distractions; the talk was generally about Paul Fadden's life and work.

After an hour, Fadden realised, with sudden horror at his own lack of perception, what was going on. The situation; the absence of anything to take his mind off the quiet conversation; even the questions. He was being fluttered, or boxed, or whatever their service liked to call it. Somewhere in the room, the microphones and sensors were picking up his words and feeding information into a most sophisticated form of PSE – a Psychological Stress Evaluator.

'You've taken a long time to realise.' It was as though the Director had read his thoughts. 'I don't know if that's a mark against you, or flattery for me and the people who set you up.'

'It's a long time since I've been in the field. I must be tired, off my guard.' He felt the answer was lame, stilted.

The Director smiled – kindly, understanding. He must have been hell to work against in the field, Fadden thought.

'Don't worry, the important questions were led in at the beginning; in case you caught on fast. Don't blame yourself. Now, if you'll excuse me . . . ' He rose, smiling, and walked to the door, and Fadden knew that he was off to check the read-back, to see if he, Fadden, was reliable, not turned, doubled, or had by the Soviets; that he was straight in every sense, and not a prey to blackmail. All the old-fashioned stuff, plus other things, such as whether he could be relied on under great stress.

It had been done before, in England, but nobody ever saw their own evaluations.

The Director was away for the best part of thirty minutes. 'We may have to sharpen up your concentration a little,' he said at first. 'I don't know; it depends on whether the President has a job for you, and if you're willing to take it. You're lunching with him, though. In private; in the Oval Office,' glancing at his watch. 'In around twenty minutes.'

Fadden had the distinct impression that the Director of the Central Intelligence Agency had wanted to add, 'And may God have mercy on your soul.'

The Director walked over to the West Wing with Fadden. They took an elevator up, and walked along a passage, the walls of which were lined with paintings of the First Ladies. Occasionally a White House Security Guard would come to attention, recognising the Director.

In the ante-room there was a middle-aged secretary, and the President's Personal Aide who stood up as they entered. 'You're to go straight in, Mr Director.' He did not even look at Fadden.

The President rose from behind the famous desk which was almost bare, but for the small plaque, the usual trappings of a tooled leather desk set, telephones and a very few papers.

Immediately, the President came out from behind the desk. Fadden was conscious of the largeness of the man, which had more to do with personality than build. He appeared more rested than he had looked on television the previous night, and the handshake was firm as the Director introduced them.

Fadden was shown to an easy chair to the right of the President's desk, while the Director was almost summarily dismissed with a 'Thank you, Mr Director.'

There was no small talk; the President got down to things

straight away by telling Fadden how much he deplored what had happened in Europe, and how he was trying to do everything possible. He said that the accent had to be on diplomacy; he asked if Fadden had heard his speech, and told him that a summit had, in fact, been arranged. In Dublin.

Fadden thought he detected a slight smile as the President said it.

'We have four weeks to do some fairly spectacular thinking.' The President paused. 'Mr Fadden, before I say anything else, or invite you to take part in what would be a most hazardous covert operation, I have some most important news.'

He went on to say that a large number of Americans, particularly those attached to embassies in Europe, had been sent home.

'Expelled. You can imagine that they are, to a man and woman, all members of our own intelligence services. The Soviets have been extremely well informed. But, naturally, they have had access to the files of agencies within the countries they have occupied. In your country, for instance, the list is pretty much the kind of thing we would expect to have been taken from your own service. However, there are one or two notable exceptions, which make us nervous.'

'Stay-behind agents?' Fadden queried, and wished he had not said it, for a frown appeared immediately on the President's brow.

'No, I'll come to them in a moment. There are one or two individuals we expected back. They have been omitted. Anyway, the people who have come are being de-briefed and analysed at this moment. One of the things that is now clear concerns the Soviet take-over of Britain.'

He paused for so long that Fadden interpolated a 'Yes, sir?'

The President continued by saying that there was now grave doubt about the story released to the world at the time of Britain's so-called treachery.

'Our people tell us there was no panic; no rioting; no barricades in the streets. They also say that the Armed

41

Forces and Reservists were called to readiness. Then, suddenly, the Prime Minister appeared on television and made the speech, which you have doubtless either read or heard.'

Fadden nodded.

'You were boxed with a PSE this morning, Mr Fadden?'

'Yes.'

'Our people boxed your Prime Minister. It is their evaluation that he invited the Soviets in under grave duress, and against his will. In other words, the whole thing was operated from Moscow within Britain. I admit the possibility that some of it was arranged by certain members of the British Government. But it is the opinion here that the so-called "peace-keeping force" of Soviet troops was let in through the back door so that fighting could be avoided. A bloodless coup, stage-managed, and orchestrated from within the British Government, but without the true blessing of either the Prime Minister or his Cabinet.'

He paused again, leaning forward and looking straight into Fadden's eyes. 'Mr Fadden would you be prepared to go back to Britain and perform a most dangerous and difficult operation for me? And, of course, for the Freedom of the Western World – your own country in particular.'

Fadden did not hesitate. 'Of course, sir.'

The President said that he must already realise the dangers. 'Your own service know you are here. Run into one of your colleagues, who may by now be playing it all by the new rules, and you're in trouble. In fact, the operation is so covert that you would be in trouble with anyone in authority.'

'Just have me briefed, sir. I'll do the best I can. But how in blazes do I get in? I understand it's virtually impossible.'

'You leave in a few days – and it will be a few days of hard work before you're ready to go.' He added the small details: that Fadden would go to Dublin as part of the United States' advance party, in preparation for the summit. There were those connected with the embassy there who thought they could get him over to Britain.

'And the operation, Mr President?'

42

The President had been through this moment once already that morning, with the German. 'You are to do a crossword puzzle; put together a jig-saw; make your way through a labyrinth so thick that I can only start you off and show you the entrance.'

Fadden began to say something about a briefing, but the President raised his hand. 'Your briefing will be mainly concerned with the situation in your country: the new regulations; rules; the way to move. The operational briefing will be done by me personally; and, frankly, there'll be precious little of it. You'll be going into the dark, Mr Fadden. But if you succeed in penetrating that darkness, black as the darkness which covered Golgotha and the crucifixion, you may bring the light of a new resurrection to Europe. Now, did you ever read a book by a man called Richard Condon – *The Manchurian Candidate*?'

'It's an old movie.'

'Yes.'

'I saw it on TV, when they did the Sinatra retrospective, after his death. I didn't read the book.'

The President opened a drawer and produced a dog-eared paperback of *The Manchurian Candidate*. 'Read it,' he said. 'It'll give you the first clue. Now we'll have lunch. After that I want to talk about our stay-behind agents in Britain, and the general nature of your operation. You see I know more about the end of the mission than anyone else in the world. In fact, I know more about the whole thing than anyone else consciously knows. Yet even I do not know the whole thing. Secrecy, and the running of a clandestine operation go hand in hand, as you know well. In this case the cut-outs in the mission do not even know they are cut-outs; yet they will lead you – with luck – without even knowing what they are doing.'

'You mean, like in the movie of this?' Fadden held up his copy of *The Manchurian Candidate*. 'A man is brainwashed and hypnotised, activated by – was it a playing card? – and would take instructions without question?'

'In that case, to kill a Presidential candidate as I recall.

Yes. In this case, the subjects are not asked to do anything. They are there simply to relay clues, which will lead you to the biggest mystery of all: and it has nothing to do with the destruction of presidents. It is much bigger than that, and, if it comes to it, *you* will be the man who pulls the trigger.'

★ 6 ★

Lunch was brought to them, on trollies, and during the meal the President did some of his own probing into Fadden's past. This time it was obvious that the Chief Executive was satisfied with whatever report the Director of the CIA had submitted. There was a sense of having been accepted without reservation, and Fadden talked, without any restraint, about his previous career – or at least those parts of it that were overt: the covert side of his life and profession was always hidden, except to those who had the right to details. Fadden carried the secrets of his other world under the floorboards of his mind, safe and secure where only he could find them.

The President was an easy and ready listener; a shrewd prompter of the mind. Fadden had not spoken of the memories of his long lost mother, who had died when he was barely twelve years old, for a long time and felt the better for speaking now.

Later, maybe even unconsciously at the time, he realised the President's psychological technique was impeccable. He was playing the game of trust – *Confidence is the only bond of friendship* – Fadden could not recall where that phrase came from; then, like an echo, he realised it was Marlborough: one hot Saturday having to write lines: five hundred times *Necessitas non habet legem*, Necessity has no law. Publius Syrus. The echoes of the form room and a disgruntled Latin master. The 'Confidence' saying was from there as well, though he had long forgotten the Latin. God help him, school was light years back in time, at the still point of the turning world.

The simple meal over, the President, with almost brusque suddenness, glanced at his watch, said he had only a short time left, and that they had better get on with matters. They would be having at least two more meetings before Fadden's departure; the Director himself would do the general briefing and explain the way in which they would spirit Fadden from Dublin to London. He was very precise about London. It was to be the venue of his first contact.

'The secret is buried,' the President said. 'Your job will be to dig it up and find out how it works. Somewhere along the line you will make the big discovery. Once you have done that, it is imperative that you take the greatest care. You will be the only one who really knows. I would even suggest a suicide pill, but I don't think that would serve any real purpose. If you're caught and interrogated after you have gone half way, the game will be either lost or won. When you have total access to the final goal, it will be up to you to contact me. By that time I shall be in Dublin, and there will be a way of making contact – either the Director, or the labyrinth you are about to enter, will see to that.'

'And the clue is here?' Fadden touched the copy of *The Manchurian Candidate*.

The President laughed. 'Oh, showmanship on my part. By now you'll have a lot of the mystery figured out anyway. You tell me what you think?'

'That there's a stay-behind secret which can change the course of world events; that there are stay-behind agents in England who can be activated by me – post-hypnotic triggers – to lead me to the big secret. And the big secret could be anything – a man, machines, an organisation. I don't know.'

The President nodded. 'It had to be buried deep, just in case this sort of emergency ever arose. Not one single person could be allowed to know the whole of it, and the whole only equals the parts. No one part is of any use without the others. I am the only person who knows it all – and even I don't really know it *quite* all. Eventually *you* will.'

He paused. 'Yes, there are stay-behinds who have the

parts, the clues, to what makes up the whole. They don't know it, of course. There are six clues which must be followed in sequence – one to six. There are more than six stay-behinds who, unknowingly, hold the clues, and the names of others, deep in their subconsciousness. It is highly unlikely that the information can be accidentally triggered. That is our first fail-safe. Only you will learn, from me, before you leave, how to dig the clues out. The people concerned can be activated anywhere, under any circumstances, and I am told they will know nothing about it. When you do activate one of the clue-holders, he, or she, will respond with two things. First, he will give you two more names – our next fail-safe in case of missing links, or names given twice. Second, the clue-giver will give you any one of the six clues you need. But one only. These people can be activated only the once. I am assured that when one of these persons is activated and has given the two names, and whatever number clue you require, the memory slate is rubbed clean. The psychiatrists and physicians we used were very good, and there is no way of delving deeper: another fail-safe. All will be clear to you once you are under way.'

He paused again, as though weighing something in the back of his mind. 'Mr Fadden, have you ever killed anyone?'

That was like a spade cutting deeply into Fadden's own memory bank. Death was no stranger. He could count those who had died by his own hand, on his own hand. Five. All unforgettable, but the mechanism of the subconscious dulls the guilt, for people like Fadden had killed in war – cold, but war nevertheless.

Assassination is not the normal way of the secret world. It is frowned upon from high places, and the death of counter-intelligence sources is always a last-resort business. If used at all, that last resort is removed, as far as possible, from the service. Sometimes it is done by suggestion; only very occasionally by a member of the service. More often, if it is the only way, it is done by a contract man who does not know for whom he is really working. Fadden's own service

47

had sometimes employed such a man, whom they grimly spoke of as The Alchemist, for some wag had coined the cryptonym, 'Because he turns lead into gold'.

Fadden nodded quietly. There were five times when he had no option but to kill quickly. Three had been terrorists and in actively dangerous me-or-them situations. The other two had been calculated, desperate even: the only way out. Once in Germany and once in Ulster.

'You may have to kill again.' The President's voice flattened, then rose. 'Cold-bloodedly. I wouldn't like it. But you've got it. You know as well as I do that some of your colleagues, many people in authority in your country, may well have accepted the situation, changed sides, become good Soviets for the sake of peace. Better Red than dead. Changed loyalties can make for strange situations. You could easily find that one, or more, of those people who are your clue-givers, have taken the easy way and joined the new regime. You've had enough experience to detect that kind of thing?'

'It's not unknown. It's not easy to penetrate. But there are ways of establishing bona fides.'

'Would you give betting odds on detecting someone like that?'

'No more than fifty-fifty.'

The President remained very silent, unmoving, for a short space of time, perhaps a minute. 'The slightest indication, Mr Fadden, the most minute hint, you trigger them, get the information and then . . . ' Another pause which Fadden understood.

'Terminate them with extreme prejudice, Mr President?'

He realised it was a bad choice of expression as he said it. The cloud crossed the President's face like a thunderhead carried on a hurricane.

At last he snapped, 'Yes. I would advise . . . '

' . . . that I triggered them and got the information somewhere safe. In the open.'

'You know your job better'n me, Mr Fadden, but I gather you people're trained to deal with that kind of eventuality:

48

in the open, away from buildings or easy sight-lines, so they can't get a parabolic device on you, or a camera.'

'And I search the body afterwards to make sure he isn't hooked into any system.'

'I think the Director will be able to help you there.'

'You mean a portable sensor?'

'He'll talk to you. In the meantime I want to be sure that you realise the absolute necessity of disposing of any possible garbage, and no regrets.'

Fadden was surprised at his own reaction, hearing his voice as though it came from someone else. 'Mr President, I won't wait for confirmation; if I get a simple tickling down my spine, I'll fix them.'

The other meetings were arranged, and Fadden was dismissed with a firm courtesy. The Director was waiting outside, in the ante-room. Tim McPherson hovered in the background, his cherubic face almost stern.

As they took the elevator down, Fadden realised, with what amounted to a near case of shock, that before the week was out he would probably be in a foreign and alien London, searching his way down a sewer, from burning brand to brand until he came to the ultimate light. Already he had a shrewd idea of what that light might possibly be, and the thought chilled him.

Myths, fables, historical legends flitted through his head – Queen Eleanor following Henry II's string through the maze at Woodstock to poison Rosalind; Theseus and his golden thread, tracking the Minotaur through the labyrinth at Knossos.

He was not surprised when the Director told him his field name and said that papers were already being arranged. Then his cryptonym. He might have been thought-reading again, or suddenly blessed with conscious ESP.

'You'll be known as Theseus,' the Director said. He gave a warm smile, 'I was overruled. I would have preferred Lazarus.'

★ 7 ★

The days shrank. Fadden suddenly found himself retraining in techniques almost forgotten – only you do not forget them altogether. Like swimming, the secret world holds you, trapped and ensnared, from the moment you enter it until the day you die. There is no real room for movement, philosophical, political, moral or ethical, once you are committed.

Very quickly he discovered his trained memory was still very active; the old mnemonics, learned years before when he was a raw junior, came back, flicking into use again like a piece of equipment that has been well stored, wrapped, lagged and greased: in working order when needed.

During long sessions with the Director he memorised names and telephone numbers (always with the proviso that, under the new regime, they could have been changed). He stored in his mental bank the places where useful weapons had been placed – in dead drops: single pieces of aid: a pistol here, a small transmitter there, a camera, ammunition: the places obvious, yet cunning in their simplicity.

The method they had devised, at such short notice, to get him into Britain, was also simple and perfectly straightforward. On arrival at Dublin he would not go to the Embassy, but to a small safe house they had along Strand Road, overlooking Dublin Bay. There he would be prepared.

'As far as we can gather,' the Director told him, 'the British police and services are co-operating with the Russians. Most of the people in authority are still there, at their desks, but all the overseeing is done by Russian ghosts. The

British establishment is a figurehead: puppets, ventriloquists' dummies. And the country is sealed, like the Wall used to be. The KGB appear to be active, and, on the face of it, there is complete co-operation with your own service and MI5. Your name and picture will be on the files, and you're almost certainly suspect before you even get in.'

The coastal waters had, they thought, been mined; radar and scanning techniques were at constant alert, so any landing, at this stage, via a light aeroplane, was out of the question.

'I know that disguise went out with Mata Hari and the old-fashioned spy fiction,' the Director grinned, 'but we're bringing it back in again.'

Because America was still technically neutral – if not the friendliest of nations – the American Embassy in Grosvenor Square was operating, and there were diplomatic couriers passing between Dublin and London all the time. 'They have clearance from the British – which is now synonymous with Russian – authorities.' The Director had a pile of documents on his desk: US passport and several other pieces of ID. 'But all of them – the couriers, I mean – are known to the airport staff and security people. We have applied for one of our couriers to go on leave, and a substitute take his place. This has been done without the knowledge of our embassies, in both Dublin and London, in case of penetration. Don't query details. The new courier goes over on Sunday, when there are not many travellers, and will therefore be more open to scrutiny. It's a piece of misdirection I particularly like.'

Fadden said he presumed that he was the new courier, and the Director pushed a passport towards him. The essentials, like height, colour of eyes, age and identifying marks were Fadden's. He did not recognise the rest. There was no photograph, as yet. It was to be done that particular afternoon, and Fadden would be surprised at the simple alterations. 'A rug, of course.' The Director tapped his hair. 'Glasses, cheek-padding. All simple, but your mother wouldn't recognise you.'

Fadden blanched.

That afternoon they did the transformation act, and Fadden had to admit the effect of foam pads in the cheeks, a reshaping of his eyebrows, spectacles, and the salt and pepper wig, changed him incredibly. Looking in the mirror, before they took the passport mug-shots, he hardly recognised himself.

'No drinking with the cheek pads in,' the Director warned. 'They make speech difficult; soak up the liquid.'

The name on the passport said *Peter Friend*. Fadden had to smile at the Director's simple audacity. Within the old Foreign Service, at the Home Office and, to some extent, with the CIA, his own service and MI5 were known as 'The Friends'.

With the 'Friend' documents were travel permits, diplomatic credentials and a number of pieces of similar identifications: Am Ex Card, two letters, a couple of photographs. That particular night, they drilled him in cover.

But it did not end with the persona of Peter Friend. He was to carry a real diplomatic bag to the Grosvenor Square Embassy. They would be told at the last minute that the regular courier had been sent on leave. He would have no detailed conversation with anyone at the Embassy. A car would meet him and whisk him from the airport.

It would be late evening, they said, and the documents would be handed over to the Duty Officer. Peter Friend would stay – as all the couriers did – at the Europa Hotel, which was almost entirely used by Embassy Staff nowadays. Friend would return for the Dublin bag on the next morning.

'But it won't be you,' he was told, the Director adding that he should not try to think, or dig too deeply, into this particular piece of covert magic. It would be done. Fadden just did not have to worry about it.

There was a midnight curfew in London, but as long as the aircraft was on time – and they usually were these days – all would go smoothly. The Peter Friend who was Fadden would dismiss the car on arrival at the Embassy which he would leave on foot.

'Do all your usual field checks,' Tim McPherson said. McPherson was the only other person working with the Director. He even took the passport photographs. 'They are almost certainly going to follow you. You'll only be carrying an overnight case. You act normal and check into the Europa as Friend, and you should be there by ten.'

Fadden picked him up. 'I have to do something before curfew?'

The Director gave a curt nod, as though he wanted to have the story told, the instructions given, without interruption. 'You have to do a great deal. You leave the overnight bag on the bed. Take the other documents, which I shall give you before you leave. Go to the bathroom, remove the wig and trimmings. You'll find a completely new change of clothes in the wardrobe of the allocated room. You change and leave. O.K., now repeat all that.'

Fadden went through it. Fast, like a schoolboy declining a Latin verb. The Director looked pleased; he nodded; a pat on the head for a good pupil. He was about to go on speaking when Fadden held up a hand.

'Sir, one point?'

Again the Director looked cross, but shrugged.

'It's my neck, sir, remember. It's been indicated to me that my first contact – Nightingale – is the *only* one hundred per cent safe stay-behind you have in Britain . . . ' They had made him parrot the list of cryptonyms backwards, forwards and sideways. The briefing, both by the Director, and the two meetings he had now attended with the President, left him in little doubt as to both the uncertainty of the American intelligence set-up in Britain, and the diabolically clever maze, hidden from almost everyone – the maze he would be blindly stumbling through.

'So?' asked the Director.

'So, if Nightingale's the only trusted person left in the field; and another Peter Friend is going to turn up at Grosvenor Square to take the Dublin bag the next day, Nightingale's going to be very busy.'

'You pray,' the Director brought his hands together, as though he was going to do 'Here's the church; here's the steeple;' for a small child. 'You pray that Nightingale *is* pure gold; and you pray that Nightingale is absolutely certain about the man who'll take your place, and do the trip back to Dublin. If not, one of two things is going is happen – very fast. Either you're going to get picked up as Friend; or the papers are going to be full of a Missing American Diplomat story the next morning. There are third and fourth possibilities – that both of those things will happen, or the papers will have a Murdered American Diplomat story. So trust and have faith, Fadden. It's all we can do. I asked you to forget about that transmogrification trick. Leave the magic and misdirection to us – at that phase anyhow.'

Fadden asked about his other identity – the one he would be using when he left the Europa.

'Yourself,' the Director said. 'Your own passport; everything, except the most recent American visa. Your passport says you're a civil servant. We'll provide the extra ID, permits and all that. We'll even tell you what to say, where you work, in case you're stopped.' He went on to explain that they felt Fadden would stand more chance, and feel happier in the role, if he played himself as soon as possible after arrival in London.

Paul Fadden saw the sense, but disliked the idea. The computers would soon throw his identity back at anyone who queried him. Even before the crisis, the police on the beat had a nasty tendency to check with the computer when they stopped someone; suspicious or not. It took the best part of a minute, from the name going through the police radio to the computer answer. Big Brother had truly arrived in the mid-1980s.

So the briefing went on, also the final meetings with the President, who only gave him hints – hints and two ordinary-looking keys. 'You'll guard those with your life,' he told Fadden. 'Keep them with you at all times. Their use

54

will be revealed as you get deep into it.'

Apart from the keys, and the list of cached equipment, they gave him only one further aid: an old watch. A bit battered, but good for its day: early sixties, he reckoned; old-fashioned, with hands and a second sweep hand. People still carried them, some even preferring them to the digitals which were in common use. On this one, the sweep hand had stopped permanently at three o'clock. Tim McPherson demonstrated that if he came within activating distance of an electronic listening device, the sweep hand would move, and he would feel a slight tingling on the wrist. The nearer he came to the device, the further round the dial the sweep hand would move, and the tingling sensation would become more acute.

Twenty four hours before Air Force Two was due to take the advance party to Dublin from Andrews Air Base, Fadden was given a morning of intensive interrogation. All the information that the Director and Tim McPherson had pumped into him was queried and questioned until they were satisfied that he had it pat. Fadden thought of school again; Shakespeare this time – *Conned by rote*; and the memory changed, the picture sharp, the words clear – in bed with Pat, one afternoon in her little apartment near Regent Street, with the rain battering at the windows, the loving over, and the pert face breaking into a grin and saying that he had learned the way to satisfy her body, like other people learned to read maps. 'You've conned me by rote, Paul – and I mean that as a compliment.'

It was also on the day before leaving, that Fadden saw the President for the last time. The Chief Executive also went through all the lessons again. He seemed anxious, as tired as ever, and said that he was going away – probably to Camp David, which had recently been refurbished – with the Secretary of State and some other advisers to 'talk things out before the summit'.

He became very serious at the end, and wished Fadden God speed and good luck. He did not pour on the drama or give a 'the world rests in your hands' speech, but his eyes showed a deep anxiety. The grip of his hand was firm when they parted, and his last words were, 'Hear from you – maybe even see you – in Dublin.'

As ever, the Director and Tim McPherson were waiting in the anteroom. There was one small last thing, the Director told him. It would not take long, but they felt he should be really fresh when he arrived. A doctor was merely going to check him out. Fadden knew then that he was, himself, going to become part of the labyrinth.

The doctor was an old man, kindly, thorough, asking the right questions. For a short while, Fadden wondered if he had been wrong. But, when the questions had been asked, and the physical examination completed, the old man asked him if he would lie on the couch for one last test.

He had no memory of what happened after that; but he knew, for there was a sense of being very alert and fresh, as though he had been asleep for a while. The doctor more or less admitted it. 'We felt you should have a little induced sleep. Hypnosis does wonders, you know. You feel less tired?'

Fadden acknowledged that he did.

'Yes, much better than drugs. Good, good.'

The Director and Tim were waiting outside. They said they were taking him out to a farewell dinner.

Fadden had an uncanny feeling, during the meal, that they were not alone. The wrist watch gave off no anti-bugging signals, but he felt they had been joined by invisible figures – Nightingale, Samson, Swallow, Sappho, Vesta, Lark and Stag.

By this time he knew that Nightingale was a woman.

⋆ 8 ⋆

Paul Fadden knew he was late, just as he knew he must not do anything that might draw attention to himself. It had gone like clockwork until his arrival at the Embassy in Grosvenor Square. There they had taken him into one of the security rooms (the sweep hand on the watch went berserk) and he had to wait for almost half an hour until the Duty Officer arrived, checked the seals on the diplomatic bag, and completed the paperwork. So he was already running twenty minutes late – they had allowed nearly fifteen for emergencies – by the time he had hurried across the Square and up into Duke Street. Then there had been a small delay about checking in at the Europa.

The room was on the fourth floor, and all was exactly as they had told him it would be, including the pair of very obvious shadows who had followed him from the Embassy. The only thing that concerned him then was that one of the men had looked Russian, and the other young and very English. They were talking to a girl in the lobby as he came down, dressed in the other clothes – which were well worn, with British labels – and without the pads, rug or glasses: his own papers, and the special new documents were safely in his breast pocket.

But now he was late.

He paused at the top of the subway steps on the junction of Regent Street and Piccadilly, glancing towards the blinding lights of the three BTR Armoured Personnel Carriers coming up fast from Lower Regent Street, circling and turning into Coventry Street. They were greeny-brown, even in the street lights, which were not as bright or vivid as he recalled; solid vehicles, armoured tops down on the mild night, the troops sitting erect, AKM rifles gripped between their knees.

Fadden noted the red flashes and numerals: 20th Guards Motor Rifle Division. The Russians seldom altered their unit badges, and the last he had heard of the 20th was when they were stationed near Grimma, in East Germany as part of the First Guards Army. But that was a lifetime ago.

Down the steps, in the circular concourse which led to Piccadilly Underground Station, and acted as an underpass below the famous Circus, there were fewer people – fewer than he remembered from even a month or two ago. Then it always seemed as though you were in an increasing fight between counter-flowing tides of humanity. Now, people moved in an orderly manner, watched by the police constables patrolling the concourse, their distinctive Metropolitan Police helmets looking antique, incongruous next to the headgear of their companions – for each constable walked his regulation beat together with a Russian Military Police private soldier, belligerent in polished calf-length boots, forage cap and khaki, belted, uniform made more distinct by the 'On Duty' shoulder boards. Unlike the constables, the Russian soldiers carried pistols in polished leather holsters.

Fadden was aware of the fatigue: that sudden downbeat of the body, together with a familiar weariness of soul and mind. The trip had taken more out of him than he realised: the hazard of being in the field again after so long. To be in your late forties was not to be old, but it was pushing it slightly on a job like this. A case officer, as the Americans called it – a controller to his own service – could go on into his sixties, but a street man in an alien country was a different matter.

He was in no doubt that England was an alien country now, and had been aware of it from the moment he arrived at Heathrow. Now he was naked and loose: vulnerable.

Fadden emerged from the underpass, up the steps, down

which the warm wind gusted, and on to the pavement on the far side of Regent Street, turning left towards the Regent Palace Hotel across the narrow road.

As he stood by the kerb, waiting for the thin stream of traffic, Fadden glanced back into Piccadilly Circus. At least the Statue of Eros was still standing, as were all London's old landmarks and buildings.

Not so the other great capitals of Europe if you were to believe the very few photographs released by *Tass* to the American Press. In Vienna, the *Stefansdom* gutted by a rocket salvo; in Paris the great Opera House smashed by a direct hit from a Frog Seven high-explosive missile on the third day of the war; and, ironically, in Berlin the splintered tower of the Kaiser Wilhelm Church, its ruin a memorial since World War Two, was now no more, while half the Ku-damm had disappeared in a mound of rubble.

There were armed infantrymen at the doors of the Regent Palace, but they paid no attention to Fadden as he passed through the main entrance. Memories chased each other around his mind of other meetings in this place, once the paradise for illicit week-ends of out-of-town businessmen and their secretaries; and, more often for Fadden, pick-up, dead-drop and brush points when he was training juniors on field technique. There was not a little irony in the situation now.

He saw her at once: Nightingale, sitting on one of the long curving plastic-covered seats which ran along the outer walls of the lobby entrance.

Nightingale – Hilary Keville, they had said. Deep cover as a writer. She was tall, very slim with long legs, crossed in a manner that seemed to accentuate the length; her brown coat hung open, draped around her, showing a matching skirt and shirt, all cut in the height of fashion for the early 1980s. There was no fashion now, no real style.

They had also told him that she was naturalised English: Hilary Keville, thirty-five years of age; a writer of far left novels which had started with moderate success and then been boosted by the establishment, so that she was totally

59

accepted by the regime. CIA-trained, and operational for the past eleven years.

Fadden knew her at once, of course, though not by the name Keville. She had always been blessed with a cryptonym when he had met her in the old days – my God, the old days, only a few months ago. She acted as a contact-breaker quite often when his own people were running anything with the Americans: contact-breaking, dropping, brushing, lurking; using the language they all used.

She used it now, as she spotted him, immediately uncrossing her legs and transferring her handbag from right to left, the old-style body talk, meaning that he could approach.

He answered, by flicking his handkerchief from the breast pocket of his jacket and dabbing his nose, while pretending to look around, spotting her at the right and natural moment.

She stood up as he approached, put her arms out and kissed him on both cheeks. How nice it was to see him again, had the journey been bad from the North? What with only three trains a week she presumed it was crowded and had arrived late at Euston.

Yes, it had been monstrously crowded and they were late. Thus were their personal bona fides established. As he pulled away from her, Paul Fadden glanced at his watch. She was clean: the sweep hand did not move.

She dropped her voice, saying they would have to leave quickly. She would only have left it another couple of minutes. It was dangerous to look as though you were loitering, or just passing the time, in this place, particularly near to curfew. A lot of junior Russian officers used the Regent Palace. They regarded any woman on her own as fair game. Taking Fadden's arm she led him towards the doors.

'You haven't brought your case?'

Fadden said, no he hadn't. Getting a seat had been unexpected, that's why she got the message at short notice.

She patted his arm. 'That's O.K., I've still got some of your things over at my place.'

The Director, and his opposite number from the National

Security Agency, who were the harder hit by the communications problems, for that was their speciality, must have worked overtime on setting that one up. It had worried him slightly when the Director briefed him, going naked into this hostile environment.

She seemed so at ease and natural, but he felt an unnatural anxiety among the welling concern and fatigue. In a split second he traced its source. He was not in a position to trust her yet, as his first contact. It even crossed his mind that she may have been lulled, like the bulk of the British people, into a giant sigh of relief because at least they were alive and had been spared the holocaust, not facing the one which would inevitably come.

As they got to the glass doors, a junior sergeant backed by a private soldier, both with shoulder boards and collar patches of the Security Police, stepped forward, barring their way. The soldier said something in Russian, which Fadden pretended not to understand.

The girl reached for her handbag, and as she did so, a man in civilian clothes stepped up to the group. 'He's asking for your papers,' the man said, holding out his hand to show a Metropolitan Police warrant card.

Hilary Keville glanced at the Englishman. 'I know what he said,' she replied, a hint of scorn in her voice before she lapsed into quiet, controlled Russian, speaking directly to the junior sergeant as she removed a pink ID card from a blue folder. Fadden glimpsed the black circle with a particular insignia stamped in the top right corner of the card. His own ID was just a plain, rather cheap piece of white cardboard with details and an official stamp. He reached for the inside of his jacket, praying that the piece of forgery would hold up.

The Security Police did not even bother with him. The junior sergeant snapped to attention and saluted the Keville girl, rapping out, 'Sorry, Comrade.' He hoped the comrade would understand, there were people who it was best to check at this time of night. All this in Russian, of course.

Hilary smiled at him, and said she would not feel safe

61

unless there were constant and vigilant security checks such as this. In the meantime, her pass would not suffice during the curfew, and it would be best if she and her friend made their way home.

There followed more bowing and scraping – Would the comrade like a taxi? It could be arranged. Yes, she said, that might be a good idea.

Fadden had already established that taxis were like gold dust and only certain people were either authorised, or had the money, to use them. Now, one appeared like magic, and Fadden stood aside while Hilary climbed in. He followed her and she gave the Chelsea address he already knew. The driver was silent, only nodding that he understood. As London cab drivers went, he indicated that he knew too bloody much and to hell with them both.

Fadden remained silent during the drive. This was not the London he knew or remembered by night. There were few people on the streets, and even less traffic. The neon advertising hoardings were turned off, and shops were without lighted windows.

The only people out in any force seemed to be Russian troops – many of them off duty, occasionally a drunk, but mainly they appeared to be behaving in a quiet orderly manner. They would have to, he thought, for there were armed Security and Military Police around in abundance, most of them in company with good old-fashioned British bobbies, or plainclothes men.

As they entered the Kings Road, a police car went ripping past them, its siren blaring. Inside, Fadden glimpsed the familiar pattern of two uniformed officers in front, and the plainclothes observer in the rear; but this last was not alone: beside him sat a young Russian officer, alert and unrelaxed, as though he sat in the car with one hand on a pistol.

Hilary Keville lived in a small mews, the kind of place beloved of American film-makers in the fifties, who thought them cute and representative of the way middle-management people lived in London. In some ways it was like a movie set. Yet, as a movie set, it would have been too small. There were two storeys only, and five rooms including kitchen and bathroom.

Fadden was distinctly uneasy. In his mind he heard the Director telling him that, of all people, he knew that Nightingale – this rather self-possessed girl, Hilary Keville – could be trusted. *There's no need to fear: she's exceptionally well-established.*

She would have had to be, for both of them to walk through a security check in which he did not have to show his papers, and the police provided a taxi.

As they entered the main room – walls booklined, a circular glass table, a settee and two armchairs, large, ornate and gilt-framed mirrors over the fireplace and taking up one wall – she must have seen the look of doubt on his face.

'You're quite right,' she said, slipping out of her coat and turning to smile at him, 'I'm part of the Russian Security Service here in London.'

Fadden automatically glanced at his watch. The sweep hand remained static. Whatever she was, there were no electronic listening devices either on her or in the room.

'So you're safe as the proverbial houses with me. I was recruited within days of the gallant Prime Minister asking for Soviet assistance. Party member for a long time. I've sweated my guts out for the bastards. That's what makes me fireproof.' Hastily she reached for the white-painted mantelpiece. 'Touch wood. There's nothing like over-confidence. You can relax, friend Theseus. It's a small risk bringing you here, but I'm not under surveillance, and I'm certainly not suspect. They've got their work cut out rounding up possible subversives, and I'm the last person they're likely to suspect – as yet.'

Fadden nodded, took off the overcoat which had been made of some synthetic fibre around the late seventies, and asked if he could check the place out – just in case. She said he was to be her guest, and that he should make a mental note of the telephone number. If he needed her during whatever operation he was on, they had better work out some double-talk code.

'You'll have to be gone in the morning. I'll risk some things, but keeping you here for more than a night isn't one of them.'

Fadden said he would get the geography straight, heading towards the glass-panelled door which led from the main room. She came up close behind him, remarking that he would probably want something to eat.

The door led to the stairs, on the right of which was a small passage ending in two steps down into a tiny kitchen. He went through, the girl following, and saw immediately that there were no exits.

She started to busy herself with a frying pan. 'We have electricity on a rota basis,' she shrugged. 'On today from noon until six in the morning. Tomorrow there'll be no electrical facilities in this area until midnight, so you're lucky,' she said, breaking eggs into a bowl.

Fadden went back along the short passage and started up the stairs, his mind still working on the enigma of Hilary Keville. They had talked a lot in Washington about who to trust, and who to approach with extreme caution. Nightingale had been the only one they said was 'known safe'; yet the weird experience at the Regent Palace, the smoothness of the operation, gave him cause to wonder.

He mounted the stairs. There was a small bathroom at the top: no windows, an extractor fan high up on the far wall. The sweep hand showed it was clean. Coming out of the bathroom, three stairs took him on to a small, and final, landing: a door to his right, another straight ahead.

The door on the right opened into a small bedroom – bed, table, lamp, chair, fitted wardrobe. On one wall an odd oil of a graveyard, the headstones looming out of mist. It could be something inspired by a Dracula movie, but he thought not, for there was no vulgarity about it, just a sombre sense of place and time.

Fadden smiled, as the words *Still Life* went through his head. There was a mounted reproduction poster over the bed – an old Railway advertisement from the thirties. That kind of thing had been very much in vogue during the nineteen-sixties, and there had been one for *Pear's Soap* in the bathroom.

He smiled again, for, to the left of the bed, a window looked out on to the rear of the mews – a small garden, walled in; the wall to the far end not more than six feet high. He tested the window. It opened easily. The drop was on to soft earth, a border, shooting spring flowers into a battle-field of colour. At least there was one escape route.

On the bed lay an open suitcase: shirts, underclothes, a couple of rollnecks, socks, ties and a pair of light canvas shoes. A dark business suit, smart in the mid-seventies, hung next to a light raincoat, on the door of the wardrobe, and a pair of shoes lay on the carpet below the suit.

For a second, the shoes caught Fadden's attention. They had been placed there neatly, in an almost military style, heels together, the toes pointing outwards. He even went and placed his own shoe in the angle made by the pair on the carpet. They were perfectly aligned. Not the way a woman would have placed them.

Turning back to the bed he reached towards the suitcase. On the top, nestling under a pair of pyjamas, was a Russian-made automatic pistol.

Fadden drew it out. One of the big old Stechkins. Deadly, with a full capacity for automatic fire. There were two spare ammunition clips lying beside the weapon. He weighed it in his hand, drew out the clip from the butt, and checked it. A full magazine. Real ammunition or very clever dummies. *Take nothing for granted*. They always said that.

He checked the firing pin and mechanism. It appeared to be in full working order. As silently as possible, Fadden pushed the magazine home, slipped the spares into his jacket, cocked the weapon and pushed it into the waistband of his trousers, at the rear. Not the correct way to go armed, but the best he could think of.

On the landing, all was quiet except for the clatter of pans in the kitchen. He pushed open the other door. Obviously Nightingale's bedroom. Feminine, with a large double bed, and a smart white dressing table taking up one entire wall.

5 65

Built-in wardrobes again. Two windows: small and not negotiable. In any case the drop was straight on to the stonework of the mews.

He was just turning away from the windows when the telephone extension on the dressing table, gave a tiny ping, as though someone had picked up the main phone downstairs.

Fadden crossed to the instrument, placed his hand over the mouthpiece, and lifted the instrument carefully off its rests: one at a time so that there would be no tell-tale click on the line.

Hilary Keville – Nightingale – was speaking in Russian, her voice low.

'Yes, I have him here . . . Yes, tonight. I'll get all I can.'

A man at the other end asked if she had the name under which he was travelling, and she said no, but she'd get it tonight. There was no need to worry, they had him firmly in the net. She would use every trick. The voice at the other end gave a little chuckle and said something about knowing her tricks.

'My instructions were to meet him and let him pass on. I haven't had a chance to talk with him. I have to brief him on the state of the ground and let him move on.'

'Then I suggest we follow,' the voice said. 'I shall have people watching by dawn.' Then, hurriedly as though worried, 'Unless you think he'll leave before then?'

'What I have in store for him will keep him until the morning,' Hilary Keville said. 'Your people can follow then. I'll report in tomorrow with anything available. Trust me, I'll get the object of his mission from him. You've no need to take him here. Let him lead you.'

'Good luck.' The voice chuckled again. 'And sleep well.'

Fadden timed his replacing the receiver at the same moment as the one downstairs. So much for their safest stay-behind, he thought. He would have to move with great care and speed. One thing was certain: if the American briefing was correct, it did not matter if Hilary Keville had been turned. She still, unknowingly, had the information he

66

needed, deep in her subconscious, ready to be programmed to him and then wiped clean – just like a computer tape.

She too would have to be wiped clean, and there was no way for him to know if the house was already being watched or not. Intrigue called for intrigue in the world which he and the Keville girl inhabited.

He left her bedroom as silently as he had entered, only starting to betray his presence by heavy-footedness after he passed the hairpin bend on the stairs by the bathroom.

She called out to him from the kitchen. 'Omelettes. I hope you like omelettes. *Fines herbes*. Bread, and a glass of revolting wine.'

'Great,' he stood in the kitchen doorway.

She had prepared two trays, and had one in her hands. His, she said, was already on the table in the main room.

It was almost cosy, sitting in armchairs with the trays resting on the table.

The omelettes were good, and the wine, as she had said, revolting – some cheap Balkan rotgut that hit his belly like fire.

'So, you're in safely,' she said at last. 'You see the gear I got you?'

'Beautiful. You got papers as well?'

'I thought you'd brought your own.'

'Yes, but they gave me to understand that you could get me the real things.'

Her hand reached out over the table. He caught the reflection in the glass top – the double image seemed appropriate. 'Let's have a look . . . ' she began.

He did not move, just looked straight into her eyes and said the trigger sentence. 'Skull a of place the.' The inverted line from the Biblical quotation.

For a second, Fadden thought the whole thing was a backfire. Then he saw that she was motionless, her eyes fixed ahead, glassy as though dead.

She spoke in a monotone. 'You need two names?'

'Yes.'

'Samson; real name Eldrich. Sir Graham Eldrich. Recently retired, Foreign Service. Recruited our service 1979. Last known address 101 Eggerton Gardens. Telephone 589–9367. Second – Swallow: real name Athay, Dr Mary Athay. Until recently research chemist with United States Allied Chemicals. Last known address 23 Kensington High Street, Flat 69. Telephone 937–0490.' She paused, as though expecting to give Fadden time to make notes. He rarely had to make notes in the field. The whole of her last sentence was safe in his own conscious memory now.

'What number do you need?' The eyes were still glazed and staring into space, not looking at him.

'One.'

'You are starting the ascent of Golgotha, then. Under the ground. Below the earth, here in England. Salvation to the occupied. Salvation through death and destruction from under the earth; and they will rise from the dead places only when you blow the last trump. You must find the last trump, and the keys you hold are the keys to either the Alpha or the Omega. The others will reveal more.'

She had spoken slowly, and Fadden, using his own system of mnemonics, took in every word, the whole thing committed and secreted into his own mind with the next two contact names.

'Calvary. Skull a of place the,' he said clearly.

'More wine,' her hand closed around his glass. 'You were going to show me the documents.'

'Oh yes.' Fadden rose, his right hand moving to the waistband of his trousers as though to get something from his hip pocket.

Instead, the massive Stechkin came out fast, his arm moving in a wide arc before she could react.

The heavy weapon caught her at the right point, low down behind the ear, on the neck. It went in so hard he could hear the bone crack and saw her jaw sag, the small white trickles of juice from the corners of her mouth, and the exhalation of death as she fell sideways.

If you are in any doubt about their loyalty, clean them and

kill, he had been told. Right or wrong, do it. He had, there, at the very beginning.

The curfew was in force; at dawn they would be coming to watch and follow. All he had were two names and addresses; a telephone in the house which he could not really trust; a pile of gibberish about something under the earth: Golgotha, and the last trump; and a dead woman.

★ 9 ★

Fadden took nearly fifteen minutes to drag the woman's stiffening body from the main room, up the stairs, and into the bedroom. He resisted the temptation to put her into night clothes, simply bundling her into the bed and covering her head with sheets and blankets. When they came – as they would – they could lose minutes by thinking she was still asleep.

He also took the telephone from the hook, intending to leave it off; but, as soon as it was removed, the sweep hand on his watch-sensor swung rapidly. He replaced the handpiece quickly. The sweep hand steadied, and he prayed that merely picking up the phone would not start the listeners worrying. If her Soviet contact decided to check up, and got no reply, they would be at the house long before dawn.

He hesitated, waiting for about five minutes, expecting the phone to ring. But there was silence.

Carefully, and with a speed learned long ago in the shadows of Europe, Fadden searched the room, going through each drawer and cupboard with care. Nothing.

When he left her bedroom, he took the key from the inside of the door, locking it from the landing, then went into the smaller bedroom in which his clothes and the suitcase lay ready.

Glancing from the window, which semed his only reasonable means of escape, he saw only darkness. The small street lamp, which had burned beyond the wall at the far end of the narrow stretch of garden, was gone. It was long past midnight. On their way to Chelsea, Fadden had noted the absence of shop lights and illuminated signs, he had also seen that only about one in four of the street lights were on, and even they burned at a reduced power. Presumably, the lights all went out at curfew – midnight.

He drew the curtains and began to think out the best action. Whatever he did meant changing into the clothes provided by Nightingale – or at least some of them. He weighed up the possibility of his description being circulated. If Nightingale had been really well turned, the Soviets would have provided the clothes and suitcase. They would be part of the description, once the Keville girl was found dead. Years ago, he had learned you should take your time, if possible, in tricky situations. He had some time in hand – presumably until around five-thirty in the morning; dawn, when the curfew would be off. But the anonymous voice talking to Nightingale on the telephone had said he would have people watching by dawn, which meant they would almost certainly be in place before five-thirty.

In his head, Fadden ran over the official papers in his pocket, and the few extras hidden in the lining of his jacket ('Sorry about this being so unsophisticated,' Tim had said, explaining that sometimes the most obvious was the best. There was no time for false heels in his shoes, or anything like that. There was not much point either. If caught, they would find the extra papers anyway.).

Slowly, still thinking, Fadden left the room and descended the stairs. When thinking, try to keep the body occupied. He piled the remains of the two meals on to one tray in the main room, and carried them through to the little kitchen.

He could change, make the drop from the bedroom window, with the suitcase, and lug the thing over the wall. Then take his chance in the hostile world just before dawn, in the hope that the watchers would not arrive too early. He did have a couple of papers that might just pass – documents allowing him to be out during curfew – as long as nobody suspected, or did a police computer check. Reason told him they probably did not have the computer fully programmed as yet. They would still be adjusting to some errors and no-shows. The reprogramming would take time, and the

Soviets, efficient though they may be, might just let him go if he did not show.

He thought about it while washing the dishes and stacking them neatly. Something else niggled in the back of his head, and it was as he placed the last plate in the draining rack that he remembered her handbag.

It was still in the main room, lying beside the chair in which she had died.

Everything came out with a clatter as he turned the bag over on to the glass-topped table, and the keys, on their little ring decorated with a worn and period piece Shell Oil symbol, seemed to leap away from the rest of the usual feminine detritus – the lipstick, compact, sachets, purse.

Keys – the ones given to him by the President, safe on his own key ring at this moment, crossed his mind. These keys belonged to a car. Picking them up he turned the ring in his hand. There was a registration number on the back of the old Shell symbol.

Quickly, Fadden crossed the room and looked around, as though memorising the layout; then he turned out the lights, closing his eyes as he did so to adjust to darkness.

He stood like this for the best part of a minute, before opening his eyes once more, and waiting until he could see through the gloom before moving to the window. He did not open the curtains from the middle, but stood to one side, pulling the drape back so that he could peer out into the empty and dark street, pressing his face as close as possible to the window.

The car was parked just forward of the house, as though it did not belong to the occupant, and, even in the darkness, lit only by a low moon in its third quarter, he could read off the number plate. It was her car without any doubt; gleaming as though kept in good condition. A Fiat 250, the low fuel consumption model, 1988, he thought. Transport, there within reach, a few paces from the door, just for the asking.

Among the other papers was a driving licence and a couple of blank vehicle permits. He might just make it. Four o'clock; maybe a little later, would be best, for that was the time of low ebb for patrols, police on the beat, people who turned their nights into day.

Sweeping the remainder of its contents back into the handbag, Fadden tossed the car keys lightly in his hand and set off up the stairs towards the bathroom. Ten minutes later, he lay in deep warm water, soaking and going through the next moves.

He needed to place himself far away from the Chelsea area as soon as possible; he also needed access to a telephone. For the second of the six clues, he had already decided on Sir Graham Eldrich. The address in Eggerton Gardens was too close for comfort – as was the other subject, the research chemist, Mary Athay – but he could, possibly, make his approach at a distance, by telephone. He even thought of trying to walk into his old service headquarters building to use an office telephone: audacity sometimes paid off, but there was too much at risk. A hotel would be the best bet. Somewhere with a nearby car park, where he might be able to stash Keville's Fiat away out of sight. Once he was away they would not just be after a description, but a car number as well. He wondered about transport from Heathrow.

It was almost half-past three by the time he had bathed, dressed in clean clothes, made out the vehicle permit with details of Nightingale's car, packed both his old and new clothes into the suitcase, and gone over all the necessary papers.

He carried the suitcase down the stairs, placing it near the front door, threw the light overcoat Nightingale had provided over a chair-back, sat down and took out the big Stechkin; he held it for a moment, then cocked the weapon and put it on to safety, placing it on the chair arm.

Fadden then tried to relax all his muscles, concentrating on the job in hand. His plans were made, and eventualities would have to be played off the cuff.

At a little before four o'clock he went through to the kitchen, put on the kettle and made some instant coffee – black with no sugar – which he drank quickly so that it almost scalded his throat, in an attempt to liven all his senses.

The first scars of light were showing in the darkness, when Fadden opened the front door, his mind running through everything, his body conscious of the weight of the automatic pistol now in a copious hip pocket.

The street seemed deserted; and, with one last check that he had everything, tightly gripping the car keys, he closed the door behind him and made quickly for the car, unlocking the driver's door, slinging the case into the rear, and with one movement, sliding into the driving seat. As he was about to turn the key in the ignition, he was aware, for one instant before the Fiat's engine roared into life, that the telephone was ringing in Hilary Keville's little mews house.

He did not need to be prompted further: slipping the gear into drive, and accelerating smoothly away from the kerb. It was only his imagination that he could still hear the ringing of the telephone as he turned out of the mews.

★ 10 ★

Alexander Suvlov sat in the window of the tall office building near Westminster Bridge looking out over the darkened city. Soon it would be dawn, and he would go down to the car pool to give the surveillance team their final instructions.

At a desk behind him, Harry Ashworth was carefully going through possible dossiers.

'You have anything, Harold?' Suvlov spoke careful English with little trace of accent. Originally he had been trained as a possible control and servicing officer for Britain and America. Now he was one of the hundred or so KGB men who were the overseers of the British Intelligence Services. He was pleased with himself, for it was he who had unearthed the few remaining deep-penetration members of the United States Service when the Soviet 'Peace Keeping Force' had moved into Britain.

'Four or five possibles.' Ashworth, a man in his midforties with a face like tanned leather, was one of the many members of the SIS who knew when the battle was lost and had agreed to go on working, hand-in-glove with the new masters. What tiny pricks of doubt invaded his professional conscience were salved by the facts of reality. The Service worked for Britain, not a political party; and Britain's security had been maintained by the arrival of a Russian Force.

Ashworth did not relish the business of working together with the Soviet Service, but his neck was safe – unlike those who had tried to go to ground, or those who had refused point blank. There was a high security camp already filled with them up in Scotland. There had been vague stories of executions, and less vague ones of very sophisticated interrogations.

Suvlov stretched out a hand towards Ashworth's desk. He did not even turn around in his swivel chair, and Ashworth had to get up and come over to him with the small batch of files.

Suvlov was about thirty-nine years old, and Ashworth thought he was more like a character from Tolstoy's *War and Peace* than a KGB officer – slim, good-looking in a Western way, a bit of a dandy, with blond hair which he had trimmed once a week at Trumpers, and, since his arrival, he sported – like so many members of the Soviet Service – clothes which even the old élite of the British Establishment had not been able to afford for years.

With his usual arrogance, Suvlov did not even thank Ashworth as he took the dossiers. When he personally appointed the SIS man as his assistant, the Russian had made it clear that it was not his way to affect natural courtesies in the office. He had other methods of rewarding work done well – things which mattered more, like passes to the better restaurants, a higher place on the new housing lists, even, eventually, there would be a permit for the *Beryozka* shops, where you could buy imported foreign goods, and luxuries for knock-down prices.

Britain was one of the very few countries left in Europe which showed no scars from the recent short war. There was little doubt in Ashworth's mind that the Britain of the future was to be used as a prime base within Europe, and this would be combined with its function as a special country in which the Soviet élite could live in style.

The armed forces already in the country were large, and the air traffic now coming in, under tight control from the continent and the Eastern Bloc, ferried essential war materials, plus luxury items, at a staggering thousand transport loads a day.

'Two of these are American,' Suvlov spoke flatly. 'I did not get the impression that this one was American. When

76

Keville told us, she maintained he would be English, which leaves us with three possibles – this man Davis; the Londoner, Morgan; and the man your service sent to Washington just before we took over Europe – Fadden. I want the photographs enlarged on those three. If the surveillance team makes a positive identification, we will be organised.'

Ashworth asked if they intended to pull him quickly, and Suvlov shrugged. No, he said, they wanted to see what the mission was. If they lost him – as they well might with an arrest – nobody would be any the wiser. The Americans would not send an Englishman just to have a look at the ground.

He flicked through the dossiers again, then gazed up, out over the city. There were occasional winks of light here and there, and, with his eyes adjusted, he could make out the shapes of buildings; the sweep of the river.

There were times when even Suvlov wondered at his good fortune of being in a position of such importance in London. Some of his friends were working with the conquered people in Bonn, Paris and Rome. They were going through hell because the intelligence services of France, Italy and the German Federal Republic, had proved themselves much less pliable than the British.

The British Services – both the SIS and MI5 – were now virtually under one joint command, with Marshal Lupaiyev at the head. Alexander Suvlov had served as Lupaiyev's assistant in Moscow. The relationship had been a happy one, and the Marshal had shown his gratitude by giving Suvlov a prime job here in London.

There had been luck also: mainly the fact that the British and American services, long suspicious of one another, had ceased to entirely trust each other by the end of the nineteen-seventies.

When Marshal Lupaiyev's men walked into the headquarters of the SIS, Suvlov had gone straight to the computers which dealt with the American Service. The printouts – similar to the pile of papers now on his lap – had given him many clues. One of them had been a serious doubt regarding Miss Hilary Keville and her possible connection with the American Service.

He was certain there were others, undetected by the British; but Hilary Keville had been suspect for a long time. More, the British had shown great discretion. During his first two weeks in London, Suvlov was certain that the Americans had no idea that the girl Keville was blown.

A skilled operator, Suvlov had personally worked on Hilary Keville. He had not needed to resort to drugs or violence. The girl stood up for a week or so, then, under the careful logic with which Suvlov was so adept, had cracked in a day.

So closely had Hilary Keville identified with her own cover, that she was psychologically ready to accept it as truth. Even Alexander Suvlov was amazed at the speed of his results. Marshal Lupaiyev had expressed doubts. Maybe, he said, it was all too fast. Perhaps they were, to use the old American term, being sold a dummy. Perhaps she was doubling. But the stress evaluator systems all came up positive. Suvlov had done the almost impossible – turned an American deep-penetration agent with unnatural speed; and it had paid off when the Keville girl had reported contact with her case officer now operating out of Ireland.

Suvlov looked at his reflection in the glass, hazy and weak against the darkness of the city. The Americans had put in a member of the British Service under cover and he, Alexander Suvlov, had the man trapped in the Keville girl's little mews house. In a few hours his best surveillance team would be able to make a positive identification, and the man – whoever he was: Davis, Morgan, or Fadden – would be tracked. It would be an undoubted coup; for this stranger among them would surely lead Suvlov to some of the few stay-behind people who the British had failed to identify.

Ashworth came back into the room. He had left so quietly that Suvlov had been almost unaware of his absence. He told the Russian that the blow-up photographs would be ready within half an hour.

Suvlov glanced at his watch. It was almost a quarter past

four in the morning. He would order his team out in twenty minutes or so. They would have the house discreetly covered by five. He was about to rise, when another thought struck him. He had purposely left the ground clear for Hilary Keville, for he knew her skills. Only last week he had tested them for the first time himself. They had spent twelve hours in bed, and her inventiveness and sexual dexterity had amazed Suvlov. He had said to her at the time that, with her talents, she could gain access to any information if her subject really trusted her. The thought of it made him hard now.

She had been with the Englishman for some time, and it was possible that she already had the information they needed. A 'wrong number, yes and no' telephone call might just quicken things. It could also save manpower. That would please the Marshal, for manpower was one of his headaches – so many of the best men were in the other European capitals.

Above, and slightly to the right, Suvlov saw the winking lights of three huge Ilyushin transports in a spread-out V-formation, turning towards Northolt. They would be the first of the day's shuttle services bringing in supplies. Soon the air around the outskirts of London would be filled with the noise of jets, as would be the East Anglian coastline. They came daily like a conveyor belt, as did the ships to the ports in the South, and far up in Scotland.

He rose. Ashworth looked up from his desk with tired eyes and asked if it was time.

'In a moment.' Suvlov smiled, not unpleasantly. 'I'm going to call the lady on a wrong number.'

Ashworth saw the point straight away, and mumbled that it could save Suvlov a lot of time. 'If he's told her enough, we can sweat him here,' Ashworth said.

Suvlov just looked through him, as though breath was too precious to repeat the obvious. He carefully dialled Hilary Keville's number.

After a minute, the slightly puzzled expression changed into a frown. Suvlov put his hands on the rests, to clear for a dialling tone, and tried again.

79

When the telephone was not answered after sixty rings, he re-dialled internally, to check with the listeners on the top floor. The log showed only that the telephone had been picked up and replaced without a call being made. The time logged was 00.48 hours.

Ashworth had never heard Suvlov shout orders before. Part of his success was the quiet painstaking attitude, the calm and unflurried exterior. His face and manner was now like the sudden cracking of a dam.

He ordered his car, a heavy team, a team from the old Special Branch – which was now padded with English-speaking Soviet police officers – and the surveillance team as a back-up, standing off. He also shouted for Ashworth to move his clean British ass. This last was yelled at the Englishman as Suvlov grabbed a pistol from the drawer of his desk.

Ashworth, still technically under probation with the Soviets, was not allowed to go armed.

Five minutes later, with sirens wailing, the small convoy was moving at speed through Westminster, heading towards Chelsea.

★ 11 ★

Paul Fadden got as far as the Hammersmith flyover before anyone even stopped him.

It was almost completely light now, and he drove carefully, well within the newly-posted speed restrictions. There was some traffic, though no crush. At major intersections he steered warily past lone Personnel Carriers, their crews fanned out in watchful combat positions.

At the Knightsbridge junction with Sloane Street and Brompton Road, there had been four such vehicles, and a lot of watchful faces: a Russian officer was standing up, the top half of his body protruding from the hatch of a Carrier. He wore a headset and started speaking as Fadden's car went by. A few yards further on, two police cars were pulled up by the kerb. Uniformed Metropolitan Police officers leaned against the cars, chatting and smoking with a pair of thickset men in plainclothes, and three or four Russian Military Police sergeants. They took no notice.

Fadden shifted in his seat, feeling the bruising hardness of the Stechkin pistol in his hip pocket. That seemed to produce an almost Pavlovian reflex, for he took his left hand off the wheel and touched the pocket of his jacket, to reassure himself that the one secret he had really retained from everybody was safe.

When they had boxed him, in Washington, nobody had asked about unauthorised papers or documents, so the matter had never come up. Fadden remained silent about it, just as he had done within his own service. In the left-hand pocket of his jacket was a cover passport, issued to him for a mission in the sixties and never recalled. Scrupulously he had kept it up to date by the many clandestine means at his disposal in the service. He doubted that there was any record of it now. A Russian passport – a fake, certainly, but well used over the years, with genuine control stamps which showed him, as Alexei Simon Gorlky, to be a Grade Three Administrative Inspector of Overseas Trade Missions. There was even a diplomatic immunity stamp on the first page. Fadden had relied on the document for years, and its very look was impressive. He had spoken to nobody about its existence, and always carried it – even when living in London in the old days; even when going round the corner to the supermarket.

It was Fadden's secret weapon, and he knew only too well, probably of more use to him now than the big Stechkin pistol.

The traffic thickened as he approached the Hammersmith flyover. It was a roadblock: three Personnel Carriers and their crews, staggered over about a hundred yards, with an old BTR-40 at each end of the stagger.

The BTRs had their turrets turned to face the traffic in both directions, the heavy Degtyarev-Shpagin machine guns constantly moving, as though they meant business.

Fadden pulled the Fiat up behind a British Leyland Austin 600, being driven by an officer in Soviet uniform. They were stopping about one car in four, and the road block had not been there when Fadden had come in from Heathrow on the previous evening.

He felt his palms, sweaty on the wheel, as they rolled forward another car length. There had not been time, he told himself. The fear that they were looking for him – him in this particular car – was simply a natural psychosis. He felt for the Stechkin, and then left it alone. There was no point in getting involved in a shoot-out. If it was him they wanted, they had him.

The people doing the checks were Soviet officers, backed up by soldiers carrying the latest modification of the Kalashnikov. There was a uniformed Metropolitan Police Inspector with each team of checkers.

82

The car in front of the 600 was stopped, and the driver and his passenger, a pretty blonde girl, were made to get out. Papers were exchanged and examined; the soldiers looked inside the car, and a sergeant frisked both of them. He took longer with the girl.

Fadden noticed they were still using mirrors on wheels and long handling poles to look under the cars.

Satisfied, the pair were allowed to pass through, and the 600 rolled up to the checkpoint. The uniformed officer merely leaned out of the window and flashed some kind of ID. The young officer in charge nodded him through.

Fadden wound down the window and drew out his Gorlky passport, as he edged the Fiat up to the group of men. He did not even give the young officer – who looked like an intelligent farm boy – a chance to speak; rattling off Russian at him calmly and without irritation.

'I'd be obliged, Comrade Captain. I am in a great hurry to meet some colleagues coming in from Berlin.' He looked the man straight in the eyes, handing him the passport, open at the page with the diplomatic immunity stamp.

The captain hesitated for a second, turned the page to Fadden's description, flicked his eyes from the photograph to Fadden and back again. Then he nervously shoved the passport back into Fadden's hand, took a step to the rear and saluted.

'Please pass, Comrade Gorlky. My apologies for the delay. We're looking for a pair of illegals who've got hold of air tickets to Switzerland.'

Fadden nodded and said he hoped they would catch them, slipped the car into drive and took it slowly through the zig-zag course between the Personnel Carriers.

On the motorway he saw plenty of other activity. At regular intervals along the hard shoulder later versions of the old ZSU-23s, anti-aircraft gun systems, stood, bedded down in regular combat readiness; their slim barrels slanting upwards, crews cooking breakfast, but always with one man up on the vehicles wearing a headset. Lord knew who they expected to try an air strike on Heathrow, Fadden wondered.

But the Russians were at least thorough.

Already one thing had become obvious: most of the military equipment allotted to Britain was old stuff, some even going back to the late sixties. That was sound tactics, Fadden considered. The latest equipment would be on the continent, where they had met with at least token resistance.

There were no troops on the departure car parks, the automatic booths manned by faces which seemed all too familiar to Fadden – the tired, disinterested look of the middle-aged, even retirable, men who were usually to be found in these places. When he drove in, collected his ticket, and passed under the black and yellow striped bar, the man in his booth did not even look towards him, but remained hunched over a morning paper.

Fadden glimpsed that it was *The Daily Express*, and felt a twinge of anguish at the strange mixture of old normality and the new repression which seemed, to all intents and purposes, to be living, almost peacefully, side by side.

He took the Fiat up to the third level and parked in a corner space where the light was not good. They would find it without much bother, but he had worn gloves the whole time, and it was just possible that someone might think he had got away quickly by air, parking in the departure area.

Nobody stopped him on the way to the old Number One Terminal; nor when he walked purposefully into the Departure area and out again through Arrivals.

Several police, both Soviet military and British airport, were on duty outside. Fadden went straight to one of the Soviets, flashed his passport, and asked, in quick fluent Russian, for a taxi.

The man saluted when he saw the diplomatic stamp, and whistled up a cab to take him the short distance to the old Excelsior Hotel. He overtipped, and the cabbie spat out of his driver's side window, which pleased Fadden, for it showed there was some spirit still around.

He did not like the Excelsior. It held nasty memories for him. When he had been forced to use it in the past, the service had been bad to the point of rudeness. He recalled a colleague, in the mid-nineteen-seventies, who had complained about his room only to receive a blistering ticking-off from the reception supervisor who had told him that he had 'made one of my girls cry'.

The girls at reception were more courteous now, particularly when he presented his passport. The girl gave him a smile and asked if he had a reservation. He shook his head, trying to convey the impression that he understood, but did not speak, English.

'Soddin' Ivan diplomat; just smile and be nice,' he heard the girl whisper to her colleague. Then she started to explain, in carefully enunciated English – as though he might be able to lip-read – that he would have one of their best rooms. They gave him a registration card in Russian, to fill in. He did so meticulously. With luck, the diplomatic number on his stamp would keep away snoops when they started to search.

There were quite a lot of people in the foyer, a good mixture of Soviets and English, but the staff still had time to provide him with a page boy who took the bag and led him to the lift. In the old days they just gave you a key and told you to find the room for yourself.

He was on the fourth floor, and expressed no surprise at seeing a security officer, a middle-aged woman, sitting at a desk as they came out of the lift. She was English, and the page boy gave her the room number. She just passed a key over the desk, gave Fadden an unsmiling nod, and said the room was vacant and had been cleaned.

There was a large bedroom, a bathroom, radio and colour TV. There was also a telephone. Fadden had told reception that he would give twenty-four hours' notice before checking out. 'Two or three days,' he said. Now, once the boy had left, again overtipped, he lifted the telephone and put the watch close to the mouthpiece. The sweep-hand did not move, but that proved nothing, for the main listening devices could well be wired into the switchboard.

The switchboard answered, and he asked, in halting English with a Russian inflexion, if he could have breakfast in the room. He had not eaten since the previous night. They said a waiter would be up within a couple of minutes. He arrived in less.

In Russia itself, Fadden had always complained to himself, about hotel service. Here, in the new People's Democratic Republic of Britain, the Soviets had obviously started out with a purge on the hotel facilities. There were no restrictions on food when he showed his visitor's permit – keeping one thumb over the name inscribed.

Within fifteen minutes the waiter returned with hot coffee, eggs, bacon, sausage, toast and marmalade. Fadden signed the bill and saw, not to his surprise, that the breakfast was costing him fifty-two pounds sterling. The last breakfast he'd had in an English hotel had cost twenty-six pounds, but the pound sterling was now, on the world market, worth a little under thirty pence so it was not unusual.

He ate the breakfast, before running a delousing sweep on the room – going over all the wall space and fixtures with his watch. However long it took them to organise things, he was certain that the hotel rooms would all have at least some kind of electronic surveillance. If the telephones were not monitored, at least the rooms would be.

The device was straightforward, rather old-fashioned, a voice-activated high-powered mike sunk into the most obvious place, one of the bedside lamps. Well, that could easily go on the blink when he made his call.

He took time re-sweeping, to make sure there were no back-up electronics, then made one call out, to the Office of Trade Delegations whose number he found easily in the supplementary telephone directory. He spoke clearly, and in Russian, banking on the old Soviet system of buck-passing.

After some initial trouble, they put him through to a secretary in the German section, and he asked who was in charge now. The secretary told him it was Comrade First Secretary Bykhov, and he said that Gorlky, the Administrative Secretary of Overseas Missions, had arrived in London and had to see Secretary Bykhov tomorrow morning. The secretary was polite and booked an appointment for eleven. Fadden told her he would telephone again if there was any delay. He had a lot of people to see in London. She did not ask for a contact address.

They would be relieved when he did not turn up. A couple of days later they may start to get worried. He would keep them on a string. Bureaucrats were the easiest to deal with, because they had a habit of chasing – and sometimes eating – their own tails.

The surveillance system in the room would monitor that call, which would give him plenty of cover for the short term. He rang down to reception and asked if they would give him an alarm call at about four that afternoon. He did not wish to be disturbed until then.

He would telephone Sir Graham Eldrich just after six.

★ 12 ★

The Marshal's car, with its pennant, stood out among the clutter of vehicles, plain and police, packed around the mews house. The whole mews had, in effect, been cordoned off, and a four-man section from Scotland Yard's murder squad was going about its methodical business in the house, under the careful eye of Menichev, who had once been Head of Homicide in Moscow.

Menichev was past his prime now, but Marshal Lupaiyev trusted him. They had been at school together.

Marshal Lupaiyev was not happy. He was particularly unhappy with Alexander Suvlov who had found the body, made a lot of mess and noise doing so, and probably muddied the waters.

When the Marshal arrived at the Chelsea mews he had to wait for nearly an hour in his car, while the murder team took photographs, did the fingerprinting, and vacuum-cleaning in the main downstairs room. He spent the hour interrogating and castigating Suvlov.

'So, you had him here, in your hands, and you left the place unwatched all night.' The Marshal had a voice like gravel which had been treated with weed killer.

'I wanted to give the girl a clear field. I didn't want him alerted . . . ' Suvlov had lost his normal poise.

'Haven't you got men who are invisible?'

'They are good but . . . '

'Alex, this was important. You've been a fool.'

'Yes, Comrade Marshal.' There was no point in disagreeing with someone like Marshal Constantin Mikhilov Lupaiyev.

'Would *I* have left the girl in that situation?' Marshal Lupaiyev did not smile.

'No, Comrade Marshal.'

'No, Comrade Marshal. No, the fuck I wouldn't. It's an elementary error. You pray, Alexei Alexeiovitch. You pray for your balls that we get on to this man quickly, that he's left some kind of clue. Thank God the British Police are wonderful,' he gave a hoarse little mocking laugh, 'and that Menichev is watching them. Who's watching for you, Alex?'

'My British man, Ashworth.'

'You trust him?'

'Yes.'

'He'd better watch his balls also.'

'Yes, Comrade Marshal.'

'In the palm of your hand, and we don't even know who he was; there is no description, no name . . . ?'

'Possibly one of three, by logic one of three . . . '

'No name. Logic has no name. No idea of why he was here. Nothing.'

'He took the girl's car.'

'Yes, and it's probably abandoned by now. He could have had another contact, one you haven't got in your pocket: one you've never even heard of. He's here for something; and not for the good of his health.'

'An error of judgement, Comrade Marshal. I acknowledge that. I shall catch him.'

'I doubt it. Menichev and the wonderful British Police Force will probably catch him. If, and when, they do, you can sweep him clean, and we won't have any accidents. Right?'

Suvlov said nothing.

'Well, what have you done so far? Apart from sending out a description of the motor car?'

'A watch on all air and sea ports.'

'For whom?'

'Anyone acting . . . '

'Suspiciously? Don't be a fool. This man's a professional.'

'I've circulated copies of the photographs of all three

89

possibles.' Suvlov paused. 'Until we've narrowed it down to the right man.'

The Marshal made a grunting noise.

Inside the house they had completed the photographs in the bedroom, and the doctor had finished his examination of the body. Ashworth spoke to the young Detective Inspector who was in charge of the case – as far as any official papers would be concerned. Ashworth, who had spent most of his intelligence career at the safe end, was not used to bodies. The house seemed to reek of death. He asked the cause, and a quiet voice came from behind them.

'Her neck was broken by a skilful blow with some heavy object.' Menichev was small and round, with skin the colour and texture of suet pudding. He spoke English well, and in his spare time was a lover of music, particularly that of Dmitri Shostakovich. Menichev added that the woman had died sometime after midnight. He then smiled and said there seemed to be plenty of fingerprints.

'Who the hell's that?' Ashworth asked, when the Russian was out of earshot.

'You may well wonder.' The DI raised his eyebrows. 'Top Ivan murder brass. You got a security problem?'

'You might say that.' Ashworth smiled, and the DI grinned. 'I say,' Ashworth called out after him. The DI came back. 'I think your London policemen are wonderful,' Ashworth said.

The DI cocked his head. 'The Moscow ones are fairly thorough as well. We should watch it, chum.'

When the Marshal was allowed in, they were taking the body out. He was fuming even more, because Suvlov had broken the news that he had allowed the British agent to be provided with an automatic pistol and ammunition.

Together with the police they sat down, in the late Hilary Keville's living room, and worked out a statement for the Press.

★ 13 ★

They rang through to Fadden's room at exactly four o'clock. He had slept soundly and felt refreshed, lying there with the Stechkin under the pillow.

He thanked the girl, and asked for tea and toast to be sent up immediately. It arrived ten minutes later, the tea Russian style, in a glass with a metal holder.

Fadden turned on the television. It was a children's pro-gramme, *Blue Peter*, and a young man in shirtsleeves was telling his audience, with the help of old film, how, earlier in the century, the British and the Russians had fought side by side against a common enemy. Now, he said, history was repeating itself. Britain had been ground down under the heel of Capitalism, but, because of the foresight of its great Prime Minister, there was a new alliance with the Russian people.

In the bathroom, Fadden soaked a hand towel, folded it, and took it over to the lamp which contained the electronic device. Then he turned up the volume of the television, lifted the lamp standard and placed the sopping towel over the microbug. He left it there for several minutes, and then gently removed it, keeping the volume of the television up, and moving around the room, going to the bathroom, cough-ing, humming to the music, then tip-toeing back to the lamp and repeating the exercise with the towel again.

It was almost five-twenty. Fadden did the trick with the towel several times. If anyone was directly monitoring – which he doubted – the effect would be that the bug was on the blink. The same thing would be thought if there was a daily play-back of the tapes. He could go through the whole business again when he made his call to Sir Graham Eldrich, though he could do nothing about the telephone if they had a wire into the switchboard.

The news came on at its scheduled time, with martial music and a symbol of crossed and interwoven flags, the Russian and the Union Jack. Incongruously, the newsreader addressed the viewers as 'Comrades'. The Prime Minister had announced he would be attending – together with his Soviet advisers – the summit meeting with the Americans due to begin in Dublin in just over a week.

They had the PM on tape saying he hoped the new alliance with Russia would not in any way harm the long-standing relationship – both in friendship and trade – between the American and British people. He also said he saw no reason why it should. Fadden saw every reason, but did not even laugh aloud.

There were several other political items and some newly announced restrictions. There followed news from other parts of the Soviet Bloc, and a story about a demonstration in Washington, against the President and his policies, before they reached a small item concerning the murder of the well-known novelist Hilary Keville.

A still photograph of her face filled the screen, then a little footage taken outside the house. It showed police, both Russian and Metropolitan, leaving. Fadden leaned forward, trying to memorise faces. The statement was terse, giving the impression that Keville had been killed by some rejected lover. There was no official police description, but you could not count on that. If they were, in fact, looking for Fadden, it would be a security matter, and they would be unlikely to publish his photograph yet.

They did add that the murderer had probably escaped in the woman's car, and showed another photograph of a Fiat with Keville's number plate superimposed. The newsreader repeated the number twice, and asked people to report any sighting of the car. 'Nobody,' he warned, 'should approach the driver as he is probably very dangerous. Instead they should telephone, or get in touch with, the nearest police or military unit as quickly as possible.'

The news ended at six, but Fadden left the set on, making a lot of noise as he went through to the bathroom and ran the taps. Then he returned, did the business again with the wet towel, and took the lamp over to the television, which he turned down slightly.

You had to dial 9 to get an outside line. There were no tell-tale clicks, and Fadden closed his eyes, bringing back Sir Graham Eldrich's number to the forefront of his mind. 589-9367. The phone began to ring at the other end, once, twice, three times, before someone lifted the receiver and answered, in a rather plummy voice, giving the number.

'Sir Graham Eldrich?' Fadden asked.

'No, who wants him?'

'Is Sir Graham there?'

'He's just coming; who shall I say is calling?'

'It's an old friend. A surprise.'

'Just one moment, I'll get him.'

Fadden waited for about thirty seconds, then an older voice came on. 'Can I help you? Eldrich here.'

'Sir Graham Eldrich?'

'Yes, who is that?'

Fadden took a deep breath, concentrated his mind and said the trigger – 'Skull a of place the.'

There was a long pause at the other end. Then – 'I beg your pardon?'

Fadden went cold.

⋆ 14 ⋆

Samson – Sir Graham Eldrich's cryptonym – was apt. Some Delilah had shorn his hair, Fadden thought, dropping the receiver quickly on to its rests.

He tried to think. Again the old habit. Do something while you think. He began to tidy up the room, taking the folded wet towel from its place on the lamp, having carried the thing back to the bedside table. Dropping the towel in the bath and dribbling water around it, spreading it out so that it looked like an accident.

Back in the bedroom he dried off the area around the microbug with a handkerchief, turned down the television – which was now showing a documentary about collective farms, followed by a discussion regarding the government's plans to merge farms in England and Wales. Vaguely, Fadden wondered why they did not include Scotland.

The voice on the other end of the line could not have been Eldrich – unless someone else had cleaned him already. If it wasn't Eldrich, what had they done with the man? Arrested? Blown? So many had been. Don Marks had staked his life on Hilary Keville, but she had all the signs of a turned agent.

What now of Swallow, the research chemist, Dr Mary Athay, who lived in Kensington High Street? If she had gone also, he was finished. If they had a wire into the switchboard – or on Sir Graham's phone – he was blown, or at least blown as far as the Russian passport was concerned. It was essential for him to go physically to the Athay woman's place, and he would have to travel light, leaving the bulk of his things at the hotel.

Fadden still took his time, not dawdling, but taking infinite care, for he was most conscious that, because of the telephone call, they might well have a fix on him already.

He went through all the pockets of his spare suit, which he left in the wardrobe, changed his shirt and tie and put a spare set of underwear and a roll-neck sweater into a carrier bag which someone had left in the bathroom.

He abandoned the shaving gear and pyjamas: if they thought he might return, the general search could at least be reduced, with people staking out the hotel. The Stechkin and light raincoat went with him, and he distributed the various documents and papers in different pockets, memorising what was where.

Lastly, he rumpled the bed, and took the chance of ringing down to reception, asking if they could provide him with a taxi. He wanted to go into the West End for the evening, but would be back before curfew.

They took a moment or two – checking no doubt on his status – then told him there would be a car waiting for him.

Fadden ordered the cabbie to drop him in Piccadilly. It was far enough away from Kensington, he considered. The man was surly and reminded him that the standard rate was fifty pounds, sterling. For a second, Fadden was tempted to take out his wallet, which had been very well filled by Washington, but decided quickly against it. Cab drivers had always been good sources of police information in London, and there was no reason to think life had changed to that extent.

The roadblock had gone from the Hammersmith flyover, and Fadden gave a quick thought to the pair of 'illegals' for whom they had been searching. Had they got through or were they, at this minute, going through some form of interrogation?

The cab dropped him opposite where Fortnum and Mason's used to be. It still had the famous clock above the premises, but the name – known world wide – had been obliterated. It was now a state shop. Crossing the road, Fadden peered in at the dismal display of goods: mostly canned foods carrying inferior brand names, though there were some pyramids of tins imported from Eastern Bloc countries. The prices were horrific, and you could tell that the ordinary British man and woman were not getting any benefit from luxuries which, he had been briefed, were being flown in daily in large quantities. They were for the military power and the new élite – those who really toed the line.

Fadden began to walk back up Piccadilly, checking, out of long training and habit, that they did not have a tail on him. It was the only safe way for him to move into Kensington – on foot.

The streets, while not crowded, still sported people, though they appeared to be outnumbered by the military. The traffic was light, again mainly military. He searched people's eyes as though looking for a hint of what that odd creature – the man in the street – really thought of Britain's plight. He thought he could detect shock; sometimes he knew it was despair.

A constable with his military counterpart, both being a little officious, stopped him for his papers near the Albert Hall. Fadden knew what they were going to do long before he reached them, for he had seen them halt two girls and question them. Then the Soviet man looked straight at him and said something to the constable who was polite, but putting on a bit of power. They would all get like that, he thought.

In the late seventies, people said it did not matter which way things went – left or right – because the police would eventually be given more control, and the end result would be more prisons, a higher rate of corruption, less crime but many new kinds of crime – like speaking your mind, or being black or Jewish, or a former royalist (nobody seemed to know, now, what had happened to the royal family, though there were rumours, which ranged from escape to Australia, to death in the Tower of London).

He gave them his real documents – the Fadden ones with the extra forged permits – and they seemed to be satisfied.

96

At least there was not an alert out for him yet. Not as Fadden anyway.

A Grand Victory Concert was to be held in a week's time at the Albert Hall; the LSO, and the Moscow Symphony Orchestra, would both be playing. He noticed that Shostakovich's 'Leningrad' Symphony was on the bill. Tonight a famous Russian quartet was to perform some of the same composer's work.

Someone, Fadden remembered, had once called Kensington High Street the most famous High Street in the world. It looked tawdry now – even more decrepit than when he had last seen it only a few weeks before. Most of the shop windows were empty; some had closed altogether. Two banks, which he had once used often, were still there, but the individual names and symbols had been removed. In English and Russian they both now carried the legend *People's State Bank of Britain.* The Soviets had moved bloody quickly.

Number twenty-three was an apartment block. The wood and glass doors to the foyer were covered by a heavy metal mesh, and there were two long banks of old Entryphones on each side. Flat sixty-nine still had a card next to it on which the name *Mary Athay* was written neatly in ink.

Fadden pressed the bell and held his breath. No immediate response; so he pressed it again. About fifteen seconds later there was a click and a woman's voice quietly said, 'Yes?'

'I'm looking for Dr Mary Athay.'

'Who are you?'

'A friend. I used to be with U.S. Allied Chemicals. There's a message for you. If you're Dr Athay.' Keville had said Dr Athay last worked for United States Allied Chemicals, and Fadden could only presume that it had been one of Don Marks' cover firms – genuine, of course, but used, as most American-owned multi-national companies were used, by the intelligence services. 'Are you Doctor Athay?' he asked again.

'Yes. Come up. Sixth floor. The elevator's working.' The voice flat.

There was a click as the security lock was operated, and

Fadden walked into the bare lobby.

He did not know what he had expected. Perhaps the name, Dr Mary Athay, had conjured in his mind some middle-aged frump: a blue-stocking; unattractive. Certainly he was not prepared for the tall blonde who opened the door to him.

She wore pink slacks, a shirt of some silky material under a matching jumper; a scarf tied neatly at her throat; the jumper, like the slacks, hugging at her waist which was slim, the slacks accentuating the long legs.

Her eyes were red-rimmed, and, from the depths of the flat, he could hear music.

'Dr Athay?'

She nodded for him to come in, blowing on a tissue, as though trying to tidy herself from the tears. 'I'm sorry,' she said, as if that explained everything.

He recognised the music, coming from the room to the right of the small entrance hall – Berlioz: The Grande Mass for the Dead. It was reaching the high point of the Dies Irae, where the strings go spiralling off into infinity, and then there is a mass of trumpets and timpani – the Last Trump and the end of the world. Last Trump, he thought. Hilary Keville's message – *they will rise from the dead places only when you blow the last trump, and the keys you hold are the keys to either the Alpha or the Omega.*

She shut the door, and Paul Fadden saw the tears still in the deep blue, large and beautiful eyes. Doe-like, some pulp writer would have called them.

'I'm sorry,' she said for the second time. 'I'll turn it off. This way.' She led him through to a large living-room, the front windows of which looked down into the street, and went straight over to the stereo unit. It was an old recording. He recognised it – the Bernstein with the two French orchestras and choir.

She pressed the key and plunged the Choeurs de Radio France into oblivion right in the middle of *Tuba, mirum spargens sonum.* Fadden had the same recording in his own collection at the house in Hampstead.

'Who sent you?' She stood, straight with head tilted, as

though trying to show pride – a woman caught at the moment of grief; unaware, disturbed at a private moment.

It was no good messing about. If he was wrong he would have to kill her anyway. 'Don Marks,' he said.

'I hope you're not lying. I tried to get a message out. Didn't know if I'd succeeded. They got Tom – my husband – on the first day. One of the many. No charges against me, of course, but he was so bloody outspoken and English.'

'But he didn't . . . ?' Fadden chanced.

'Work for Don? No, of course not. They got him because he was anti-government, anti-state, anti-every-bloody-thing. No trial. Two coppers came, with a Russian. They said he had been tried. The bastards shot him.'

'Is that why . . . ?' He indicated the stereo unit and her own face. She gave a little laugh.

'No. No, I'm sorry. I shed a few tears for Tom, but . . . No, there's only so much you can take. I was conducting a private requiem for someone else. An acquaintance really. I only heard tonight. An acquaintance got herself murdered.'

Oh Christ, thought Fadden, not another one. Then he saw it, above the face mantelpiece, the oil painting – the graveyard, the headstones rising from the mist. The same painting that had been in the room Hilary Keville allotted him in the Chelsea house.

She was speaking to him. It took a second for him to realise that she was repeating a question.

'I said, what's your name?'

'Just call me Paul, for the moment. The friend who was murdered? It wouldn't have been Hilary Keville, would it?'

Her eyes brimmed again and she bit her lip, nodding.

'Don't waste your tears. She finked on Don.'

'She was . . . ?'

He crossed to the windows and looked down.

'It's O.K.' Mary Athay seemed to be more in control now. 'I'm in the clear. They questioned me: about my husband's politics. Everything. They knew that I disagreed with him, and they know I've retained my American citizenship – not that they give a shit for that now – but the dogs are off.'

99

Fadden turned. 'Sit down,' he said quietly. 'Then we can talk about it.'

She sat, rather primly, on the edge of the settee, hands clasped between her thighs (body talk for a woman deprived? he wondered), eyes still wet from the crying and shock.

'Are you getting me out?' she asked.

'Maybe.' He knew that it must be done now. Get hold of the information and then talk. Looking directly at her he said, 'Skull a of place the.'

Her body relaxed slightly, eyes losing their glitter. Then the monotone he had noticed in Hilary Keville when she was triggered. 'You need two names?'

'Yes.'

'Sappho. Real name Cork Halstead, freelance journalist; specialist in political and military affairs. Lives in a village near Oxford. The Elms, Cumnor. Telephone Oxford 3786. Second: Vesta. Real name Janet Fain: first woman director of the National Theatre. Private address, Flat in the Barbican Building in the City of London. Ex-Directory telephone. Can be approached at the National Theatre . . . What number do you need?'

'Two.'

'You may need to take notes. If so you must cipher them afterwards. There are many numbers. Tell me when you're ready.'

Fadden did not like it, preferring to trust his memory, but this was a once only chance with no repeats. He felt inside his jacket and took out the little black notebook, which was virgin empty, then uncapped his pen.

'I'm ready.'

'There are thirty-five co-ordinates. I shall start when you count from one to five.'

He counted and she began immediately after he had said ' . . . five . . . ' A series of co-ordinates which he recognised at once as map references. Six-figure series, probably for ordnance survey maps. It was a good job, Fadden realised, that they had built in the bit about notes which he would have to cipher afterwards. If the references were as important as he suspected, it was impossible for him to rely on memory alone at one hearing.

At last she finished, and he wiped her clean with the trigger – 'Calvary. Skull a of place the.'

There was only a slight pause before she asked again if he was getting her out; the voice normal now.

'I said, maybe. I'm in a tricky situation myself. They might just be looking for me.'

She rose and went to the window, just as he had done. 'You weren't followed?'

'I've got nobody watching my back, but I'd say not.'

'Then you'll be safe here. They'd have to break down the street door, and mount a large flushing operation to get at you. The phone was disconnected after they took Tom away.' As an afterthought she asked if he was hungry.

'I'm sorry,' she always seemed to be apologising. 'I'm not a good hostess. Probably one of the reasons Tom took to the little tarts he used to hang around with.'

Fadden's mind flashed back – it seemed a long time ago – to Pat, and the final argument – the one that really did it, a few weeks before the actual farewell in that hotel room. She had taunted him. She always did. As far as Paul Fadden knew he was still impotent from her taunts. He knew she had been with at least two other friends of his – not in the trade – both small men known for their promiscuity, both indiscriminate, taking anything of any age. There was usually money involved somewhere. 'You prefer little male tarts to me,' he had shouted at her. 'At least they know what to do with it,' Pat retorted, screeching, her mouth smeared red: a target he would have liked to smash in.

'It happens.'

'I know. It happened to me. I wanted out before the balloon went up, but Don wouldn't hear of it; and it was not as if I did anything.' She turned suddenly, a flush of anxiety in her eyes, mouth open a little. 'Oh Jesus, that's not it, is it? You haven't come to make me work in this godforsaken country?'

'You were never a sleeper, Mary. You're a trained officer. If they had a special job for you, you'd be doing it now. No, I'll get you out if I can. I've got to get myself out,' he paused as she went towards the door, and he added, 'Eventually,' just as she asked if he would like to come into the kitchen with her.

They both laughed. 'Sure. What's Mary got in her pantry?'

The tears had gone. 'Not a bun, that's for sure. Come on.'

Her kitchen cupboards were stacked full – canned goods, preserving jars full of eggs and vegetables; a deep freeze filled to the lid.

'I'm a hoarder,' she gave a pretty shrug. 'Tom said it was coming: coming soon, and I should be prepared; so I hoarded. You can be shot for it now. Did you know that.'

'I'd heard, but there're so many rumours.'

'That's no rumour. The first week they shot over two hundred women in East London alone. God knows how many elsewhere. One or two out in the country districts, but a lot in the cities. The first couple of weeks saw most of the purges. The pogroms: hoarders, looters, theft, corruption. The Met. dragging people into vans with the lewd and licentious soldiery standing by with guns – like those old pictures of Europe under the Nazis. The country's in shock now. What's your fancy, Paul?' She grinned at him, as though a true good humour had suddenly returned, re-placing a disease, like a patient once the crisis of an illness is over.

'You have amazing powers of recuperation, Mary.'

One slim hand rested on the table. She looked at him hard, dry-eyed now. 'Of course. It's contact with another human being. I've been frightened to go out much. Contact with one from the real world. You have come from the real world, haven't you, Paul?'

'I think so.'

'Then let's eat, drink and be merry, for tomorrow . . . '

'Never comes.' He grinned back, and they chose the meal. As she worked, he slipped in one casual leading question.

'You know of a Sir Graham Eldrich? Retired Foreign Service?'

She had been opening a can, and did not pause. 'Tom knew him, poor bugger.'

'What's happened to him?'

'Arrested, when they got Tom. Same club and all that sort of thing.'

'And shot him?'

She shook her head slowly. 'Not according to the papers. He's got life in one of those imitation Siberias they're building in Scotland. God knows what they do to them up there.'

Paul Fadden felt a little dizzy. The man at Eldrich's number had identified himself. One of them. Not only would they have got to the hotel by now, but also they would have the trigger words: and they had Eldrich to try them on. Two possible future contacts might well be blown. If not now, then within the next few hours. He had two clues; there were four to go. Every name mattered from now on, and there was no way of telling what names had been locked in Sir Graham Eldrich's head.

'Mary.' He could hear the gravity in his own voice. 'Hate to spoil your fun, but what you've just told me makes a lot of difference. We'll eat, I promise you. But I have to go out now, for a short time at least. I'll leave my things.'

'Shit,' she said, the voice almost bitter.

'I'll be back. Before curfew, and we'll eat. I swear.' Already, in the far reaches of his head, he was wondering how he could get to the National Theatre, and if Janet Fain – a tough lady in anyone's book – would see him.

★ 15 ★

Marshal Constantin Mikhilov Lupaiyev seldom actually used the high-rise block near Westminster Bridge, once the sole preserve of Britain's Secret Intelligence Service.

He preferred to operate from his suite at the Savoy Hotel but on this occasion he had decided he should be as near to the action as possible. Alexander Suvlov, whom he had trusted for many years, had been slack, in allowing a perfect opportunity to slip through his smooth fingers. This hurt Lupaiyev more than it angered him. He was a hard and tough man, but would be the first to admit that failures were inevitable. Unhappily, under the pressures of the new state of affairs in Europe, the High Command and the Politicians would countenance no failures.

Like so many senior officers and politicians, Lupaiyev knew how far-stretched the Soviet forces had become. Lines of supply were always a problem for armies, that was why he – with military and political advisers – had personally managed to bring the whole British business to a satisfactory conclusion by clandestine and overt manipulation, so that no shot had been fired to gather Britain into the Soviet Bloc.

The policy was to make Britain a base of action, but – possibly more important – a show state. A man who had great weights of secrets buried within his soul, Marshal Lupaiyev knew the truth concerning the difficulties which the Soviet armies were experiencing in the rest of conquered Europe, and how disappointed the politicians had been when the President of the United States refused to attend a summit in Britain itself. There were hopes that the President would allow a short visit to London during the Dublin summit; but time was running out. They could not keep up the inflow of materials and goods at a high rate for much longer. There was little doubt, also, that the military presence had to be drastically reduced as quickly as possible.

This was the main reason that the capture of the infiltrator was so important. The lists, which Suvlov had taken from the computers at the SIS headquarters – and other men had filched from the MI5 and Special Branch tapes – were incomplete. To control subversive elements, and reduce the number of men needed to hold Britain secure, they needed to be certain that *all* known agents of foreign powers – particularly the United States – were either expelled, in the Scottish camps, or dead.

Suvlov should have made certain that the intruder was controlled from the moment he came into contact with the Keville girl.

Lupaiyev did not care what happened to the infiltrator. Eventually he would end up dead, of course, but what the Marshal wanted, above anything, was to have the man under surveillance – quickly.

Sitting now in Suvlov's office, with the suet-faced, quiet, Menichev turning pages of print out dossiers in silence, and Alexander Suvlov looking worried, pacing the room, Marshal Lupaiyev sighed. He took another vodka, lit a cigarette, and thought about what he could be doing at this moment.

Back in his suite at the Savoy, the waiters would have set the table for two. He glanced at his watch. The girl would be arriving at eight. Now, shortly after seven, he would soon have to ring the Savoy and give orders for her to be entertained until he returned.

The silence was broken by Menichev. 'The man you are looking for is this one.' He held up a photograph of Paul Fadden.

'You're sure?' The Marshal sounded dubious.

'No, I'm not sure, but if I was to make a bet, my money would go on him.'

'Why?' An angry whiplash from Suvlov. He was angry with himself; they all understood that.

'Because he has the right qualifications,' Menichev spread his hands wide. 'There is no evidence – I mean hard evidence: the kind we would look for as police officers. But the logical evidence, the man's past, his training, experience, geographical position at the time of the invasion; his outlook, his professionalism – they all point to him.'

He went on to explain that the other two suspects did not have either the experience, or the qualifications, to operate in this manner.

'As a police officer, what would you say he's after?' Suvlov was more calm.

'You know that yourself. You have virtually told me already.' The little detective looked at him with weary eyes. 'He is here to make contact with United States' operatives who you have not yet uncovered.'

Suvlov asked if that was all, and Menichev shrugged, saying that he doubted it. 'There is probably something else. Instructions for the formation of covert resistance cells within Britain. Isn't that happening in the rest of Europe?'

Lupaiyev frowned, and Suvlov gave him a questioning look. 'Is there still resistance in the rest of Europe, Comrade Marshal?'

Lupaiyev gave a small flick of the head, muttering that there was a little. He did not wish to go into details concerning the series of bombings and shootings in Germany, France and the Low Countries; even in Italy and Spain. He certainly was not going to mention the assassination of three very high-ranking military governors, all of whom had died during the last week.

Suvlov was about to probe his senior even further, when Ashworth came in looking excited. 'They've found the car,' the Englishman blurted, and they all waited while he told them where and when. 'It could mean that he's got out. Disguised somehow, and got away on an aircraft. There would be some kind of contingency plan.'

'There would be.' The Marshal smiled benignly. 'But I doubt if he's gone. This man is still around – probably

106

somewhere near Heathrow, using forged papers, perhaps posing as one of us.'

It made sense to Suvlov, who nodded agreement and commented that the intruder might even be waiting for someone to contact *him*.

The Marshal asked Ashworth to pass him the telephone. He had to give instructions to his staff at the Savoy. 'A vital meeting. It will have to be delayed.'

As his hand moved towards the instrument, it started to ring and Suvlov sprang towards it like a cat. He spoke quietly into the mouthpiece and listened, nodding; then snapped his fingers at Ashworth, instructing him by nods and silent mouthing, to give him some paper and a pen. He then went on listening and nodding, holding the receiver against his ear, with his shoulder hunched up against his cheek, leaving the hands free to hold the paper and write.

Finally he spoke again and put the telephone down, turning to Ashworth and almost snarling at him to get the print-out on a man called Sir Graham Eldrich. 'I know he's in Camp Fifteen because I put him there, but we'll need his details.' Suvlov then turned to Lupaiyev. 'I think we have him.' The smile showed satisfaction as he added, 'And more.'

'Well?'

Suvlov quietly explained the latest news. A recently retired Foreign Service officer – Sir Graham Eldrich – had been on the SIS lists, as a possible American recruit, when Suvlov had scanned the computers during his first week in London. They had arrested Eldrich and kept him on ice, in Scotland. He had two men in Eldrich's old apartment in Eggerton Gardens – 'Just going through things and answering his telephone. Within the last hour they've received a strange telephone call.' He repeated what had taken place.

Lupaiyev frowned and spoke the words aloud – 'Skull a of place the?' his voice rising in query.

Menichev shifted his body slightly, like a man making himself more comfortable in sleep. 'The Christian Bible. The place of a skull. Golgotha. One of the gospels. Golgotha,

107

the place where Christ was crucified.'

Ashworth blundered back to say the printout would be down in a minute.

'Why reverse the words?' Suvlov spoke as though to himself.

Lupaiyev smiled. He had a fair idea why. 'Try it on this Eldrich man, and we'll see. Do we know who made this odd telephone call?'

Suvlov's face lit up as he inclined his head. 'Our man, I think. A guest at the Excelsior Hotel at Heathrow. They have a trace machine on the spot in Eldrich's apartment. I have several in the houses of possible American agents we're holding in custody. The call was very short, but they got a reaction, and rang the hotel security. The man is registered under the name of Alexei Simon Gorlky. He has a Soviet passport; very official.'

'And he is there now?' Menichev asked quietly.

The expression on Suvlov's face only changed slightly. He spoke evenly and with confidence. 'You were apparently correct, Comrade Menichev. The description is that of Paul Fadden.'

'Is he there now, though?' repeated the detective with a hint of steel in his voice.

Suvlov appeared unconcerned. 'He will return. All his things are there. My people missed him by a few minutes – ten minutes or so – all his things are in order, but he went, by taxi, to Piccadilly. He will be back before curfew. He has to be. He thinks he is safe.'

Lupaiyev rose, his face masked in anger. 'He had better return, Alexei Alexeioivitch. Your men did not think of getting the taxi checked? Trailed from the motorway once they knew? It should have been the first thing . . . '

'They were not fast enough. There were telephone conversations, but they were not fast enough. I think they were doubtful about using their own initiative.'

'Then see to it that someone who knows his job gets out to this Excelsior Hotel, so that we can control Comrade Alexei Simon Gorlky. And pray, Alexander. If he does not return, you will be up to your eyes in the shit.' He picked up his uniform cap. 'In the meantime, have this man Eldrich separated from the other prisoners in Camp Fifteen. Arrange a fast flight for the pair of us first thing tomorrow. Get the best men possible – Kalshinyev if he is free – to organise the surveillance of Fadden. Do not alert him; pass his description, but make sure that he is not stopped.' His voice rose. 'I want him watched every minute. I want to know where he is, who he sees, when he breaks wind, or takes a piss.'

'We'll have him, Comrade Marshal. He cannot evade us, it is impossible now.' Suvlov sounded very certain of himself.

'See to it then.' Marshal Lupaiyev did not look back. Suvlov was a good man, and would not make a second mistake. What the Marshal needed now was the meal they were providing at the Savoy, the company of the woman he had met last week, and the sexual pleasures that would follow. The evening and night ahead would set him up nicely for the work they would be doing in Scotland tomorrow.

★ 16 ★

The clothes Fadden wore did not draw undue attention in the vast foyer area of the National Theatre. It was a first night at the Olivier Theatre, but the mixture of dress just made him one of the herd. True, there were glittering ladies and men in evening clothes; many of the men were in uniform – both Russian and British. But there was also a good seeding of people in jeans, denim jackets, faded, shabby, suits, and even roll-necks under casual jackets and slacks.

Janet Fain had been appointed Director of the National Theatre only last year – angular-looking, a brilliant theatrical director since leaving university, she had made her mark with productions at the National very early in her career. Now, at the age of thirty-five, she had attained the pinnacle of success after three years at the Royal Shakespeare. The critics, Fadden recalled, had often accused her of being conservative – in the theatrical sense – and he had no doubt, when the appointment was first announced, that it was a left-wing socialist move. For all her astuteness, Janet Fain had always been content to direct the classics, or modern plays, with a left-wing bias.

Her famous production of *The Tempest* at Stratford-upon-Avon, for instance, was seen by everybody as a reading which accused Capitalism, and stood up for Marxist ideals.

For Janet Fain, tonight was another coup. Before the Soviet invasion of Europe she had enticed Lord Hall of Akenfield out of semi-retirement to direct a new version of *Hamlet*. The production had been held up, but the Soviet authorities had now given permission for its staging. Tonight, by fate, or coincidence, was the night when, at eight-thirty,

Lord Hall's *Hamlet* would get its official public airing.

Fadden had taken the risk of flagging down a taxi on his own initiative – waiting until he had walked briskly past the peeling, down-at-heel, building which had once been the Royal Garden Hotel, turned, by the last but one Socialist government, into a hostel for the homeless, as, indeed, had so many other large hotels, though they had been careful to leave places like the Savoy, Ritz and Dorchester intact.

The driver had been doubtful – Fadden would not show him a pass – but took a twenty pound note as bribery. Fadden disguised his voice and tried not to let the cabbie see his face. Now, in the concourse of the great grey bunker-like National Theatre, his face was in full view. He believed, however, that at functions like this, unless there were professional surveillance men at work, people just did not notice faces unless they were internationally famous.

Almost as soon as he entered, Fadden caught sight of several great names from the old world of theatre and cinema: Dame Vanessa Redgrave, walking with care, using a cane, and escorted by a Colonel General in the dress uniform of the Soviet Air Force; Sir Trevor Nunn, still looking surprisingly young for his years, talked with the elderly Roy Dotrice, who was now also forced to walk with a stick because of arthritis.

As he pushed his way through the rush, Fadden saw the aged Richard Harris go over to join the small group. Then, through the crowd and crush, he caught sight of Lord Hall, the grizzled beard and noble head turned towards the young and abrasive Janet Fain. Their companion was a now hardly-recognisable Sir Christopher Plummer, trapped in a wheel chair, a pretty nurse in attendance.

Golden lads and lasses must, like chimney sweepers come to dust, Fadden thought, sadly. Around him the crowd seethed and buzzed. A young British star, who had made his name in a few successful, left-wing orientated, movies for television, was coming in, besieged by a crowd of young people. Fadden smiled wryly to himself; for the youngsters had failed to notice the two other men escorting young girls,

111

a fraction of their ages, behind the popular figure. The two men still looking spry for their own advancing years. Unlike many others they were quite recognisable: Ringo Starr and George Harrison.

The five-minute curtain bell rang, and Fadden pushed harder into the crowd, heading to where Janet Fain was planting a kiss on Lord Hall's cheek, prior to going into the auditorium. He reached her as Lord Hall was saying, 'Thank you, Janet. God how I hate this.'

'Miss Fain, I'm sorry to bother you . . . ' Fadden began.

'Then don't,' she snapped, living up to her reputation of brash rudeness, moving away from him.

'Vesta,' Fadden half-whispered, so that it would catch her ear only.

The Director of the National Theatre stopped, as though by a thick invisible wall. Then she turned slowly to look at him. 'What did you say?' She came close to him now.

'I need to speak with you; most privately and urgently. Vesta.'

'Who sent you?' Her voice dropped, but she kept her face in repose, placid: a tall and very thin lady; angular, with a body that seemed to be made up of sharp points – nose, chin, ears, elbows; even the small breasts, exaggerated by the tight dress she wore, looked like pyramids. Janet Fain was a deceptive person physically: unattractive, asexual, yet Fadden could, even now, feel the immense static power that seemed to flow from her. Her unflagging energy was well-known, and her power of concentration legendary.

Again, Fadden knew he had to take risks. He glanced at his watch; the sweep hand did not even tremble. 'Don Marks,' he replied.

'One moment.' Janet Fain turned and called back to Lord Hall, who had now been joined by his wife, Lady Jacqueline. 'Peter, I may not be with you until the first interval. Something's come up in the Cottesloe.'

Fadden had noticed they were playing Ibsen in the Cottesloe, and Chekov in the third auditorium.

'Come.' Janet Fain strode ahead of Fadden, leading

through pass doors, up stairs, until they came to the administrative corridors. There was little noise; the offices were all empty. At last they reached the one marked, simply, *The Director*. She took him through the small ante-room, into the large office with its windows looking out over the river towards the Houses of Parliament.

As the door closed, Fadden glanced quickly at his wrist watch. Still no sign of devices.

Janet Fain stood her ground, head lifted arrogantly. 'Don't tell me they actually want me to do some work for them at long last?'

'Just sit down, Miss Fain.'

'Who are you?' She slid into an easy chair as she asked, and he did not even answer her question, speaking the trigger as soon as her body was in the chair.

Her reaction was the same as the other two women. A drowsy relaxing, after a momentary pause; Then the monotone stating that she required two names. Fadden said he did, and she began:

'First, Sappho. Real name Cork Halstead, freelance journalist; specialist in political and military affairs. Lives in a village near Oxford. The Elms, Cumnor. Telephone Oxford 3786 . . .'

Oh Christ, Fadden thought, they're doubling back on each other. He should have thought about that. The President had told him the cutouts would overlap their information regarding other contacts. At least one name out of each two, once he was at this point, would be new. She went on speaking.

'Second, Lark. Real name James Furnivall-Wells. Industrialist with good cover as a Socialist. Well thought-of by the Socialist governments, for his work in attempting to deal with the economy. Address: 40A Rutland Gate; business address Wells Holdings, 84 Farringdon Road; home telephone number 937–8350; Wells Holdings number 374–8696, twenty-eight lines. Suggest contact in open, or at home address.'

'Good.'

'What number do you want?'

'Three.'

Fadden concentrated hard, for she rattled the information off at speed:

'The co-ordinates will only be of use to you when in conjunction with a particular document. For safety, this document has been duplicated and placed in seven locations. It would mean nothing without the co-ordinates, and the locations are easily accessible. The document is sealed into the spine of copies of Walt Whitman's *Leaves of Grass* – as it has been computed this is the least borrowed book in any British public library; it is also unlikely to be removed by restriction. A treated copy will be found in three London Public Libraries – Marylebone; the Kensington and Chelsea Public Library; and Fulham Public Library. If access is unavailable, treated copies are also in Oxford Public Library, and the libraries at Hungerford and Ashford, in Kent. In the event of all these being denied, there is a further treated copy in the British Museum.'

Fadden paused for a moment – letting the information sink in. Then he wiped her memory clean. She took up where she had left off, asking who he was.

He told her to call him Paul, and she said she was taking one hell of a risk with him.

'And I with you. We don't know who's been turned or seduced.'

'Well, you can be bloody sure about me. What's the message? Can I start something? I'm itching to get at the buggers.'

Paul Fadden shrugged. 'I'm sorry, Miss Fain. The message is that you must keep the faith, and string along with them. Do as they ask. Co-operate. Things are happening.'

'Things are bloody hopeless.'

Fadden assured her that they were not. 'You'll be seeing me, or someone else, again soon. Things are far from hopeless.'

'We need some rabble-rousers. The British people have been in shock since before it happened. They're in deep trauma now. Even the Trades Unionists see their folly – wages cut, slave labour. And those silly fools who've sat on the fence for so long, going with the tide: bring back flogging and hanging. Well, they've got it with a vengeance now. We need a rabble-rouser; a resistance leader, and I happen to think I could raise a sodding army, Paul, whatever your name is.'

'You might just be asked to do that. I'm here to sound you out.'

'Is that all? You disappoint me.'

'Two other favours.'

'Speak away. I *am* in the giving vein today,' she hunched one shoulder up. Richard III in drag. An old movie came into his head – *The Goodbye Girl.*

'Is there a telephone in this place that's one hundred per cent untapped?'

'Of course. I've always had a special line. Untraceable. Had it done last year when I found the government were listening in to see if we were squandering their bloody money. Bypasses all switchboards. You want to use it?'

'If I could please.'

'And the other favour? My body?' She arched an eyebrow, and seemed to think it amusing.

'It's kind of you, but . . . ' He grinned.

'Pity,' she seemed suddenly serious. 'You're a nicely set-up man. What's the second thing?'

'I need some transport. Just to somewhere easy – like behind the Albert Hall. But transport in which I'm not going to be traced.'

'Easy.' She produced a key ring, and unlocked a drawer in her large desk. There was a telephone inside the drawer, and Janet Fain took it out, placing it on the desk. 'Dial away, Paul. I'll go and fix the transport.'

He picked up the instrument, then paused to ask if she had a code book.

'I thought they went out with Mata Hari.'

He explained it was a dialling code book he required, and she tossed one to him from a stack of directories balanced on a chair, then left, closing the door firmly behind her.

Fadden looked up the code for Oxford. He already knew about Cork Halstead – at least his reputation – for a couple of years ago he had run a trace on the journalist. There was talk of recruitment, but obviously the Americans had got there first; which probably meant the Soviets had him in their system by now – or dead. Unlike Eldrich, Fadden would know the sound of Halstead's breezy voice. He also knew the names of his beloved dogs, Wolfie and Emma. Halstead knew him on the telephone also, under an assumed name, of course. To Halstead, Paul Fadden was Dougie Shelving, a chinless wonder who had something to do with the Canine Defence League – dog lovers to the uninitiated.

He dialled the Oxford code, and then Halstead's number. The voice at the other end was unmistakable: gruff, hearty, even truculent – 'Halstead.'

'Cork, old chum,' Fadden affected the voice he used for chinless wonders.

'Who the hell's that? Just having me dinner.'

'Oh, sorry to bother you, sport. Haven't kept in touch. Dougie Shelving here. I'm checking all our members and associates – Canine Defence League, and all that. Wondered how Wolfie and Emma were faring under the new order of things.'

'Good God, "Bookie" Shelving. Nice to hear. The dogs're fine. Feeding them rabbit mainly. Snares you know, but . . . '

Fadden triggered him – 'Skull a of place the.'

116

⋆ 17 ⋆

The first name that Cork Halstead gave him was Mary Athay. The double-back again. The next was a shock, sending doubts clawing up into Fadden's head.

'Second, Stag. Real name Rupert Graves. Flat 5A, 7 Norham Gardens, Oxford. Telephone Oxford 6398. Recruited our service six years ago. Loyal in spite of outward political affiliations.'

He would have to be, Fadden thought. Graves had served in two Socialist administrations. The last he had heard, Graves had retired to write a book on the political future of the West under Socialism. If it was really all tied up, Fadden had to take off his hat to Don Marks and the men at Langley. They had placed the agents with cunning accuracy.

Halstead asked what number he required. Fadden told him number four, and the voice at the other end began its parrot-like speech.

'You may need paper for this. Destroy when you've completed. You already have thirty-five co-ordinates. They have not been given to you in order of precedence. You will need the order when you get to the goal. I shall read you the correct sequence, so that you can place the co-ordinates against their proper number. Are you ready?'

Fadden pulled out the notebook, which still contained the co-ordinates *en clair,* for there had been no chance to cipher them. He asked for a moment, uncapping his pen and holding it ready against the first co-ordinate, before telling Halstead to continue.

'The first you were given is really number five,' the voice droned on. 'I shall just read numbers from now on. Eight . . .

twenty-three . . . thirty-one . . . twelve . . . '

Fadden placed the notations next to each of the map references. If anyone picked him up now, they might just have something; but the President had been correct – he was starting to see light in the labyrinth. Dim, but there. What he saw was both hope and horror.

When Halstead completed telling off the numbers, Fadden took a deep breath and used the 'Calvary. Skull a of place the' wipe.

Halstead went on talking, as though he had not been interrupted . . .

'Snares. Probably illegal, but we've got to do our best for the dogs, "Bookie". How're things going in the cities?'

'We have our problems, Cork. Tussles with the Min of Environment as ever. Nothing's changed under the new order. They're still difficult to convince. You know there's talk of a bill to do away with all domestic pets? Gas the lot?'

'Been on the books for years, old boy. But they'll never do it. Not even with the Ivans leadin' 'em by the nose.'

'Look, Cork, you're eating, and I've got to phone a lot of people.'

Halstead laughed, 'Yes, the shepherd's pie's getting cold. Nice of you to think of me. Please let's hear again soon. I've got your number, I think.'

'I expect so.' There were a few more words of farewell chatter, then Fadden closed the line with a sigh.

He put the telephone back into the drawer, and went over to the door which led to the ante-room. Janet Fain sat there, a coat thrown over her shoulders. She asked if he had finished, and went back to lock the drawer.

'The transport?' Fadden asked.

'Do it myself,' she said. 'Safer. Nobody's going to question me here. I come and go as I please. You fit?'

He said he was ready.

'Let's just check where they've got to.' She turned the knob on a loudspeaker which stood on the desk. Immediately the sound came crackling through from the stage.

He recognised the voice of the famous young actor play-

118

ing Hamlet. They had reached the first ghost scene:

Be thou a spirit of health, or goblin damn'd,
Bring with thee airs from heaven or blasts from hell?

Apt, thought Paul Fadden, as Janet Fain clicked off the speaker. She nodded.

'Somewhere behind the Albert Hall, you said?'

'Do me fine.'

'Good. I'll be back to join Peter for the second half.'

He followed her down the stairs, and nobody, not even the Russian military security people at the doors, took any notice of him. They only had eyes for this great young lady of the Theatre – all skin and bones and jutting angles; but there was a strange quality which made people aware of her and drew their attention like magnets.

Again, Fadden thought how well the Americans had chosen their people.

She dropped him off in Prince Consort Road, and he left the car without a word. They could not have spoken anyway, except by shouting, for a huge old Antonov airliner was making its Heathrow approach too low, its ancient turbo-props shrieking for more power to boost it the further ten miles or so to touchdown.

Fadden walked quickly, hands in pockets and head lowered, up Queen's Gate and into Kensington Road. He would be glad to get back to the safety of Mary Athay's apartment. In the meantime his head buzzed with information; the notebook was burning a hole in his pocket, giving him the sensation that anyone could see through the cloth and on to the pages inside.

Nightingale – Hilary Keville – had given him the first clue, that it was his task to blow the last trump on the Soviets. The something which lay, sleeping, under the earth of Britain could only be wakened by him. Now there were map reference co-ordinates, which had been placed in a particular order; so, presumably, they would inform him where the sleeping instruments of death lay.

119

The document, hidden in the spine of a little-used book, would, he was sure, give him the true locations. There must also be some kind of control centre. The keys, given to him by the President himself, would be the keys to that particular kingdom, and there were still two more clues to trigger. Both of them had far left-wing cover, and would, he hoped, still be at large: the former politician in Oxford (though how the hell would he get out of London to Oxford?); and the business executive with the smart address in Rutland Gate.

For all the clever cut-outs and choices of agents, Don Marks – or whoever – had been taking a risk, placing most of the contacts within the London area. But there were, he supposed, technical reasons for that.

A police car, followed by a black Russian Volga saloon, sirens blaring, entered Kensington High Street, going at speed. As Fadden crossed the road, bringing himself nearer to Mary Athay's apartment buildings, he watched the two vehicles disappearing.

He did not know that they contained Metropolitan Police officers, together with the detective Menichev, Alexander Suvlov of the KGB, and his SIS assistant, Harry Ashworth. He did not know they were heading out to oversee surveillance on a man called Alexei Simon Gorlky at the Excelsior Hotel, Heathrow.

In turn, the occupants of the two cars were oblivious to the fact that they had just streaked past their quarry, whose photograph was now in the hands of most civil and military police, and army security personnel, in the London area.

He buzzed the Entryphone and Mary Athay answered.

'I didn't think you'd come back,' she said, her face still white, the eyes showing the same red rings. 'I really didn't, Paul.'

'Then you must learn faith.'

Without warning, she threw her arms around his neck and clung to him, like a child coming out of a nightmare. After a few moments she broke away, asking how long he planned to stay.

'As long as it takes. There's work for you to do.'

'Like making food?'

'To start with. Mary, have you got a library ticket?'

'For the one up the road? The Kensington and Chelsea? Yes.'

'Good. I want you to use it for me tomorrow. I also need to talk with you. We have to find a way for me to visit Oxford.'

'Can I come?'

'I reckon you'll probably have to come.' He leaned forward and kissed her lightly on the cheek.

She thanked him for returning, and he made some remark about her being his only hiding place. 'You'll be my legs, and voice as well, before we're through.'

'Anything.' She went on to say that she would get a meal, and clean up a bit. She must look terrible.

Absently, he told her she looked great, but his mind was on many things – putting the map references into cipher, and the problem of how he was going to contact Mr Furnivall-Wells. He felt that Furnivall-Wells should be the next port of call. Oxford had to be left until last.

Mary Athay had disappeared when he looked up, coming out of this reverie; and, for the first time since the horrors, so long ago now, with Pat, he felt the stirrings in his loins.

Slowly, he took out the notebook and began to turn the letters and numbers into a cipher which only he could break.

★ 18 ★

It was almost four in the afternoon in Washington, and Don Marks, Director of the CIA, had been closeted with the President for the best part of an hour.

In another office within the White House, the Secretary of State waited patiently, getting on with vital work, until called into the conference.

There was little that Marks could report, except the known facts that their agent, Theseus, was in and running; and that he had received a surprise flash, from a source in Dublin, that Nightingale was dead.

What Marks really wanted to talk about was the entire global situation. The information was still sporadic, but there seemed to be hope in the news of an upsurge in resistance attacks within the continent of Europe.

'For all their might, the Soviets are under pressure,' Marks repeated several times, ticking off the available facts on his fingers. They now knew, from the Dublin sources, that the vast airlift of essential supplies and luxuries into Britain – both to maintain the military and make the country a 'show state' – gave signs of dwindling.

'They're in trouble right across the board, and another month'll see them strapped for oil and gasoline. Napoleon and Hitler both failed to get to Moscow because of supply lines and the weather. Now it's going to work in reverse.'

'Can we help slow them down?' The President plucked at the papers on his desk. He looked, the Director thought, full of years and the weight of life.

Marks said that communication was the problem; just as it had been since the beginning. The hard information was not coming in at a higher rate. 'Because of the real fighting in Europe, it'll take months for them to get industry working – years maybe. I'm also told that the Middle East oil supplies are likely to be hit by so-called terrorists. Our own off-shore fuels are O.K. – which I suppose makes us the next prime target – but the Soviets were after territory, minerals, oil, and space to use advanced industrial technology. They have to maintain their occupation armies, and, without support, they'll either lash out at us or go to the wall.'

'And the Chinese?'

'You'll have to speak with the Secretary of State. Our communications with them are very good. They should not be underestimated. The Chinese are well organised within Europe, and it wouldn't surprise me if they're behind much of the resistance going on. They're certainly backing moves to hit the Middle East oil fields.'

They went on to speak about arrangements for the Dublin Summit. Tim McPherson was already there – 'Watching out for Theseus,' as Marks put it. 'If Golgotha gets really set, how much notice will you have, Mr President?'

The President thought for a long while, steepling his finger tips to his lower lip, in a characteristic manner. 'Depends on our man's freedom of movement; but the so-called Golgotha satellite should be sent into orbit on the day I arrive in Dublin. There is another way I can be alerted, but nothing's going to work without that satellite up there. The timing's crucial.'

They talked some more, and the Secretary of State was finally asked to come to the Oval Office. He brought good news. The Chinese had agreed to go public on the first day of the Dublin Summit. They would, at the appropriate moment, stand up and show themselves as allies of the Americans, repudiating the non-aggression pact with the Soviets. 'I've also had official confirmation that the Soviets have agreed to the other Heads of State being present – the British Prime Minister, France, all you wanted, Mr President.'

'Rome?' queried the President.

'His Holiness has agreed to a private audience, and we've got clearance from the Soviets. Air Force One'll be allowed into Rome, and you'll be given security to and from the Vatican.'

The President spoke for some time about the acts of resistance within Europe. It seemed the Secretary of State was even better informed than the Director of the CIA. 'We know there have been bombs, and acts of sabotage, on a large scale. You know,' he nodded at Don Marks, 'that at least three of the key Soviet military governors have been taken out. More appear to be planned.'

It was obvious to all three men that, if the pressure was continued, the Soviets could find themselves in a precarious fuel and supply situation within a matter of weeks. 'If your scheme works, Mr President, we'll have the Mexican stand-off of all time once you get to Dublin.'

The President did not smile. The old head nodded a fraction, and he murmured, 'Pray God it works.'

*   *   *

In London, the police car and the unmarked Volga drew up in the service area behind the Excelsior Hotel at Heathrow. They had turned off their sirens on reaching the M4 Motorway. Few people paid attention to them.

The Marshal had asked for Kalshinyev to take over the surveillance of the intruder, Fadden, because he was the most experienced officer in this field among the KGB team which now ran intelligence and security throughout the People's Democratic Republic of Britain. Kalshinyev was already there, at the Excelsior, waiting for them.

He came out of the service doors, walking slowly over the tarmac parking area to meet Suvlov and Menichev as they climbed out of the Volga. The British police officers got out of their car and waited for instructions.

Suvlov could have done without this chore, but after all the errors of the past twenty-four hours, he knew his presence was essential. If anything else went wrong, if they did not get Fadden under some proper control quickly, he would take the responsibility and the blame. Marshal Lupaiyev would be powerless to help him, and it would mean an immediate posting to one of the more difficult areas of Europe: a posting, and, almost certainly, some kind of demotion.

Kalshinyev was a small, nondescript man, like most of his particular breed. He spoke eight languages, was a wizard with electronics, and could easily pass as a native of any European country. He certainly did not look like a Russian, a quirk due to his mixed parentage. His father had been the product of a union between a French girl and a Russian officer. Kalshinyev's mother had been English.

Suvlov thought that Kalshinyev was like a chameleon. As he shook hands he could feel the dry, almost reptilian, touch of the surveillance man's hand. Suvlov said he had come to see what was being done, and Kalshinyev responded with a shrug which said, better than words, that there was really no need.

'We have done everything.' The surveillance man spoke in his soft, confident voice.

Suvlov asked if there was any doubt about the identity of the intruder, and Kalshinyev told him there had been the most positive identification. The man who had checked in at the hotel with a Russian passport, under the name of Alexei Simon Gorlky, was the Englishman, Paul Fadden. He looked up to see the face of Ashworth, concerned, behind Suvlov's shoulder.

'You are familiar with Fadden?' Kalshinyev asked Ashworth.

Ashworth nodded, 'I've met him. He's most experienced. Very experienced.'

'Then he's a worthy opponent.'

Suvlov scraped his toe along the ground, his right foot prescribing an arc. The shoes were Italian and beautifully polished. 'You are certain he's not alerted? That he'll return here?'

Kalshinyev smiled. 'Who can be certain? All I can tell you

125

is that my teams are here, and we have put our most sophisticated equipment into both his room and clothing. The girls who worked on reception when he arrived – in fact every member of the hotel staff who came into contact with him – have been removed to a safe place until we have him. There is no way he can escape once he returns. There is also little chance of him realising that he is being controlled.'

'If he returns,' Suvlov said, almost to himself.

'Quite.'

Menichev coughed, uneasily, clearing his throat before speaking. 'Comrade Kalshinyev: what do you really think? What are the true chances of the man returning?'

'I think he will come back. He is a stranger in his own country. He must know that we are looking for him, and he will be aware that the British police work with us. His resources will be limited. As far as I can see, he has left all his clothing here, together with his toilet gear. A man like Fadden, provided with such a high-quality passport, is probably also supplied with some other form of identification – and possibly a ticket, to get him out. He chose this hotel, so logic says he has an air ticket. I have men in the terminal buildings.'

'The chances, then, are in our favour?' Suvlov made it clear that the question was rhetorical. He wanted to believe that Fadden would be picked up and controlled from this hotel at the airport.

Kalshinyev said he felt the chances were much more than even. He then went on to ask for instructions, should Fadden try to board an aircraft and leave the country.

Suvlov was dogmatically firm. On no account must Fadden be allowed to leave. He was to be kept under control while he remained in England. If they wanted him picked up, Kalshinyev would receive a personal order, either directly from Marshal Lupaiyev or Suvlov. The order would come by a code phrase which Kalshinyev must pass to all his men. There must be no mistake, and the phrase would be relayed to all military and civil police units engaged in the search. The phrase would be, *Money is coined liberty.*

Kalshinyev and Menichev smiled to themselves. Ashworth looked puzzled. The Russians had immediately recognised the quotation from Dostoevsky. The whole phrase would have read – *Money is coined liberty, and so it is ten times dearer to a man who is deprived of freedom.*

Ashworth, punctilious about these matters, and knowing that it would probably be his job to issue the order when the moment arrived, made a note of the phrase in his standard issue paper-covered notebook.

On their way back into London, Suvlov felt happier than he had done since that morning, when he had shattered Hilary Keville's bedroom door and found her dead. He was confident that Kalshinyev would do the trick. When they got back to the building near Westminster Bridge he would pass on the code phrase for Fadden's arrest. The chances were more than even.

It was Menichev who took this small joy out of life. Sitting in the back of the Volga, Menichev appeared to be lost in his own particular brand of thought. At last he said, 'Comrade Suvlov, a word from me, as just an ordinary policeman. The British used to have a little cliché, that the murderer always returned to the scene of his crime; it is a phrase much used in British detective fiction of a certain woolly kind. Also it is not true.'

'So?'

'So, the only crime this Fadden has committed at the Excelsior Hotel is that of using false papers – a forged passport ... '

'Punishable by death.'

'True. I fear, though, that my instinct tells me Fadden has led us a small dance. Personally I disagree with Comrade Kalshinyev. I don't think he intends to go back to that hotel, or anywhere near Heathrow.'

At the very moment Menichev said this, the car was passing along Kensington High Street, almost abreast of the apartment buildings where Paul Fadden sat over dinner with Mary Athay.

★ 19 ★

Fadden thought Mary Athay's hoarded food was the best he'd tasted in years.

In spite of her protests that she had not expected him to return, she had not remained idle. There was a game soup – which came from a tin – followed by steaks, new potatoes, haricots verts, and a side salad, excellently dressed. All these things came from the freezer, as did the lemon sorbet. The wine was a 1982 St Emilion. 'You'll have to thank my late husband for that,' she told him. Tom had been keen on wines and laid down as good a cellar as he could, though the cellar in this apartment was, in reality, a small broom cupboard near the kitchen door which led to a fire escape. As for the freezer, the power cuts and rota system of electricity supplies, while harsh, had caused no catastrophic damage to the hoarded food.

Over dinner, Fadden prised from her the essentials concerning her undoubtedly unhappy marriage. He was going to handle her like a case officer and the information was important to him. She had only just qualified as a research chemist when the young politician began to court her. 'I knew it was a mistake as soon as I said yes. We didn't marry for nearly a year, and I kept my job – I kept it the whole time really. Isn't it funny, life? You can know something is going to work out badly, but you allow yourself to be hauled on into it; you don't resist? It was as though Tom had some terrible power over me.'

Fadden sat there eating, making only occasional comments, prodding her story on.

'In my head I was dragged down the aisle, kicking and

screaming. In reality I walked calmly, just like any other bride. Then, it was all over in a matter of months.'

Fadden expressed surprise that they had gone on living together. She said it was a trap, plus a good deal of habit. Tom owned the apartment, and she didn't want to go back to the States. 'I'd been recruited by then, and couldn't go back anyway. My case officer was a really clever customer. There were times when he specifically used my unhappiness with Tom to the advantage of the service. They were always dangling carrots – you know, "Do another year: stick at it, then we'll see about getting you home to the States."'

Fadden knew the way services handled agents – carrots, prizes, reward and punishment: all the psychological ruses. He nodded again.

'Tom always hinted that things would be better if I gave up my job: became a politician's wife full-time. But he wasn't a real politician, Paul. Anyway, my cover was in the job, and I was a bloody good research chemist. If I'd given that up, things would have been worse. I'd have just sat here and brooded.'

The red circles had disappeared from around her eyes: the face carefully made-up, and hair silky-smooth. She had changed into a linen dress which showed off her figure. The physical and mental attractions of this girl were without question.

As if reading his thoughts, she asked if he found her attractive – the question being at once naïve and candid.

'Come on, Paul. Tell me. You can't hurt me any more. Just tell me the truth.'

He said she was not just attractive, but desirable, and she laughed. 'Poor Tom didn't see it. I *know* I'm attractive and desirable. Women *do* know. But you have doubts when your husband tells you he doesn't want you, and it's your fault; that it's you who's unattractive, and asexual, and undesirable.'

'He said *that*?'

'That's what Tom said. He wouldn't even sleep in the same bed.'

129

Fadden made a motion meant to depict that the man had been a fool.

'It saps confidence.' She took a little sip of wine. 'I don't know what I am.'

Fadden said he understood, telling her some of the story about Pat and the way she had undermined his own masculinity.

'Book-ends,' she said when he finished. 'That's us, Paul. Book-ends.'

They talked about her work; music; the more recent books, before the Soviet attack; older books they had liked, enjoyed or hated. Paul Fadden began to weave his own questions into the conversation. At one point he asked how she managed without a telephone, and she said it was quite easy. She had a pass key to one of the ground floor flats that was vacant. 'They're supposed to be starting work on it soon – but that was last year. It's got plumbing and wiring problems, so they've never rented it since the last people left. But the phone's still working. I just use it.'

That was one problem solved. Gently he began to explain what he would require of her on the following day. They would both go down to the unused flat. She could make the call while he prompted her. Then he would need her to get the book from the library.

She grinned – they had reached the sorbet. 'What's in it for me?'

'The usual carrot. Back to the States, if everything works out.'

The look in her eyes became serious. 'You really mean that? Or just playing with me?'

'I really mean it. If everything works, I swear to get you back.'

She played with her sorbet, pushing it with her spoon, prodding at it, just as he was prodding at her mind.

'You said something about going to Oxford?'

'Yes. Another job for you. How to get there with the minimum bother. I gather that the trains are scarce nowadays.'

'They went back to steam – oh, years ago . . . '

'Over ten years ago. I'm English. Remember?'

'Well, it's only the long distance stuff that's scarce. You have to book weeks ahead for the North and Scotland. It's been like that for a long time.'

'I know. What I'm getting at – is it worse under this lot?'

'I think so, but places nearer to London are easy, I think. There wouldn't be any hassle getting to Oxford by train.'

'And security? What's security like at the stations?'

She paused for a long time, still pushing the sorbet around her plate, before saying that she honestly did not know. 'I told you. I've hardly been out of the flat since they took over.'

'Think you could manage a trip to Paddington, to do a recce for me tomorrow?'

She said of course, and they went on to talk of other things. Mary Athay kept going back to Fadden's last affair, with Pat, and the similarities between the way it had left him, and the mental and physical anguish her husband had heaped on her. Without being explicit, she conjured into his mind great sexual fantasies, so that he could almost see the pair of them coupled. She described the physical and mental despair of a woman in her situation ('I have this thing about not being promiscuous: and I really have to *want* the person. That's probably why I stayed with Tom. I wanted him so much. Nobody else.') Her nights were fevered, and the imagination ran riot with the idea of other bodies; what was possible; what was impossible.

Fadden wondered if it was the wine. Her eyes were calm and deep: dark blue and bottomless. She looked at him over her spoonful of sorbet – her tongue licking the dessert from the spoon slowly, then circling her lips.

He wanted to touch her; hold her close. Part of his mind knew he was being seduced; because he was there, and she liked him, and had need of him.

'Paul . . . ' The voice throaty.

'I know, Mary . . . ' He felt his body shaking, his hands trembling.

'Don't be afraid, Paul my dear. You've been sent to me.' Then, as though suddenly afraid, 'You will, won't you? I like you. It's not just any old quick thing to get relief. There's been nobody else for so long. Not love, or that folly . . .'

'I know,' he repeated, rising from the table and feeling her body close to his.

She told him she loved him, after the first time, as they lay in her bed which had been so badly used by her marriage. Gently, he said that love was a big word. She did not know him.

'I know enough,' she kissed him on the mouth, and the throat, and then, lower, under the sheet that covered them.

When they finished, she said again that she loved him, placing her fingers over his lips to stop him denying her the pleasure of saying it. 'There is an old French proverb,' she said quietly. 'Try to reason about love, and you will lose your reason.'

Fadden was elated because the devil, who had clung to his mind and between his legs since Pat, had now left him, and he would grant Mary any pleasure. They made love again, in a way she said she had always wanted, and it was better than he had ever remembered it in all his life. He supposed that, while most of this was lust, and the salving of bodily needs, there was a kind of love in it also.

So they dozed, woke, fondled one another, kissed, entered each other, drew together becoming one person, then dozed again.

The world outside: Britain defeated from within; Europe enslaved; the desperate labyrinth of Golgotha, lay far away. For a time they rested in the oasis of her bed, floating from reality. Reality would return quickly enough with the dawn. And while they slept, desperate things were happening in the world,

★ 20 ★

While Paul Fadden and Mary Athay loved and slept, there were eruptions in the world. Along the whole great oil-producing areas of the Middle East, vast explosions rocked wells, pumps and refineries – great blasts which set oil wells ablaze, and sent volcanoes of fire through the pipes which carried the precious fuels to the refineries.

The same thing happened to fuel storage dumps, from one end of Europe to the other, and among the off-shore rigs in the North Sea.

The Chinese had trained men – Europeans – for years now, to take this kind of action if necessary. Because the Soviet intelligence services had concentrated mostly on their counterparts in Europe, the Chinese operation had gone undetected. Now, even Mother Russia was not safe. Eight of her main vast fuel dumps were raging infernos by the morning.

That was not all. Terrorist attacks came, with death and stealth, among the Soviet forces throughout Europe. Only Britain remained clear of these assaults. Aircraft on the ground were set ablaze; troop concentrations were bewildered by the sudden triggering of well-placed napalm devices; and over three hundred mobile nuclear launch-pads were spiked, the controls to move the giant caterpillar launchers blown away by relatively small charges the guidance systems were smashed with similar apparatus. The crews of these important strategic battle weapons were machine-gunned, caught by surprise. The resistance terrorists melted away into the night, as though they had never been.

The same thing happened in major cities: buildings occupied by military command staff in Paris, Brussels, Rome, Madrid, Lisbon, Oslo, Berlin, Amsterdam and Stockholm were gutted.

The Chinese had worked on this kind of action for years, and not necessarily to thwart a Soviet act of aggression in Europe. In the beginning, the teams were trained secretly as a plan to bring down the already failing Western economy. Now, it had more far-reaching effects.

* * *

Marshal Lupaiyev was advised of the carnage, and crippling spear aimed at the Soviet heart, in the early hours of the morning. His night had been more successful than he had dared hope, the girl most pliable, and conducive to certain sexual peccadillos in which the Marshal revelled. The telephone, when it rang, was an intrusion into his special privacy. But when the extent of the news was given to him, he became wide awake very quickly.

His opposite numbers in other countries were running in circles; arrests were being made on a large scale. Blame had to be pinned somewhere, and local possible agitators were the best bet. Nobody really thought of the Chinese. They did think of the Americans. Marshal Lupaiyev was told that the propaganda departments were working on suitably-worded texts which would, by inference, point fingers at the United States.

For the first time, Lupaiyev was a little frightened. If it was the Americans, then this could be the true reason for the infiltration of the intruder, Fadden, into Britain. It was possible, even probable, that Fadden was there for the sole purpose of activating cells similar to the ones which had caused such havoc throughout the rest of occupied Europe.

He telephoned Suvlov, who sounded depressed. He too had heard the news, which was not being released through any public channels until some blame could be apportioned.

But the mainspring of his present low spirits was the message he had received from Kalshinyev. Fadden had not returned to the Excelsior Hotel, either before curfew, or, covertly, during the night.

The priority was obvious. A jet would be waiting within the hour to carry the Marshal and himself up to Scotland, to Camp Fifteen, where Sir Graham Eldrich was being held. They would see what that interrogation would produce.

The Soviet 'Peace Keeping Force' in Britain had done incredible things in a very short time, within the borders of their new satellite island. Through some of the old ways of legislation, and the British constitution – which had been slightly amended – they had brought in draconian repressive measures against all forms of crime, both civil and political. The old prisons could not cater for the victims of the new laws, so, within ten days of the new regime taking effect, work was started on what were known with awe as the Scottish Camps. There were four of these only, though they were numbered Ten, Fifteen, Twenty and Twenty-Five. All were set in remote areas: in glens, and at the foot of mountains, renowned for their beauty. All thought of beauty was swept away with the building of the camps. None of them was yet complete, the prisoners being forced to build under the direction of Soviet specialists and guards. The only one which was running well, and almost finished, was the political Camp Fifteen.

The camp was situated in a bleak area of the Southern Uplands, that part of Scotland made up of rolling moors and rocky cliffs, which is subject to one of the heaviest rainfalls in Britain.

To old people, and those who had seen the film and photographs which came out of Germany and the occupied Europe of the 1940s, the very sight of Camp Fifteen was enough to stir memories of long-lost horror.

With its high electrified fences, observation towers, drilled rows of prefabricated huts and administrative blocks, Camp Fifteen could have been a film set replica of the repulsive Nazi Concentration Camps – those great dark blots which would forever stain the history of man's inhumanity.

Outside the main perimeter fence, a long metalled runway and helicopter pad had been built. It was to this destination that the small Yakovlev military executive transport took off from Northolt Airbase, on the fringes of outer London.

Marshal Lupaiyev and Suvlov sat together, heads bent in serious conversation. Harold Ashworth had been left in London, but the detective, Menichev – who looked more suety than usual, because of his aversion to air travel – went along for the ride.

They roared off the main Northolt runway just before eleven-thirty. At eleven thirty-five, Paul Fadden and Mary Athay were entering the empty flat on the ground floor of the apartment block in Kensington High Street.

*   *   *

Fadden had explained, in detail, what he wished Mary to do. She dialled the number of Wells Holdings, in the City of London, and told the switchboard that there was a top priority call for Mr Furnivall-Wells from the Central Trade Delegation Offices. No, he wasn't expecting it, but the urgency was so great that, in his own interests, he should accept the call.

There was a thirty-second delay before Furnivall-Wells identified himself on the line.

'I have the First Secretary for you,' Mary said, and Fadden took the instrument from her hands.

'Mr Furnivall-Wells?' Fadden distorted his voice into a nondescript accent.

'Wells here, yes. First Secretary, Trade, they said.'

'It's quite a *lark*, isn't it, Mr Wells?' Fadden stressed the word lark (the cryptonym given by the triggered Janet Fain), crossing his fingers, in the hope that Wells was as quick on the uptake with words as he was with business matters. In the back of Fadden's mind he was also conscious of the major risk he now ran. But it was the same

136

with all of them: any one of the contacts could have been turned, as he was certain Hilary Keville had been.

'You require?' The two words seemed, over the line, to be an indication that Wells understood.

'An urgent meeting.' Fadden wanted to keep the conversation as short as possible. He knew there might be a direct tap on Wells Holdings' switchboard. If this was the case, he prayed there would be no immediate traceback to the telephone from which he spoke, and no connection, in the minds of listeners, with himself. He was certain that, by now, whoever was in charge – following Hilary Keville's death – must have made a positive identification. By using the Russian passport at the Excelsior Hotel he had left himself wide open.

'You want to come here?' Furnivall-Wells was fast, clipped – the traditional businessman under pressure, used to making quick decisions.

'Your place, I think. In the gardens, perhaps. A stroll outside would be pleasant.'

'I'll be there by five. Come to the house. If the weather stays fine, we'll have tea in the garden.'

'Good.'

'See you then.' The line was closed abruptly, signifying to Fadden that Wells equally desired to keep the conversation to a bare minimum.

He turned to Mary Athay, who began to ask what it was all about; she had done so several times, and he had been forced to caution her to remember her training. 'Need-to-know is a principle of all tradecraft. There is no need for you to know. Just obey, and, if everything goes well, I'll get you back to America.'

'Now,' he snapped, 'out fast. Back upstairs first, then the trip to the library.'

She nodded, pausing only to give him a small kiss on the cheek.

Within ten minutes, Fadden was waiting, alone, in her flat while she took the short walk up to the Kensington and

Chelsea Public Library, to withdraw their copy of Walt Whitman's *Leaves of Grass*.

If she could get it, he would spend the next few hours taking it apart, examining the document sealed into the spine, and seeing what sense he could make of it, in conjunction with the reference co-ordinates ciphered in his notebook. Mary Athay would be out for most of the afternoon, having a look around Paddington station and seeing about trains to Oxford.

Then, if the meeting with Furnivall-Wells went without hitch, there would only be Stag – Rupert Graves – in Oxford. Get him, and Fadden would have all six clues: the labyrinth of Golgotha would be negotiated; he would know what to do next.

He paced the room, waiting for Mary's return, his mind, flashing like one of those old neon signs, between the pleasures and joys – the rediscovery of last night – and the urgent, life and death matters in which he was so deeply involved.

Occasionally he glanced out of the windows, down into the High Street. There seemed to be a lot of activity. Military traffic had been passing, in a series of convoys, all morning. There were two patrols of military and civil police, moving up and down the pavements on both sides of the High Street, stopping people, it seemed, at random; checking papers.

It was not far to Rutland Gate, but he would have to give himself plenty of time, and take the greatest care. He was so near to the final goal, and yet so far from it.

Mary Athay took just over half an hour. She returned, with the book clutched tightly, like a baby, to her breast. She had been stopped once, she told him. It seemed to be purely a routine check on identification papers; but she had noticed that more men than women were being approached.

Fadden put the book to one side, and they ate together, quickly. She had taken bread, cheese and butter from the freezer in the early hours. There was electricity in the area for this day, so she also heated another of her hoarded cans

138

of soup. They drank Perrier water, of which she appeared to have a vast supply. Fadden insisted on no alcohol. Both of their heads must be clear for the afternoon's work.

Just before they sat down to eat, unknown to either of them, the Yakovlev jet containing Lupaiyev, Suvlov and Menichev, was making its final approach over the scrub and moorland, down on to the threshold of the runway running alongside Camp Fifteen in Scotland.

★ 21 ★

The Commandant of Camp Fifteen was a big, raw-boned Colonel: a man whose face showed his ancestry lay among the old peasant families of Russia as plainly as if he had displayed a label on his chest to proclaim the fact.

The Commandant, a career officer of the Soviet Army, had no sentiment about the job he held in Scotland. To him, the orders were there to be obeyed. He obeyed them to the letter. If the General Staff, or High Command, issued a directive saying he was to shoot all the prisoners, he would have done it without turning a hair. Equally, if the order was to shoot himself, he would have taken a pistol to his head immediately.

When the directive had arrived, the previous evening, to separate Sir Graham Eldrich from the other prisoners, the job was done within ten minutes. Half of that time was taken up in checking Eldrich's name against his prison number. Prisoners at Camp Fifteen lived without names.

Some knew, or recognised, each other; but they all carried numbers stencilled on to their drab grey overalls. It was forbidden to use real names.

When he was called, prisoner 44533A had been eating his slice of dark bread, dipping it in the cup of dishwater soup that was his evening meal, and two armed guards led him away to a block half a mile from the main concentration of huts.

While the whole camp ran on a high-security basis, with four electrified fences surrounding it, this small, concrete block, set in one corner of the complex, was cut off from the rest of the camp by an extra fence. From the air it looked like a small square in the top left-hand corner of the huge rectangle.

Sir Graham Eldrich – Prisoner 44533A – looked an old man; gaunt, with shaking hands; the once famous shock of white hair now thin and unkempt, while the normally erect stance had disintegrated to a shambling and stooping attitude, through the meagre diet and back-breaking work forced upon him so suddenly. In fact, Graham Eldrich was only fifty-six years of age. He looked seventy. He also looked as though he was dying.

The cell, where he slept for that one night, was more comfortable than the stinking barrack block which he normally shared with fifty other inmates. There was a bed and blankets; privacy; a decent toilet and – to his surprise – a reasonable meal waiting for him. The Commandant knew the value of presenting prisoners in moderately good condition when senior KGB officers wanted to see them. This prisoner was also provided with a shave and haircut, by the military barber, and an entire change of clothes.

At least he looked, and smelled, clean, fresh and slightly rejuvenated when they unlocked the cell, telling him to follow them down the short corridor leading to a bare room, equipped only with a table (screwed to the floor) around which stood four, equally immovable, chairs. The guards told him to sit down, their English confined only to the simple words, 'Sit there. Stand when officers come.'

Graham Eldrich felt no fear. He had accepted death as the natural outcome of his arrest, from the moment the military had bundled him into a car and driven him, wordlessly, to the station. He was not so happy about the secrets he held safe – that he was a recruited agent of the United States Central Intelligence Agency – though he thanked his God that he had few names to give them; even under the use of most sophisticated drugs.

One, or both, of two things would happen to him now they had brought him to this part of the camp. Either a death

141

warrant would be read and he would suffer the penalty quickly; or they would interrogate him at length. He longed for the first, not relishing the second, but knowing the odds were in favour of both.

He had slept with few nightmares in these new surroundings; undisturbed by the male animal noises of men, close-confined in bad conditions. They fed him late, and he heard aircraft noise shortly before the guards took him to the room where he now sat, trying to compose himself, averting his eyes from the two soldiers who stood by the door, their Kalashnikovs crooked under their arms like men on a game shoot.

There was hunger in the soldiers' eyes: the hunger to kill, for most of the guards at Camp Fifteen resented doing eternal sentry and watchtower duty. They would have preferred to have been out in more dangerous places. It was not their idea of soldiering, though this was the precise thinking of the senior officers who had sent them to the Camps. Battle-starved troops would always shoot first and ask questions afterwards. One clash with the prisoners would dissuade even the bravest among those incarcerated in Camp Fifteen, from causing further trouble.

Footsteps echoed down the short passage. There was the harsh clang of locks, and the metal door opened. The two soldiers came to attention, and the Commandant entered, followed by three men in civilian clothes – the Marshal, Suvlov, and Menichev.

Prisoner 44533A rose, tried to square his shoulders, and remind himself of his background, his family, and the place he once held in his country's service.

'Sit down, Sir Graham. My name is Constantin Mikhilov Lupaiyev. I hold the rank of Marshal in the Komitet Gosudarstvennoy Bezopasnosti. This exalted rank makes me the chief of this organisation within the Peace-Keeping Soviet Forces operating, at the request of your legal government, within the People's Republic of Britain. You understand?'

'I understand, but do not recognise the People's Republic.'

Graham Eldrich forced his voice to come out strong and without waver.

'Of course not.' Lupaiyev smiled pleasantly, then turned to the Commandant and spoke in Russian, telling him that neither he nor his guards would be required. The guards could wait at the end of the passage.

The Colonel Commandant saluted and gave a sharp order to the pair of soldiers. The three men left, and, with the same politeness, Marshall Lupaiyev introduced Suvlov and Menichev, gesturing that Graham Eldrich should sit.

Menichev took out cigarettes and offered one to the prisoner, who refused, saying he had not smoked since schooldays. Suvlov asked how he was being treated.

'I'd be more comfortable at the Reform.'

The three men seemed to enjoy the little joke. It showed spirit.

'Seriously, Sir Graham. How do you find it here?' Menichev asked. He even sounded really interested.

'It's foul. The food, what there is of it, stinks. The conditions are not fit for cattle.'

'Yet it is newly-built,' Suvlov spoke absent-mindedly.

'And fouled by bad sanitation and overcrowding. Your people have created the conditions out of psychological purpose.'

Lupaiyev spread his hands, and said they had business to discuss. 'Business,' he said quietly,' which could have you out of here, and into a decent job in a matter of hours.'

Inside his head, Graham Eldrich noted the bait. This was simple, elementary, stuff. Play to them. 'Anything in particular?'

'What does the name Fadden mean to you? Paul Fadden?' asked Suvlov.

'Nothing.' It was true; he had never heard of Paul Fadden.

Suvlov continued. 'Can you honestly tell us, Sir Graham – and I should stress the honesty, for we know a great deal already – that you have not worked for any intelligence service? British? American?'

Eldrich shook his head.

'Aloud please,' Suvlov still spoke quietly.

'The answer's no.'

'You realise that we could hook you to a device that would tell us if you're lying? In fact we do not need wires. For all you know, this room is monitored. Again, do you, or have you ever, worked for any intelligence service?'

'Not worked for them.' Graham Eldrich had been trained how to play interrogators. The maximum truth with the minimum information.

'Not worked for them.' Lupaiyev leaned over the table. 'What does that mean in precise terms, Sir Graham?'

'I was approached. Recruited. But never actually worked.'

'For whom?' Suvlov spoke again.

'The Americans.'

'And who did the recruiting?'

'I did not know his name. I knew no real names.'

'And you refused to work for this service?'

'No.'

Suvlov sighed. 'But you have just said you have never worked for an intelligence service.'

'Correct.'

'You were approached and agreed. You have said this.'

'I was never used. I have never *worked* for them.'

'They talked to you?'

'Yes.'

'How many times?'

'Several. I didn't keep count.'

'One person?'

'Three or four.'

'And you did not know them?'

'I did not know their names.'

Lupaiyev touched Suvlov's arm, to signify that the next question was his. 'Did they train you? Take you to some centre? Give you some course?'

'Not as such; no.'

Lupaiyev continued, 'They just talked to you?'

144

'That's correct.'

'Did they speak of any acts of terrorism, these name-less Americans?'

'Certainly not.'

'And when was this?' Suvlov asked.

'Many years ago. Long before the present troubles started.'

'Be precise.' Suvlov snapped hard this time.

'Around about 1979.'

There was a silence, filling the room, for a few seconds which felt like minutes. Then Lupaiyev asked if he really expected them to believe the Americans had recruited him as long ago as 1979, and never used him.

'It's the plain and simple truth.'

Both the KGB officers looked at the foxy, experienced, Menichev, who shrugged and nodded, indicating that this, together with Graham Eldrich's demeanour, had all the hall-marks of truth.

Lupaiyev tried once more. 'At no time were acts of terrorism, within Soviet countries, or possible occupied countries, discussed?'

'Terrorism does not figure in the American intelligence field.' Eldrich took a short breath. 'I'm sorry, gentlemen, the straight answer is no. I was approached, agreed to work for them, but was never used.'

Lupaiyev turned towards Menichev and gave him the pre-arranged signal. They had decided that Menichev would say the words which had been reported by the men monitoring Eldrich's telephone in Eggerton Gardens. Suvlov reached for his notebook and pen.

Menichev leaned forward, looking hard at Sir Graham Eldrich. 'Skull a of place the.'

Eldrich relaxed, eyes dulling. Then, in a monotone, 'You need two names?' he asked.

Menichev remained calm. 'Yes.'

'First, Vesta. Real name Janet Fain: first woman director of the National Theatre. Private address, flat in the Barbican Building in the City of London. Ex-directory telephone. Can be approached at the National Theatre. Second, Lark. Real name James Furnivall-Wells: Industrialist, with good cover as a socialist. Well thought-of by the socialist governments for his work in attempting to deal with the economy. Address: 40A Rutland Gate; business address, Wells Holdings, 85 Farringdon Road; home telephone number 937-8350; Wells Holdings number 374-8696, twenty-eight lines. Suggest contact in open, or at home address.'

Survlov wrote furiously. There was a mildly shocked expression on Lupaiyev's face.

'Good,' Menichev said.

'What number do you need?' asked Graham Eldrich.

The three men looked at one another. The silence lengthened.

Eldrich repeated the question. Desperately Lupaiyev tried to make some calculations. By now he realised what was happening: that Eldrich was one in a chain of people who had secrets locked in their subconscious minds – secrets which could be released by this strange form of words. They had the names of two people who were part of the chain, though heaven knew whether either had yet been approached by Fadden. Hilary Keville had been killed. Slowly Lupaiyev argued, in his mind, that Hilary Keville's death could well mean that the first person in the chain had not given up her secret. He held up one finger to Menichev.

The policeman opened his mouth, as though to argue, then thought better of it. 'One,' he said.

Graham Eldrich repeated, word for word, exactly what Hilary Keville had told Fadden on that first night in London:

'You are starting the ascent of Golgotha, then. Under the ground. Below the earth, here in England, Salvation to the occupied. Salvation through death and destruction from under the earth; and they will rise from the dead places only when you blow the last trump. You must find the last trump, and the keys you hold are to either the Alpha or the Omega. The others will reveal more.'

Suvlov still wrote frantically. Lupaiyev held up two fingers.

146

'Two,' Menichev's voice was hardly raised above a whisper.

Eldrich remained seated, relaxed, the eyes still staring out, dull from his head, as though no brain or intelligence lay behind them. He did not speak.

'Two,' Menichev repeated; louder this time.

★ 22 ★

Fadden waited until Mary Athay left the apartment block to go to Paddington Railway Station. He briefed her thoroughly – not simply about train times and delays, but especially the amount of security operating at the terminal.

Over lunch, she flirted with him, pretending it was all a game. He knew the symptoms well enough, the marks of deep fear. The flirtation turned to invitation. She wanted to feel him within her again, before venturing into the world. He was gentle, telling her there was no time. In his own mind he held the unspoken thought that it may take a long while to deal with whatever was hidden, sealed, in the spine of Whitman's *Leaves of Grass*.

She tried right up until the moment he said she must go, being by turns seductive and petulant. She sat, at one point, facing him with her skirt pulled high; kissed him, placing a hand between his thighs.

Fadden's body reacted, his mind whirling between the immediacy of desire, and the urgency of the work which had to be accomplished.

Just before he ordered her to leave, reinforcing the fact that priorities must be observed, she began to talk lewdly. 'Tell me about your first woman, Paul? Go on, tell me. I won't be jealous.'

For a second the distant memory returned: night; darkness, and the shrubbery on the hillside. The girl small and very young, as he had been, ruled by her body, as he worked her into submission. He could not see her face, or her body, now all these years later as the act flashed through his memory.

'I'll tell you about mine,' she said, coming closer.

'Mary, no. Tonight. After we've both done what has to be done today. Tonight we'll talk and do anything you want.'

He said he would be leaving soon after four. That she was to wait for him and not worry. At last, she accepted the situation, held on to him, hard and long, leaving quickly, turning her face away so that he would not see either the fear or the tears.

Alone, Fadden took the book, and his own notebook, to the table in her main room. He sat down and began to strip off the binding with care, using a sharp cooking knife from the kitchen.

It had been done with great skill: the spine removed, a false pocket sewn on to the inside, and then the whole sealed up before the spine was replaced. Nobody could have detected the join in the leather.

From the pocket, Fadden gingerly removed the long, thin, folded paper, opening it up to its full size, spreading it on the table in front of him. It was about the size of two sheets of what they used to call A4 paper, or, in earlier days, almost foolscap size, so thin and soft that it would probably tear easily. It was a highly-detailed map of what used to be known as the British Isles, the whole overlaid with grids, but in a scale Fadden had never seen before. The map, its scale and grid system, would be an unrepeated one-off job – the plates smashed once the few copies were taken.

The reference co-ordinates, ciphered and numbered in his own notebook, would mean nothing on any other map.

Slowly, Fadden worked out the references, all thirty-five of them. At first they appeared to have little pattern; and even when he did find one clue to some of them, it did not apply to the others.

Some of the references took him directly on to spots which he knew had been United States bases before Britain had made the Americans withdraw from her shores – Alconbury, Mildenhall, Lakenheath were there, as were Greenham Common, Upper Heyford, Woodbridge, and others. These made sense, but there were further pinpoints, which seemed random until Fadden thought deeply about it.

Those which were not near, or on, old United States NATO sites, were all in areas not readily accessible: remote places; the middle of forests; pieces of land far from any beaten track. The more he looked at the map and its reference points, which he numbered appropriately, and lightly, in pencil, the more he understood.

It was almost four o'clock when he folded the map into its original shape, and placed it within the spine of one of Mary Athay's books, shelved down the wall to the right of her electric log fireplace.

He chose a copy of Graham Greene's *Journey Without Maps* – she had a whole set of Greene, in the nice old Bodley Head matching edition, and Fadden smiled at the ironic choice.

He checked the Stechkin. The sun still shone, but, looking down into the street, Fadden could see, by the way people walked, that there was a light, and probably chill, breeze.

He put on the raincoat, thrusting the Stechkin into the right hand pocket. Below, there were quite a few pedestrians in the street, but no sign of the police and military activity of the morning.

It is often better to go naked and without disguise. He heard the words of one of his old training officers, from way back, echoing in his head. *If many people are looking for you, few will have a truly distinctive picture of your height and manner in their heads.* Fadden knew this to be a reasonable risk. In his mind, he had worked out the route with care, taking mainly back-doubles, and unlikely crossing points, to Rutland Gate. He waited until almost twenty past four before leaving.

★ 23 ★

They worked for over an hour on Graham Eldrich, but with
no effect. Lupaiyev became agitated, telling Menichev to try
every possible number. Eldrich did not respond.

'Just as there was a phrase to unlock his mind, there must
be another to bring him back,' Menichev advised. 'We
should have a doctor. The man is mentally suspended. He
answers no questions. Reacts to nothing.'

Both Lupaiyev and Suvlov urged the detective to try
variants of the 'Skull a of place the' phrase. Nothing worked.
Referring back to the notes of what the man had actually
said, Suvlov suggested they added the word Golgotha. It was
no use.

At last, Lupaiyev, out of impatience and frustration, and
full of the knowledge that they had at least two names to pull
in London, said a doctor should be brought – 'A specialist
who knows about these things: post-hypnotic suggestion:
hypnosis in general,' – and they should take off for Northolt
immediately.

Suvlov wanted to telephone Ashworth to set the ball in
motion – have the police, or some of his own men, bring in
Janet Fain and James Furnivall-Wells for questioning.
Lupaiyev was tempted, but the catch was so important, and
the flying time so short, that he refused to risk a telephone
mention of the names, even on a closed and secure line.

The Commandant was told that his prisoner was in a post-
hypnotic coma, and a doctor was ordered to fly up from
London. They were not to know that, built in to the subjects
was a time key which released them from the hypnotic state

six hours after entering it, should something go wrong with the un-triggering.

At just before three-thirty, the Yakovlev jet rotated, and lifted off the landing strip beside Camp Fifteen. The only concession Lupaiyev had made was a radio order, for Ashworth and a team of Suvlov's men to be waiting for them with cars and a police escort, at Northolt. Their flying time from Scotland would be under an hour. With luck they would be snarling through the evening traffic by about four forty-five.

On the aircraft they discussed the priority of the names they were to arrest for questioning. Then they turned to the more serious business of making sense of the Golgotha and Last Trump speech which Eldrich had repeated.

Menichev joined the two KGB officers at the small table, fitted into the executive cabin of the aircraft. Lupaiyev was explaining the ramifications of the news which had reached them that morning, concerning the widespread and devastating attacks throughout the Western world.

'I am told we can only regard these acts as American-inspired and organised.' The aircraft lurched slightly, in a patch of high turbulence. 'Much planning went into these attacks, and Britain is almost the only country unaffected.'

Suvlov frowned. 'There were reports of fuel dumps being destroyed in Russia itself. Some of the old satellite states – Poland, Czechoslovakia, Yugoslavia, Bulgaria – have not been hit though. Nor has Greece or Turkey.'

Greece and Turkey, by mutual consent, had both become satellite states of the Soviet Bloc in the mid-eighties, as a result of a bungling attempt by the American Secretary of State, of that time, to bring peace between the two countries. The Soviets had stepped in and produced a peace plan which resulted in both countries being made part of the spreading Eastern Bloc.

Menichev gave Suvlov a sly look. 'You're suggesting that these assaults could have been inspired within our own states?'

'Not at all. I'm stating facts aloud. Putting the record

152

down; sifting the evidence, just like a detective.'

Menichev nodded, as though he had been reproved. 'Marshal, you are suggesting that these acts of terrorism are all American-organised, and that the man we seek – Fadden – is on a mission to activate cells to carry out similar attacks in Britain? Here, among us?'

The Marshal nodded. 'It seems obvious; just as it is obvious the Americans have cells already here, unknown to us, and, it would seem, hidden from the British Intelligence Services.' He gave a quick glance at Suvlov; for it was Suvlov's responsibility to comb the British files.

'We were aware that the British must have missed a few of their people.' Suvlov had hardly smiled since hearing Eldrich's Golgotha message. 'But not on the scale needed for these sort of attacks.'

Menichev coughed drily and apologised. It was the air conditioning in the plane, he said. It always made his throat dry. He continued, 'Perhaps they do not need many people to carry out such acts. That would appear to be the gist of this strange talk about an ascent to Golgotha.'

'The images are all Christian.' Lupaiyev stated the obvious.

'Indeed.' Menichev did not need to look at Suvlov's notebook. He was long trained in memory. 'The secret imparted by Eldrich is the kind of semi-poetic, allegorical, and obvious spoken cryptogram which both the British and Americans have used for years. Break it down.' He coughed again. 'Fadden is sent to ascend Golgotha – the place where Christ died on the cross, only to rise again three days later.'

'Three days would have a significance?' Suvlov asked.

Menichev shrugged. 'Who can say? But there are things of greater significance. The message talks about salvation coming to the occupied, from under the earth.'

'Death and destruction from under the earth,' Suvlov read from his notes. 'They will rise from the dead places when you blow the last trump – that is when Fadden blows the last trump.'

'The end of the world,' Menichev said coldly. 'And

153

Fadden had to find the last trump. That is the reason for the other names. There are people with clues who can be triggered by a use of certain words – the words we used. They will lead him to the last trump. He has keys, these could be real, or the clues. The information in these clues will bring Fadden to the hiding place of the last trump.'

Lupaiyev looked tired. He said, wearily, that Fadden was, presumably, programmed, like the others, to 'blow the last trump'; which might mean simply pressing a button.

'To bring about the end of the world?' queried Suvlov.

'Either the Alpha or the Omega,' Menichev quoted. 'Biblical. Greek. The beginning and the end. The beginning or the end.'

'So what are your deductions?' Lupaiyev already knew.

Menichev gave one of his characteristic shrugs. 'If the Americans were responsible for the attacks during the night, they could easily have planned something far more devastating for Britain. They tend to become petulant with the British when they do not co-operate. Look at history: in 1949, after the Great Patriotic War. When they feared we would turn upon Britain, the Americans were prepared to sacrifice her.' Even all these years and decades after World War II, they spoke of it as the Great Patriotic War, with a sense of pride.

Suvlov nodded. 'Didn't they refuse to assist British colonial aggression in Egypt?'

'In the 1950s, yes.' The aircraft engines altered their pitch as it banked into a change of course. For a second, Menichev's eyes flickered fear.

Lupaiyev gave another of his weary smiles. 'What Britain has done in the past months has only angered the Americans more. They would be quite prepared to see the world end as far as this island is concerned.'

'Then you think . . . ?' Suvlov began.

'I think that Fadden does not know it, but he is an agent of suicide. We have large forces here. Someone – the Americans probably – has proved they can hit targets, like fuel dumps in Russia itself. I believe that, before they left

154

Britain – maybe a long time before – the Americans placed nuclear weapons underground at strategic points. I believe few people consciously know of this: they have used an ingenious cut-out system which involves hypnotic suggestion. Fadden is the key. When he has made all his contacts, he is programmed to blow the last trump: press the button, wherever it is, which will turn Britain – and so a large part of Europe – into an area of nuclear horror.'

The logic was undeniable. Suvlov said something obvious about catching Fadden, controlling him, as quickly as possible. Menichev, for all his fear of flying, calmly suggested that the Marshal should pass on his analysis to what he called 'the highest possible authority'.

He continued, 'Marshal Lupaiyev – Constantin – there are two ways we can prevent this holocaust. One is by catching Fadden, or breaking his chain of contacts before he can find his way to whatever activates the last trump. The other is a solely political exercise. Already a summit meeting is arranged with the Americans. You have to persuade the President of the Supreme Soviet to advance this summit: to get the Americans to hold their hand.'

'A compromise?' Suvlov knew the President and the General Staff would be dismayed at the very thought. To have made such progress in the world, only to be baulked by some American suicide plan, would be to lose credibility within their own country, and those they had brought into the fold.

'I agree this bringing forward of the summit is essential. But the President of the Supreme Soviet must go into that summit knowing that we have Fadden in check, or his chain broken.' Lupaiyev suddenly seemed to make a decision. 'Suvlov, on landing you will apprehend this Furnivall-Wells, while our good friend Menichev arrests the Director of the National Theatre. I shall be doing other things. Whatever resources we possess – the scanning satellites, for instance – must search for possible places, under Britain, where these nuclear devices are placed. That is possible. At the same time I shall have to make a report which will be carried straight to the President of the Supreme Soviet,' – he gave a quick smile – 'the Steel Man himself: urging him to do as we have decided.' He drummed on the table, two small rattles with his fingernails. 'I shall have to put my head on the block, however. I shall have to guarantee that we will break Fadden's chain or capture him, before the summit begins.'

They lapsed into silence, as the steward came from the aircraft's flight deck to say they would be late landing, because of heavy incoming traffic at Northolt. They were now in some holding pattern.

Marshal Lupaiyev began to shout at him, ordering that he tell the pilot to radio Northolt. 'This is a flight of the utmost priority. He can tell them that. Unless they give us clearance to land now, they will be held responsible to the Supreme Soviet itself.'

Even though the delay was minimal, the Yakovlev jet did not touch down until almost four-forty.

★ 24 ★

Fadden made Rutland Gate by five minutes to five. It took him a little less time than he had anticipated, and the worst part, for him, was the short and hurried walk in the open, up Kensington High Street and past the mouldering Royal Garden Hotel, into Kensington Gardens.

Fadden felt this was the best back-double of all – the wide open space of the great park which, at this time of day, was full of strolling people. There seemed to be no security patrols in evidence, and Fadden walked in a quick and very wide arc, which finally brought him out at Prince of Wales Gate, leading to the main thoroughfare of Knightsbridge. Loitering for a moment, he spotted a military patrol steadily working their way, with police support, up the opposite side of the road.

Fadden turned casually, walking back into the park, completing another, smaller, sweep, so that he could view the progress of the patrol as it passed Prince of Wales Gate.

When they had gone, he strolled out into Knightsbridge and crossed the road. It was less than five minutes' walk from there to the turning into the cul de sac which was Rutland Gate.

Number 40A was the ground floor of one of the great houses in this, once most fashionable, mall. The houses had, for many years now, been too big for city dwellers. Since the 1950s, most of them had been converted into offices or elegant flats. Exactly at five o'clock, Fadden rang the bell next to the small nameplate showing this was the residence of James Furnivall-Wells Esq.

'I have only one other person who lives here,' Wells said,

opening the door and nodding at Fadden's muttered 'Lark?'

'He has been sent out for a short walk. We can talk in the garden.'

Fadden watched the sweep hand on his watch. No electronic surveillance in the house. No movement or tingling sensation in his wrist.

They went through a room which looked as though it had come straight out of the 1960s. Middle Biba period, Fadden thought; or early Habitat. All except for one thing – the reproduction hanging, almost hidden, on a wall near large French windows that led to the garden. It was the same picture – the one he had seen before – of the graveyard. He certainly knew the significance of the paintings now; but the eerie quality of the marshy mist and the tombstones rising, like pieces of wrecked ship from a sea, produced a calming element. Fadden had no fear of what he was doing. A sense of genuine pride had replaced any nervousness. The United States was making a dangerous gamble to save Europe, to give back to individual peoples their own choice to make political errors or successes, and remove the dogma of dictatorial ideology – no matter how fair some might think that ideology to be.

There was a red-brick terrace immediately outside the windows. Steps led down from the terrace to a long lawn – around fifty yards of it – bordered by beds of flowers and shrubs.

As they went out on to the terrace, Fadden instinctively took note of the sight-lines from the house; the straight sweep of the lawn, and the cover of trees and bushes along the wall at the end of the garden. To the left of this end wall was a small wooden door, dull green and in need of painting. He asked Furnivall-Wells if the door was a hazard to privacy, and the businessman told him it was locked and bolted most of the time. 'It's open now,' he said, as though letting Fadden know he had the sense to take the right kind of precautions.

Wells was dressed like an old-fashioned London businessman: a striped suit of good heavy material, but now showing signs of wear: shiny patches on the sleeves. His shirt collar also looked on the verge of fraying, though the dark blue, polka-dot tie was immaculate. He was a short man, stocky and going to fat. In his mid-fifties, Fadden thought, even though he looked older as he gestured to one of the metal chairs, white painted, a relic of much better days.

There were three other such chairs, and a matching table on which Wells had set out a tray with cups, teapot and the usual accessories, including a plate of plain biscuits.

'Sorry I can't offer you a proper tea,' Wells said, as though by way of explanation. 'Cake and the cucumber sandwiches. Can't be done these days.'

'Don't worry.' Fadden wanted to get it over quickly. He sat opposite Wells, giving the trigger phrase as the man was about to reach out to the teapot.

The stretching arm withdrew, and Wells relaxed, going through the same procedure as before. The two names he gave were Rupert Graves and Mary Athay. Repeats, as Fadden had expected. Then –

'What number do you require?'

'Five.'

'Take special note. You must remember this: picture it in your head. I am going to describe the Last Trump.' He paused. Fadden counted about five heartbeats: it was the kind of timing they would have put into the programme, giving just enough space for the recipient to compose himself.

Wells continued, 'Picture a metal control board. It has the minimum number of controls on it. Spartan, but effective. Immediately on your arrival you will activate the board. There is one switch for this. Unmarked, the only switch on the board: it lies in the top left hand corner. Next to the switch are two circular lights. The one nearest to the switch will give you the condition. Red means that the board is working, but there is no contact from outside. When contact is made. and the things you control are live, this light will automatically change to green.

'The centre of the board contains two banks of push

159

buttons: two rows of seventeen buttons to each row. The buttons are numbered and correspond with the numbers you already possess. Each button has a small light under it. When contact is made these lights will come on. They will show red. Each numbered light is the control for six assets. Remember, there are six to each number. Six items at each reference you possess. Numbers one to seventeen are military; numbers eighteen to twenty-eight are civil. Number twenty-nine – I repeat: twenty-nine – has special significance – one asset only. If you are required to blow the Last Trump you will press number twenty-nine at the signal which is yet to be given to you.'

He paused again. Then –

'Numbers thirty to thirty-four are specially targeted to seek out specific objects whose positions may change. All the assets were maintained and targeted on . . . ' he gave a date which, Fadden deduced, was roughly two weeks before the United States' forces had to pull out of the NATO bases in England. Fadden wanted to ask desperately what had happened to the thirty-fifth reference; but Wells was still speaking:

'The instructions signals – the orders – are not complex, but will be given to you by another. The second light to the right of the main switch, together with a sounding device, will be used to convey these instructions. Once you reach the Last Trump, and throw the main switch, you must stay by the board twenty-four hours a day. In a drawer to the right of the board you will find drugs that will enable you to remain awake for long periods – up to one week. As your instructions are passed to you, so you will press the correct button. If the six assets, at the represented co-ordinate, operate correctly, the red light under that button will change to green after ten seconds. If it does not, you will reactivate by pressing the button again. A second failure is final, and you will pass on to your next instruction. Good luck.'

Fadden sat, silent for a few moments, picturing the simple piece of equipment in his mind. By now he knew what had happened to the thirty-fifth map reference. He knew what was expected of him: what Golgotha truly was, and how devastating it could be if used correctly. So much depended on the skill of the man who would be controlling him – the President of the United States – once he found the board which they called the Last Trump. Wells had seemed to speak those two words using capital letters.

He had the picture vivid in his head now, so, without hurrying, he brought Furnivall-Wells out of his trance.

'How do you like your tea?' Wells asked, and Fadden said just as it came.

Wells gave a short laugh. It was how everybody had to put up with it these days. 'How can I help you?' As he spoke, the tea was dribbling into Fadden's cup. The cool breeze winnowed down the garden. With it came sounds that made Fadden suddenly edgy. The noise of cars screeching to a halt, somewhere behind them, at the front of the house. Doors slamming, and voices, carried on the air over the roof. Russian and English orders, shouted loudly.

Wells said very calmly, 'Sorry. We're rumbled. You get out, I'll hold them back. The gate.'

As he said it, the house trembled with a furious knocking at the door. The knocking turned into the more sinister sound of splintering wood. The front door was being broken in.

Fadden was up and running almost before Wells mentioned the gate. He did not look back, but zig-zagged down the lawn, out of habit, in case any of them made the terrace before he reached the gate, which grew larger with every second.

Panting, he reached it, grabbed the latch, pulled at the handle and stepped through, closing the gate softly behind him. He was in a narrow alley with the rear of a house facing him. The alley ran to openings on either side which, with a fast deduction, Fadden realised must bring him out into Tower Place, or somewhere near it. There were plenty of streets in which he could lose himself from there.

Back, from behind the wall, there were more shouts. Without hesitation, he turned right and began to run. Five paces in, he knew his mistake. A black Volga saloon pulled up at the point where the alley emptied into the street ahead.

Hand diving for his pocket, fingers closing around the Stechkin, Fadden swivelled and began to run back the other way, hoping they had not been too thorough and sent cars to each end of his only escape route. Behind him the car doors slammed, and there was a shout – clear, in English – 'Halt. Fadden halt.'

He went on running, the alley's junction rushing towards him like the light at the end of a tunnel.

The warning shot whined over his head, clipping the brickwork somewhere to his left. He knew a burst of fire would follow, and, in the confines of the house and wall, he would not stand a chance. He slipped the Stechkin from safety to automatic fire. Twenty rounds in the magazine, his brain said. Only give them bursts of five. Still moving towards the exit, Fadden whirled round, catching a picture of four or five men, at least two in Soviet uniform, crowding and thudding after him. He pressed the trigger twice, quickly, and saw the first two men go spinning backwards, one of their faces dissolving into a red spray. There was a scream from the group, all of whom seemed to be cannoning backwards, like a row of skittles.

The second burst must have done more damage. He was only six or so paces from the end of the alley now. Turning, Fadden plunged ahead, pushing the Stechkin back in his raincoat pocket.

He did not see the wooden door to Furnivall-Wells' garden open. Nor did he see Suvlov step into the alley, glance at the pile of men: some still, and some struggling from the heap. Suvlov raised his pistol.

The shot came just as Fadden got to the street.

★ 25 ★

The street was deserted. No chase car at this end. But before Fadden could duck away from the alley, he felt the stinging pain as a bullet grooved the side of his leg, spinning him around, making him stagger from the alley, out of sight from another shot.

He hauled at the Stechkin again, without thinking he could be met by a hailstorm of bullets, and swung back into the alley entrance, pressing the trigger once. He caught sight of the man who had fired from Wells' garden doorway. The man had his pistol raised, but leaped back as Fadden's burst ripped and ricocheted from the walls and ground.

Fadden began to run as he had never run before, moving by instinct, overcoming the burning pain in his leg by turning his mind to the need for survival; not his need, but that of so many others. He thought of faces: mainly people he knew or had known; his mind filled with pictures of conquered peoples, of men and women in chains – from the dawn of time – being dragged through streets by their captors; of prisoners dying for their faith or beliefs; of the Spanish Inquisition; the tortures and torturers of the world – hideous, Boschian, montages; the concentration camps of Nazi Germany; the so-called mental hospitals of the Soviets; Lubianka gaol; faces, faces and more faces. Pleading. A forest of arms and hands stretching out to him in supplication.

Then, almost suddenly, he found himself in a back street; empty, but with the sounds of traffic nearby. The pain in his leg was more of an aching throb now, and Fadden paused to take a look at the damage.

The bullet had ripped a slash, about the length of his middle finger, from his right trouser leg, mid-calf. There was not much blood, for the slug had run a neat red groove on his calf; a red indentation, as if someone had placed a red-hot poker to the fleshy part of his lower leg.

What blood there was Fadden cleaned off quickly, with a handkerchief, which he then folded, binding it around the wound. The area would be crawling with police and military. The only way he could possibly get back to Mary Athay's apartment block was by walking straight through, using every possible back street and cut he could find. It was impossible for them to cordon the area completely - at least this quickly.

He could walk without a limp, and soon found that he was in Trevor Street, which emptied out into Knightsbridge, almost directly opposite the famous barracks.

If he reversed his course, he could get back among the crowds of Brompton Road, which formed a triangle with Knightsbridge and the broad Exhibition Road.

There were plenty of side streets that would carry him through that triangle; and the view along thoroughfares like the Brompton Road should give ample warning of possible road blocks. If necessary he could lose himself in one of the museums which lay along that path - the Science Museum, or the Natural History. There was no reason to suppose they had been closed to the public.

Those shops and businesses that were still trading under the new regime were closing, the employees beginning their various long, or short, marches home. Brompton Road was full of pedestrians. A police car led an ambulance, at speed, through the moderate traffic, their sirens wailing. Fadden wondered if that was some of his handywork being rushed to intensive care.

To his relief, they had not got around to checking people by the time he made the intersection with Exhibition Road; but Fadden decided to go on, up Cromwell Road, which ran almost parallel to Kensington High Street, until he judged there was a suitable series of streets which would take him out almost opposite Mary Athay's building.

He found such a street – Marloes Road – which he knew, from his old London experience, would bring him through the relatively quiet backwaters of Cheniston Gardens and Wright's Lane. Getting to Marloes Road took him nearly twenty minutes. The leg burned and throbbed, but he kept to the rules: pausing, loitering; showing indecision; watching faces, and hoping they did not watch his or reappear. Nobody seemed to be following.

Then, half-way up Marloes Road, Fadden began to feel the instinctive prickle at the back of his neck. He glanced around. A man in civilian clothes was crossing the road, going in the same direction as himself. Ahead of him there was another man carrying a briefcase, walking slowly. There was something about the man behind him – the cut of his smart casual clothes; the neatness of his hair.

Fadden had not spotted his face in the crowds, but, somehow, he knew the man. He turned into Cheniston Gardens and saw that the man with the briefcase had disappeared. If it was a pincer movement, he was probably standing, under cover, at the entrance to Wright's Lane. That man's back now also seemed familiar, and, with a sudden roll of the guts, Fadden realised that the person, quite far behind now, was the one he had glimpsed in the doorway of Furnivall-Wells' garden: the one who had shot at him.

He closed his hand around the Stechkin, flicking the catch to single shot, remembering that there were only around five slugs left in the magazine. If the one in front was waiting in Wright's Lane, the man behind him would increase speed as soon as Fadden was out of sight.

He braced himself as he entered Wright's Lane, and immediately knew he was correct. The man had lost his briefcase. He stepped out, smiling, an automatic pistol pointing straight at Fadden's guts.

'Hallo, Paul,' said Harry Ashworth. 'Haven't seen you in yonks, as they used to say. You've led us one hell of a dance.'

★ 26 ★

Fadden did not even recall Ashworth's name. In the split second he simply recognised him as a junior SIS officer he'd seen around the Westminster Bridge building.

So braced and ready was he, that he did not even give the automatic pistol a thought. Speed was essential, and he closed immediately, putting Ashworth's pistol to the left of his own body. The SIS officer merely looked surprised at the sudden proximity of his prisoner. The look of surprise turned to one of severe agony as Fadden's knee came up, so hard that the man's testicles must have been dislodged.

The pain was obviously so great that Ashworth could not even scream. His face contorted; his mouth opened wide. Fadden's elbow under the jaw put Ashworth to sleep for a long time.

Scooping up the pistol – thinking that an extra weapon would be of use – Paul Fadden ran again. This time he knew that the other officer, the one who had shot at him, could not be far behind. It was a matter of trying to make the High Street, crossing it, and getting into Mary Athay's building, before he was spotted. There was no way he could do that. Thinking on the hoof, Fadden did exactly what his former colleague – Ashford, or Ashwell, or whatever his name was – had done: dodging into the nearest doorway, which happened to be the entrance to a shop, bolted and barred, the windows boarded over.

He switched the new automatic for the Stechkin, and reversed it in his hand. The street remained deserted, but he now heard the hurried approach of feet. One man. The one behind – pausing for a second at Ashworth, then starting at full stretch up Wright's Lane in the hope of catching

Fadden in the relatively open country of Kensington High Street.

He passed the doorway, and Fadden stepped out, matching his run to that of the blond, neat, man. His arm swung back as his quarry realised, too late, that he had someone on his tail. The blond man, Suvlov, slowed and half turned his head.

He saw Fadden's face for a fraction of time, before the butt of the Stechkin caught him behind the ear and blotted out light.

When the light returned, there were two policemen bending over him, one of them raising his head.

'Just lie still, we've sent for an ambulance,' one of them said.

Suvlov groped around for his gun. It had gone, and he began to shout a stream of abuse at the policemen; first in Russian, then English, feeling in the inside of his jacket for his ID.

'Oh shit,' said one of the policemen when he saw the KGB card.

'Did you get him?' Suvlov kept repeating.

The policeman asked who he was talking about and, even in the pain and fogginess of his condition, Suvlov pulled out the photograph of Fadden they were now all carrying.

'Oh Christ,' the other policeman said.

'Did you get him?' Suvlov asked again, feeling the world sliding away from him, and hearing, far away, the sound of a siren. As the world diminished he thought he heard one of the policeman say something about keeping quiet. He thought the man said, 'That was the bugger who tipped us off about two men badly hurt down Wright's Lane.'

*　*　*

Mary Athay bathed and dressed the wound. Fadden was content just to lie still and rest. It had all been too close for comfort. They knew him; he had got to Wells only just in time. Yes, he could work out where the Last Trump (he thought of it in capital letters now) was located. If he used his intelligence, he could probably deduce the signals by which he would be commanded to operate it. But, in reality, he needed whatever the final clue could give him. That meant Oxford, and Rupert Graves. If they had got that close to him at Wells' place in Rutland Gate, God knew how close they would be to him in Oxford.

As she bandaged the wound, Mary told him that Paddington was swarming with security people. Almost everyone was having their papers checked, on and off the trains, which ran, direct to Oxford, at a rate of one every three hours. The first train left at nine the next morning. What he needed, Fadden reasoned with himself, was a new identity. There was no possible way they would let him get through a railway station cordon.

Boxed into a flat above Kensington High Street, Fadden's mind traversed every possibility. Mary cooked for them, and he rested the leg. She would come into the main room as often as possible, leaning over to kiss him, telling him, in plain words, exactly how she felt, and what she wanted. He needn't worry, she understood about his leg, knew he must be feeling rough; but it was such a pleasure to have him there.

Tired as he was, an idea started to form, like a pin-point of light, at the back of his mind. Mary cooked steaks again – 'They're easiest and I've got a lot in the freezer.' Over the meal, she said this was what she would like for ever: just to be there, with Paul, in the flat. There was so much they had to learn about one another.

At nine o'clock the news bulletin announced the Summit Conference with the Americans might possibly be brought forward. 'Urgent events in the People's Republics throughout Europe have made a meeting of world leaders essential.' *Tass* had issued a statement that the President of the Supreme Soviet, Mr Alymnov, had sent a note to the President of the United States, asking that the planned Summit Conference, in Dublin, be brought forward, in an attempt to reach some understanding and avert further bloodshed, or armed conflict. The newsreader gave out the statement in a flat, almost disinterested, voice.

It was a terse and typical piece of propaganda, which brought a leaden sense to Paul Fadden's heart and mind. He had worked far more quickly than even he expected. But there were now attempts to alter the Presidential schedule. He wondered, anxiously, what the urgent events throughout Europe could be? Were they connected with him? He also knew that if Mr Alymnov – the Soviet President – was making noises, they would be made from strength. Alone, Alymnov had whipped up the military and civil forces of the USSR, and her satellite states. They did not call him The Steel Man for nothing. Elected after the Grand Purge in 1983, Kiril Alymnov had altered the whole pace of world affairs with his Doctrine of Leadership, declaring that Russia, and the whole Soviet system, alone was destined to lead the entire world.

If the Dublin Summit was now imminent – and the newscaster predicted it would now be held in a matter of days – it was even more essential that he get to Oxford quickly.

Mary told him to rest his leg. She would do the kitchen chores. When she returned, laughing, he saw that she had stripped to her underwear.

'Trying to turn you on, Paul.'

Fadden smiled and said, probably, but later. Could she put a robe on as he wanted to talk seriously to her? She was, he knew, the last way he could make any contact. She saw the gravity in his eyes, and went quietly to the bedroom, returning with a towel robe covering herself, the tie pulled tight around her slim waist.

Fadden patted the settee, indicating that she should come and sit beside him. He started by asking about her status. 'You are still an American citizen?'

She told him that her marriage with Tom had made the situation ambiguous. After the marriage she held two passports – British and American. They had confiscated the British passport when they took Tom Athay and shot him. She had not disclosed the American papers, but they would know. Yes, legally she was still an American citizen.

'Then why haven't you tried to get out via the American Embassy?' he asked, checking all loopholes.

'I've been waiting for my case officer. His last promise was that if I performed one more service I would be taken out.'

'And he hasn't shown.' Fadden spoke softly, almost to himself. 'Did he forbid you to go to the Embassy?'

Not exactly forbid, she told him. Her case officer maintained that unexplained, or unnecessary, visits to the Embassy were insecure.

'I think you can regard me as your case officer, now.' Fadden put an arm around her shoulders. 'I can't tell you anything as yet. You know that.'

'I know it's all dangerous.'

'It's also urgent. Mary, you're to go to the Embassy tomorrow, and wait there until you've made contact with one particular person. He may have to be flown in to see you. Maybe from Dublin.' Fadden gave her Tim McPherson's name, and briefed her about the techniques she should use to avoid being picked out by any Soviet infiltrators within the Embassy. Then he carefully went through his requirements from Tim McPherson.

Breaking cover, like this, was a risk. But just as the President of the United States was gambling with the world, he saw no other way but to gamble with his security.

They went to bed, and Mary Athay made love to him. He did not protest. Whatever difficulties she might have had with her husband, Mary had learned techniques instinctively; her methods of arousal and bringing them both to climax, again and again, came whirling up from her own fevered nights of imagination. She even seemed a little surprised at her own success, her confidence growing throughout the long period of pleasure. At last they both sank, exhausted, into sleep.

Fadden woke twice after that, his leg wound stinging, and nightmare thoughts chasing each other around his brain. Again, in the wider world, there were horrors and chaos.

* * *

During the night, the European agents of the People's Republic of China carried out more attacks. As before, fuel dumps and refineries, pipe-lines and plants, were blown; more Soviet equipment was damaged – this time only inside Russia itself. The attacks were carried out with even greater ferocity and daring than before. Some of those who the Soviets called terrorists were killed; a few were caught, though none lived to talk, for they had been schooled in courage, conditioned by the techniques of thought reform which the Chinese had begun to perfect so many years before.

On capture, the European Chinese agents each activated a small bomb, taped to their chests, blowing themselves – and, in most cases, their captors – to fragments.

Before these assaults took place, Marshal Constantin Mikhilov Lupaiyev visited the injured Suvlov at the Lenin Hospital (formerly St Mary Abbots Hospital in Kensington).

Suvlov had suffered concussion, but X-Rays showed that the skull was not fractured, as the doctors had first feared.

Lupaiyev looked grim and concerned as he sat at Suvlov's bedside. 'I've had Comrade Menichev transferred to our service, officially,' the Marshal said, keeping his voice low, even though they were in a small private ward. 'He's now in charge of the affair. I've even taken his advice. Fadden's photograph will be on the front page of every newspaper by the morning. It will go out on the late television news tonight.' He glanced at his watch. 'About now.' It was almost eleven. 'Every soldier, policeman and member of our service will be looking for him.'

'And me?' Suvlov, his head feeling like a split melon, knew he was in trouble. Lupaiyev shrugged.

'Alexei Alexeiovitch, we are both in the same boat. If Fadden is caught – preferably alive – and we get some kind of a statement, and details of what the Americans are going to do, then we will be in the clear. If not, it depends on the success of the politicians and how badly certain people's ulcers are playing up when they go through the files.'

Suvlov tried to nod, but found it painful. 'And the other business?'

'Which one? Finding any information on the scanners? Or my advice to Moscow?'

'Both, I suppose.'

'I am reliably informed by those whose job it is to analyse the satellite information, that, prior to Eurostrike, no hint of nuclear or neutron material showed up under the surface throughout the length and breadth of Britain.' Eurostrike had been the uninspired code word for the operation which led to the Soviet control of Europe.

'More,' the Marshal continued, 'I asked for the most recent scannings, and the experts say nothing shows. They maintain they could tell if underground devices were in place and shielded. There is no sign of anything having been done in the last seven years or so.'

'They could be very small devices.'

'The experts say no. If what we believe is true – that the United States is willing to sacrifice Britain, by making it into one huge atomic explosion that will put nearly the entire continent at risk for the next twenty or thirty years, then the devices would have to be numerous, and large.'

'We could be wrong.'

'Pray we are. But the evidence we had from Eldrich is strong.'

'Moscow?'

Lupaiyev's face became shrouded in anxiety. 'I did what we agreed. The Steel Man himself acted at once. He has asked the American President to meet him – with other world leaders – in Dublin within four days. It went out on the *Tass* wires earlier this evening. Even Alymnov was worried. The attacks the other night have seriously disrupted essential supplies. The threat of Britain being a massive nuclear bomb made him distinctly edgy. I spoke personally, on a secure line, but I did not like it.' The Marshal had a horror of discussing anything on telephone or radio lines, even if they were supposedly secure. He did not trust the things, probably because he knew how easily they could be tapped.

'Comrade Alymnov made it very clear to me. He has to go into this Dublin meeting with genuine evidence that, whatever the threat may be, it is overcome. He said that he could promise nothing for the entire system if he went in cold.' The Marshal even allowed himself to tell Suvlov that Premier Alymnov had seemed unnerved by the evidence. 'He asked if Lead Leo should make a special trip over.'

'Jesus,' said Suvlov. Lead Leo – as they all called him – was Leonid Vereshenko, the supreme Director of the KGB: probably the most feared man in the Soviet hierarchy since the dark days of Beria.

Lupaiyev smiled and shook his head, telling Suvlov he must not worry. Lead Leo had his work cut out trying to trace the sources of the previous night's attacks. He did not know, then, that Vereshenko would be under even more pressure by the morning. 'A note of strong protest has gone to the United States President. I've seen the wording – Alymnov is all but ordering him to Dublin to explain himself. That will be in tomorrow's newspapers also, with a shaded-down account of the atrocities.' He raised a quizzical eyebrow.

Before the Marshal left, Suvlov had the grace to ask about Ashworth's condition.

'Let's put it like this.' Lupaiyev did not smile. 'Ashworth will never father children. He'll live the rest of his life as a most frustrated man. The desire will be there, but the means will not.'

*   *   *

The President of the United States sat in the Oval Office with the Secretary of State and his Chief of Intelligence, Don Marks. They awaited the arrival of the Chinese Minister, K'e Hu-We, the man who acted as their go-between with the People's Republic of China.

K'e Hu-We did not normally come to the White House.

Information and agreements were usually carried out in the most strict conditions of security. Don Marks had men who did this job in conjunction with trained people from State.

The situation, however, had altered so drastically that the Chinese Minister agreed to be picked up and brought into the White House, under cover. Only when Marks' people assured them that K'e Hu-We was definitely clear of any foreign surveillance, would he come – driven in a small closed car with blacked-out windows.

While they waited, the President discussed strategy. He was glad now that he had demanded the new communications satellites to be ready quickly for launching. At the time, he imagined it would be a good six weeks before they would be needed. The fact that they were ready for launching at any time now helped him a great deal.

'The Golgotha satellite must go first,' he told Marks. 'That, and the launching of the new communications satellites at ten-minute intervals, will be your first concern. Nothing must go wrong. You start launching the moment you hear I've touched down at Dublin Airport.'

'It's as good as done. NSA has it organised.'

'I need news of Theseus.' The President gave a quick sideways glance at the Secretary of State, who should not really be present while this subject was under discussion.

'There was a flash, via Dublin, from Tim McPherson in London, earlier.' Marks looked concerned. 'Theseus is under great pressure. They know him, and nearly got him. There's no way of knowing how advanced he is. Because the Dublin summit's been pulled forward, I've ordered Tim back to Ireland. He's reluctant to go.'

'I shall certainly need him there.'

'I've made a concession – told him to go tomorrow night, their time. Something might just break by then. Apart from that, we pray.'

The last words appeared to stir something in the President's mind. 'You've cleared the earlier arrival at Rome, and the Papal audience?' he asked.

Both the other men started to speak at once. The President would leave the day after tomorrow – a Wednesday; there would be a night stopover in Rome where he would see Pope John Paul IV. Air Force One would reach Dublin by the Thursday evening. They had now definitely agreed the start of the Summit talks at noon on the Friday. The President thought it should have been a Good Friday, that would have been really appropriate.

One of the phones rang on the President's desk. The Chinese Minister had been cleared, and arrived at the rear entrance to the White House.

K'e Hu-We was one of the youngest men holding any power in the People's Republic of China. He was only thirty-nine years of age, but looked what he was – sharp, razor-minded, and agile at negotiation. Tall, for one of his race, he was – like Suvlov in London – an afficionado of Western clothes: always impeccably turned out, with suits and casual clothes made by the best New York tailors. His personality matched his clothes – precise, smooth and unduly polite.

The President treated him with great deference, and K'e Hu-We was at pains to act most correctly towards the President.

'I think I understand your problem,' the Chinese Minister began.

'Would you care to read the Soviet note?' The President motioned towards the Secretary of State, who passed the document over to the Chinese politician, who read it carefully.

'Might I see your reply?' K'e Hu-We put down the paper which protested at what the Soviet Premier had called 'acts of diabolical aggression organised by the American military forces.'

The Secretary of State looked at the President for permission, and passed a further document to the Chinese.

'You can do no more and no less.' K'e Hu-We returned both documents. 'I am so sorry you have been at the wrong end of the Soviet wrath; and I fear they will become even more tough by tomorrow.'

'You mean . . . ?' began the Secretary of State.

The Chinese Minister nodded. 'There will be more; during the night, in Europe. They have to be put at a disadvantage – a real disadvantage – before the final revelations in Dublin. Might I suggest that, if they start rattling their swords, you again deny these actions most strongly, and suggest that the Soviet's allies – ourselves, the Chinese – be allowed to examine the problem. What else can you do? You will be at the meeting. Be calm, Mr President, Tai Yen-Sen, our leader, will be beside you at the conference table. So will our Premier, Shih P'eng Te. What they will have to say is going to shift the balance completely. You also have a secret matter . . . ?'

'Which I can discuss with nobody.' The President's voice was bland, though difficult to control. 'Our alliance remains fast – steadfast. Our arrangement with you on military matters can only be reinforced by this other matter. The timing must be perfect.' He spread his hands towards K'e Hu-We. 'None of us wish to start a holocaust from which Europe may never recover.'

'If it can be avoided, it will be avoided. No, of course, we do not wish to devastate Europe, unless it is the only way. As you say, the timing must be perfect.'

'Then I think' – the President looked at his Secretary of State and the Director of the CIA – 'I think we should be alone for a short while. What we agree can be passed on to the appropriate people.'

K'e Hu-We bowed his head. There was the ghost of a smile around his lips.

★ 27 ★

Tim McPherson had been worried from the moment they brought him the instructions to return to Dublin.

In the little office, with its adjoining bedroom, that had been his home in the London American Embassy for the last couple of days, he looked at the morning's newspapers and felt a wave of nausea.

He knew how serious the acts of sabotage and assault had been throughout Europe. It was clear they were so cleverly and strategically carried out that the Soviet war machine across the continent had been dealt a staggering blow.

In the middle of the night, the Duty Officer, who he knew could be trusted, had wakened him to bring news of further acts. The Soviet powers would be reeling through lack of supplies – oil, other fuels, and ground weapons. The situation at sea, however, was a different matter. European waters were patrolled by nuke submarines capable of delivering devastating attacks.

Now he saw that the British – Soviet-run – papers had produced a scaled-down version of the first night attacks, passing them off as pin-pricks, but naming the Americans as the source of sabotage which had been directed, not just at Soviet installations and troops, but at women and children in towns and cities. 'The American Government, and Military Forces,' said the London *Daily Express*, 'are unquestionably behind these acts of terrorism, and Mr Alymnov has called upon the United States President to account for these cloak and dagger, cut-throat, tactics.' The President, the piece went on to say, had agreed to answer the charges by coming to Dublin for the conference much earlier than already planned. He would be on his way to-morrow. The Soviet Premier would be stopping in London, briefly, on his way to Dublin. The British Prime Minister was standing by to be in Dublin, as were other Heads of State, including those of their glorious ally, the People's Republic of China.

All this sickened Tim McPherson, but the thing that really turned his guts was the large photograph which seemed to overshadow this dramatic lead story. Paul Fadden's face stared out from the page, with bold lettering asking, in characteristic old-style English journalese, HAVE YOU SEEN THIS MAN?

There was only a short story under the photograph, but its content was enough. The man, it said, was a traitor and murderer: a former British officer who had run berserk. The police had been searching for him in connection with the murder of the famous novelist, Hilary Keville. Yesterday afternoon, Fadden had narrowly escaped arrest by shooting down four police officers – it was stressed that two were British – and seriously wounding a fifth. He had also attacked a pair of private individuals – one Russian and one British – without reason. Both were seriously ill in the Lenin Hospital, Kensington. Fadden was undoubtedly a maniac, and should be approached with great care. He was probably armed. Anyone seeing him should get in touch with police, or military, as quickly as possible. This was not a political matter, and Fadden could be classed as the most dangerous man in Britain. He must be caught.

They'll get him with that, McPherson thought. Wherever he's holed-up, we've failed. Fadden would not dare show himself on the streets. There was no way of knowing what progress he had made. Now, pinned down, and with the Dublin Summit suddenly changed, and almost upon them, Paul Fadden's mission – whatever the details – was blown.

McPherson had been in the secret world for a long time. He knew one had to accept failure just as philosophically as one accepted success. Perhaps he would be able to serve the President better in Dublin after all.

178

Now it would simply be a time for attempted concessions; though he gravely doubted if Europe would survive. McPherson knew, before he left Washington, that if the President failed at the conference table, the Chinese would insist on a fast and conclusive premeditated strike.

'And may the best man win,' he said aloud, putting down his paper to start packing.

Then the telephone rang. It was the same Duty Officer, who was doing a midnight-to-midday stint. 'There's a young American woman – at least she carries a U.S. passport – at Passport Control and Visas, who says she has to speak to you. They can't make head nor tail of her. She just says she's an old family friend and she won't leave the Embassy without talking to you. I've spoken, and told her you've been posted out. She simply said, 'Post him back by first-class mail because I'm not leaving until I've seen the old bastard.' I don't want to let her go without some kind of protection; the papers have sparked off a demo right across Grosvenor Square.'

'She used the passport to get in?'

'Yes.'

'Her name?'

'Mary Athay. Dr Mary Athay.'

'Anything else?'

'Says you owe a friend of hers some golden string.'

McPherson grabbed at his coat. The legend of Theseus, using the golden string to penetrate the labyrinth and kill the Minotaur. 'Get her up here without any fuss. Don't make a production number of it.'

He knew Mary Athay's face from photographs on the Washington files, but there had been no name to her, only the crypto – Swallow.

'Good morning,' McPherson said, calmly. 'Now who are you?'

She smiled sweetly and asked for his ID. He showed it, and she seemed satisfied, so he asked her again.

Once more she smiled sweetly and pointed to her arm. Incongruously, strapped to her most feminine wrist was the

179

heavy watch they had given to Paul Fadden. The sweep hand was going wild.

McPherson nodded, motioned for her to follow him, and took her to one of the screened rooms which could not be penetrated by even the most sophisticated electronic gear.

'Now, who are you?' he asked for the third time.

'Swallow,' she said, sitting gingerly on the edge of a chair. 'I bring greetings from Theseus.'

★ 28 ★

At a quarter to three that afternoon, a middle-aged couple stood in the queue for the three o'clock Oxford train. Paddington Station dealt with fewer passengers than in recent years, but things were much slower than usual this afternoon, because of the extensive police checks being made, at ticket offices and at the barriers. Every person, male or female, adult or child, had their papers examined at least twice. Some were being searched. There had even been a few arrests – mainly small-time criminals, recognised by British police officers.

There were only about sixty people travelling on the 3 p.m. to Oxford, but, as they stood in line, awaiting the inspection of their various papers and permits, all of them knew there was a grave risk that the train would leave at least half of them behind. Trains did not wait for security officers.

The middle-aged couple finally got to the barrier and handed over their papers. Both were dressed in shabby clothes, which had once been smart and fashionable. The man had stooped shoulders and rather bushy eyebrows, also slightly prominent teeth; his hair was iron grey, and he walked with exaggerated care. The woman, who carried a suitcase – old and battered – had hair which could have been pretty if she had taken trouble with it: instead she seemed to prefer a severe style, braided and plaited over her head, like a German girl. She wore thick pebble glasses and had hardly any bust.

The Soviet sergeant who took their papers, ran his eyes over them both and thought what poor specimens they looked. He passed the papers back to the British police officer who stood behind him.

'You are Professor Folden?' the British police officer asked the man.

'Folden,' the man said. 'Richard Folden. Professor of Modern Languages.'

'You teach at Oxford?'

'At Trinity.'

The policeman nodded wisely, as though he had graduated from the university himself.

'What languages in particular?' As though they had all the time in the world. The hands of the big clock on number one platform jumped to ten minutes to three.

'French, German, Russian,' the man said, wearily.

At the mention of his own tongue the Soviet sergeant livened up, speaking a sentence quickly. 'What is the purpose of your visit?'

'We're going home. We've been in London just for two days. To see some friends,' the man replied in fluent Russian.

'What friends?'

'Just university friends. They were getting married.'

'You have permits?'

Professor Folden inclined his head towards the papers held by the policeman. The Soviet sergeant took them, examined the photographs on the identity cards, the travel permits, and other documents, then returned them with a salute. 'Teach good Russian, comrade.'

'I try to do that, Comrade Sergeant. It is the language of the new world.'

It seemed to please the sergeant who saluted again, and nodded at Mrs Folden, waving them through.

'We're not out of the wood yet,' whispered Fadden as they walked slowly up the train, looking for an empty carriage. 'If they're really on the ball, they could catch us out when we get to the other end.'

'Don't remind me.' Mary Athay was trying to walk with the unsteady gait Fadden had prescribed for her. It was not

182

difficult, because she could hardly see through the pebble lenses.

Tim McPherson had provided the documents, and elements of disguise, before smuggling Mary Athay from the Embassy. 'Paul won't like the idea of disguise, if I'm any judge of the man,' he had laughed. 'But there's no other way; and, for Christ's sake, tell him to go unarmed.' He had given her other, blank, documents, and a polaroid camera with built-in flash, so that they could provide their own photographs for the identity documents. 'Paul will know how to age them,' he said.

Mary Athay was surprised that she managed to get back to the Kensington flat without being stopped once. There were many more patrols about than usual. Oxford Street, she heard, had been sealed off at each end, as had Regent and Bond Streets.

There were mobile patrols as well as those on foot; armoured cars and personnel carriers, cruising the streets: stopping suddenly to round up a group of pedestrians, some of whom they took away. There appeared, she thought, to be more tension in the streets today than at any other time since the Prime Minister had made the dramatic announcement about calling in a Soviet peace-keeping force.

Once back at the flat it had been plain hard work. While Paul briefed her, giving instructions regarding disguises, he had cursed solidly. As McPherson predicted, he did not like working with disguise. 'Bloody fancy-dress games.'

To her dismay, he also refused to go unarmed – 'If only for both our sakes,' he said, a coldness freezing in his eyes. It was the first time she had been truly frightened of him.

Even though Fadden expressed hatred of disguise, Mary Athay saw, within a few minutes, that he was an expert who could totally change his, or her, appearance with a few deft strokes.

There were spare hotel permits, together with other blank identification papers. Fadden said they should be two sets of people. One for leaving London; the other for Oxford, and, maybe, afterwards. The second personas had to be made up first, and needed the bare minimum. 'We can't go around looking uncomfortable. We have to be as young as possible for the second pair,' he said, telling her to brush her hair out, showing her how to model it; to go without a bra; make up her eyes in a different way.

He simply altered his hair parting, used some dark glasses, and put pads in his cheeks. He looked younger, and vaguely American. They took pictures of themselves like this, and made out the ID in the names Bob and Carol Hunter.

The Folden disguises took longer, and, for Mary Athay at least, were more uncomfortable, particularly the severe hair style, and the way he made her bind up her breasts. 'They won't give you a second look without tits.'

While Mary's Folden disguise was a question of hair, glasses, binding of breasts, and wearing a frumpish collection of clothes, Fadden's change of identity to the Professor of Modern Languages, had to be slightly more elaborate. Special dentures (which were not well-sized) fitted over his own teeth, a powder to grey his hair – 'They used to have stuff you washed in. Took two hours to soak out. The powder's easier' – and false eyebrows which bushed out over his own, and were attached with precise care. Even close to him, Mary could not see the join.

When they were both satisfied with the Folden disguises, they again took pictures of each other with the Polaroid, cutting the head and shoulders sections from the fully-developed photographs to the prescribed size, and doctoring blank identity cards.

Other clothes, changes of underwear, the things they would wear as Bob and Carol Hunter, Tom Athay's toilet gear – which Fadden was using – make-up and other necessities, were put into the most decrepit suitcase Mary could find, the spare documents hidden under the lining, which Fadden slit open with a kitchen knife.

Just before the packing was complete, Mary was surprised to see Fadden toss one of her books on top of the clothes: Greene's *Journey Without Maps*. 'Guard that one with your life,' he told her, and she asked no questions.

184

Last thing, before they left the Kensington flat, Mary dressed Fadden's wound. The blood had dried to the bandage, but, when cleaned, the wound looked healthy enough. 'I've got fast-healing flesh,' he said. Mary took no chances, salving it with antiseptic ointment. She even remembered to pack spare bandages and the ointment.

It had taken a lot of time, but they still managed to make Paddington Station by two-thirty.

Having successfully negotiated the security barrier, they found an empty compartment, relaxing a little as the giant old steam engine gave its nostalgic shrill whistle, roared into life, and, disgorging a great gush of smoke and steam, took up the strain and slowly pulled out of Paddington.

Mary wanted to go up the corridor and change, straight away, into the Carol Hunter character, but Fadden held her back. 'We don't know how they're handling the security.' He sat next to her, occasionally glancing from the window. 'Did you notice there was a guy taking notes about each passenger at the barrier? For all we know they're checking people off at their supposed destinations. They may even be running people like Folden through the computers.'

She said McPherson had told her Folden's name would show as O.K. on any security computer.

'Well, that proves my point. We have to be clear of Oxford railway station before making any changes.' Fadden went on to detail his plan, cautioning her that speed was essential. 'If I'm right, we might have to be out of Oxford before curfew.' The Hunter documents showed them as a pair of surveyors – a husband and wife team – working for the Soviet military. One of the papers gave them priority to travel in restricted areas, though Fadden had left part of it blank until he knew, for certain, that his guesswork was correct.

Each of them would, in turn, need the suitcase to make the change of disguise. Mary would go first into the nearest public convenience, once out of the station, and make her change.

'I'll meet you outside the old Oxford Playhouse,' Fadden

directed her, 'near the Randolph Hotel.' He asked if she knew Oxford well enough to find her way. 'I'll take the risk of carrying the case to the Randolph and doing my change there. We separate when I go to change.'

They would meet again exactly ninety minutes after this last separation. He went through the body talk and signals. She had to preserve all the old tradecraft and technique she knew – watching, double-checking that nobody was following. He would do the same. If it was not safe, he went through alternate meeting points: fall-backs at half-hour intervals.

The first meeting place would be the Martyrs' Memorial; the fall-backs were the Bodleian Library and Magdalen Bridge. Mary Athay, smiling, let him know that she probably knew Oxford as well as he did, when Fadden began explaining the topography.

It was five o'clock when they met outside the old Playhouse (Now a People's Theatre with a student production of *The Cherry Orchard* billed), Mary now looking far removed from the severe bluestocking Mrs Folden. They stood outside, gazing at the cheap photographs of the cast, and stills of the production. 'Brother, my suffering brother.' Fadden quoted the tramp in the play who, in turn, quotes the poetry of Nekrasov.

Mary smiled at this travesty of Fadden, still in his Folden disguise, then completed the quotation. '*Come to Mother Volga, whose groans* . . . Isn't that just after they hear the strange noise?'

Fadden nodded. 'A distant sound, as if coming out of the sky, like the sound of a string snapping, slowly and sadly dying away.'

'You know your Chekhov.'

'I watched Russia for a long time. All the people we had there wanted to use Anton Pavlovich Chekhov's quotes as passwords. The string snapping in *The Cherry Orchard* was his prophecy about the revolution. Like Eliot's "This is the way the world ends – not with a bang, but a whimper." The string's snapped, Mary. We're just waiting for the whimper, only it may be a bloody great bang.'

He touched her shoulder, his hand resting, almost fondling her. 'Ninety minutes from now. If I don't make any of the meetings, get yourself back to London and into the Embassy. Kick and scream if you have to, but contact McPherson again.'

There were not as many troops, or checks, in Oxford as in London. In fact the city had changed little. Fadden was reminded that a friend once told him Oxford always looked like an industrial town with the beautiful old colleges thrown down into it, 'like a maniac hurling darts with roses tied to them.' The friend said he always felt the presence of the university, but it seemed overshadowed by the classless and faceless industrialism. It was all much the same as in the 1970s, when Fadden had last been there.

He knew there was a small risk in carrying the suitcase, but, having successfully changed into his Bob Hunter clothes, it was a chance Fadden was willing to take.

Norham Gardens is a quiet backwater, a cul de sac off the Banbury Road. The cul de sac led into Lady Margaret Hall, years before the only woman's college of the University. Times had changed.

He found number seven easily enough – a large house, divided into many small flats: some simply bed-sitting-rooms. Number 5A was on the ground floor, and Fadden recognised the elderly man, with his hawk-like profile and big domed bald head, as soon as he opened the door.

'Rupert Graves?' As he asked, Fadden got an arm inside the door and glanced at the watch, which he had retrieved from Mary. The sweep hand remained still.

Graves nodded without speaking. Fadden thought he saw a small glint of fear behind the old politician's eyes.

'I'm looking for a stag,' he said, using the cryptonym – Stag.

The old man smiled and nodded. 'There're few of them left. You'd better come in.'

He had two rooms and a small kitchen. 'I share a bath-room with a pair of nubile young women students,' Graves chuckled. 'They bring back memories of my youth, and they know it. Hussies.' He growled an almost lecherous laugh. 'Always leaving their underwear to dry in the bathroom.'

The room was piled with books and papers, a table by the window held an ancient manual typewriter and a stack of manuscript paper. Fadden asked how the book was going.

'You haven't come to talk about the book.' Graves indicated a chair, throwing a pile of papers from it on to the floor. Fadden sat, and the old man took the stand chair from in front of his typewriter, turning it so that he could face Fadden.

Fadden triggered him immediately.

Relaxed, and with the glazed expression, Rupert Graves asked if he wanted two names. Fadden said no. He required number six.

'You are almost at the end,' Graves parroted. 'You may know by now that the co-ordinate given to you as number thirty-five is the location of the Last Trump. You have two keys. You will find the place in ruins, except for the West Wing which is shored up and secure. Key A opens the door. Insert the key, turn it three times clockwise and once anti-clockwise.

'In the kitchen there is a loose flagstone – somewhere in the centre. Prise it up, and you will find the keyhole for Key B. Key B should be turned three times anti-clockwise and once clockwise. It opens a small box containing a combination lock. Make a note and memorise the combination. Set to zero and turn to the numbers, alternating clockwise and anti-clockwise. The combination is seven – fifteen – twelve – seven – fifteen – twenty – eight – one.' He paused. Fadden reckoned on about five heartbeats. He had the combination scribbled into his notebook. Some familiar connection niggled in his mind.

Graves went on, 'You will hear a click. Push hard to the right. A section of the floor will slide back. There are steps down to the cellar, which contains all you will need – including the Last Trump. That has been explained to you, except for the signals. Signify if you understand.'

Fadden said he understood.

'The operation signals will come to you through the second light to the right of the master switch. All lights will come on when you activate. All except the second of the two by the master switch. When the condition is imminent, the light will come on. Red. There will also be a small sound-tone – steady, like the light. The first signal will be to operate button number twenty-nine. The tone will suddenly alter to a rapid bleeping. That is the stand-by signal. You will then hear a vocal command. This is all computerised and on tape. It will simply tell you to fire. You then activate number twenty-nine. The tone will return, and one of two things will happen within twenty minutes or so. Either the tone will suddenly cease and the second light will go out – in which case you will switch off the master control and wait until somebody arrives; or the bleeping will start again. If the latter occurs, it is a warning that you are to activate the rest of the panel. The bleeping will cease, and you will receive vocal, taped, orders giving you a sequence of buttons to press. You will continue obeying these instructions until either the entire board is clear, or the orders cease and there is no tone, voice, or light.

'If this happens you will switch off at the master control, and wait for somebody to arrive. Signify if you understand.'

Fadden said he understood.

'One last thing,' Graves droned. 'Hill green a was Golgotha.'

In the split second that followed, Fadden realised that, forwards, the words spoken said 'Golgotha was a green hill'. He also knew that, by some ingenious act, he had also been triggered. He felt as though he was plunging down a terrible, dark and infinite abyss. Layers of rock pressed in on either side of him, and he started to see visions and hear voices.

★ 29 ★

The visions ranged from the old Salvador Dali painting of the crucifixion – the great down-sweep of the cross, disappearing towards a lake shore – to a nuclear rocket, cleaving the stratosphere.

What he first imagined were voices became one voice which he recognised. It spoke clearly, slowly, and, while it told him things, it was as if Fadden could see the words – the whole function and history, the aim of Golgotha passing before his eyes.

Just as suddenly as it began, so the sensation ended. There was no way of telling how long the state had lasted, but it could only have been a few minutes. He was still sitting opposite Rupert Graves in the small untidy room in a quiet Oxford street. But he now knew everything. The knowledge both dazzled and horrified him. He sat, for a second or two, assimilating the new sensation, before using the words which would both bring Rupert Graves back to his normal state, and wipe the deeply-planted information from the old man's subconscious.

'You haven't come to talk about the book,' Graves repeated, as though he had never said it before Fadden triggered him.

'No. Those we work for said you might be of help.' Fadden knew what he needed, holding his breath, hoping Graves had access to his need.

'Fire away.'

'I need a car.'

Graves laughed. 'With permits and gasoline supplies as they are?'

'I have permits. Have you any ideas?'

Graves slowly rose, walked to the table which served as a desk, opened a drawer and tossed a set of keys to Fadden. 'Mine,' he said. 'I have no permits, but it has a full tank of petrol, and I've started it, and let it run for a minute or two once a week. It's in reasonable condition. Should get you a hundred miles or so. Maybe more.'

If they had planned it, Fadden thought, they could not have chosen better. For some time he had suspected where he would end the trail, and he knew the area well enough from his schooldays. He knew the exact reference point of the thirty-fifth co-ordinate. If Graves' car was working; if they could avoid patrols and roadblocks; they would make it on one full tank. After that, he presumed, it would not matter. It would be success or failure; and if failure nobody stood a chance.

Slowly he removed the spare permit from his pocket, where he had placed it, and the other documents, while changing into the Bob Hunter persona. He asked Graves about the car's log book, and copied the licence number on to the vehicle permit.

'It's in the garage at the side of the house,' Graves told him. 'I'll go to the bathroom when you leave. I won't see you take it. If anyone gets on to me, I shall say it was stolen, you understand?'

It made no difference. Fadden shrugged. Strictly he should have snuffed out Graves as he had done Hilary Keville – though for different reasons. Graves was certainly no traitor. But, if they came to question him, the answers would be the same. They would either find a body, or a man willing to say that his car had been stolen.

'Only if they search,' Fadden warned him. 'I'll close the garage doors. You tell them only if they discover it's gone. But I don't expect you to be receiving guests. Nobody's on to you as far as I know.'

Graves nodded and pressed his hand. 'Good luck, whatever it is.'

The car was an ancient Rover 2200, kept in very good

condition – if fuel was not scarce, it would be a collector's item now. Around 1976, Fadden judged by the model. About six years before the motor industry had ground to a halt in Britain, and nearly all vehicles had to be brought in from Germany and Italy – except for the new small American models which drank minimal amounts of fuel. This motor had the one drawback of being easily spottable. People would not forget seeing a '76 Rover on the road.

She started first time. He backed out, closed the garage doors, and set off gently, getting used to the unfamiliar controls, heading back towards the centre of Oxford.

Mary had a ten-minute leeway instruction on all meeting points. He had left her eighty-five minutes before, and she should still be at the Martyrs' Memorial by the time he got there, providing no nosey policeman, or security patrol, decided to turn him over.

He reached the meeting point at just after six-thirty. She was there, surprised to see him in a car, as he opened the door and called her name – 'Carol.'

'I didn't understand for a moment – too used to Mary.' She settled in beside him. 'Where're we going?'

'If anyone stops us, we have special orders to report to the military commander at Newbury – and pray heaven they've got a small garrison there.' He was turning the car on to the ring road, and Mary said he had missed the Newbury exit at the roundabout.

'Yes, we're going to be a bit lost if anyone asks.'

'You're not telling me where we're going?'

'Nearer Marlborough – my old school – than Newbury.'

He concentrated on the road. 'We're going to get ourselves lost in the Savernake Forest.'

* * *

Lupaiyev had moved from the comfortable suite in the Savoy, and taken the largest office he could find at the top of the building near Westminster Bridge. There was a cot pushed into one corner; a whole battery of telephones, teleprinters, and communications systems lined the walls. The

Dublin Summit was now imminent; the reports from the rest of Europe indicated that the damage done by terrorist attacks was strategically high. Lead Leo badgered him, constantly, on behalf of the Premier, for news of the intruder, Fadden. The Marshal needed to be close to the action.

Menichev used the office next to his, and Suvlov would not be out of hospital for a week.

Every time the Marshal put his head around Menichev's door, the foxy detective would look up and shake *his* head sadly. Now, in the early evening, it was Menichev's turn to come cautiously into the Marshal's office.

'News?' Lupaiyev asked.

Menichev raised his eyebrows in a 'maybe-perhaps' gesture. 'In a few hours the United States President will be leaving Rome for Dublin. In a few hours, our own Premier, our Man of Steel, will be here, heading for Dublin. Time shrinks, Comrade Marshal.'

The Marshal made a remark suggesting that it would shrink quicker if Menichev did not come to the point.

'I do not like hurrying. It's not good. You miss things.'

'Menichev, we cannot afford to miss things.'

'Precisely.'

'Well?'

Menichev explained what the Marshal already knew – that Fadden seemed to have disappeared from the face of the earth. 'With his picture all over the place, and a general alert out for him, I believe you can relax, Comrade Marshal.'

Lupaiyev told him to speak to Lead Leo next time he was in touch. 'It's like talking to a computer. All he asks is, have you got him? Why not? When will you get him?'

Menichev suggested the Marshal should lie. 'At least it'll get Leo off your back. Say Fadden's been stopped; killed. I shall go on searching. After all, the man cannot move; cannot do anything. All my senses tell me he has gone to ground, his mission aborted.'

Lupaiyev toyed with the idea. After a while he muttered that he could at least tell Leo, and even Premier Alymnov, that their first fears appeared to be unjustified. There was no evidence to support the conclusion of Britain being a vast nuclear time bomb. 'No evidence at all,' he repeated, as though to convince himself. Then, sharply, to the detective, 'With all your skill, you've found nothing?'

'Nothing definite, just some tiny straws.'

'I am a drowning man. Give them to me so that I may clutch them.'

Menichev said he had been through all the old SIS computer tapes again, to see if Suvlov had missed anything. 'I went back over almost twenty years.'

'And?'

'Three very small items. I am having them double-checked now.'

'If only that fool Suvlov had not shot the Furnivall-Wells man. We could have sweated him.'

'He would have nothing to tell. The Americans used extreme caution with their cut-out system. That should be obvious from the Eldrich business. The key people are unaware of each other. The need-to-know principle. The Fain woman will be deaf and dumb also – believe me.'

Lupaiyev asked again about the small straws, and Menichev told him that, according to the tapes, several years ago, the SIS had done some limited surveillance on three people they suspected of having what, at the time, they called 'love affairs with clandestine Americans'. Lupaiyev asked for their names.

'I must stress that the SIS called off the surveillance, and cleared all three. They were 'antiseptic' they said.

'The names,' Lupaiyev pressed.

'Strangely, one was an American – a woman married to a British amateur politician called Thomas Athay. You had him shot. Her name was Mary Athay. Suvlov cleared her.'

Lupaiyev nodded, asking for more. Menichev said there was another woman – a girl in the Foreign Service, an Edith Middleton. 'And a real politician.' The detective's lips curled. 'Rupert Graves. A famous Socialist. He has been given a student's flat – the last British administration did this – in Oxford. He is writing a great political work on the rise of Socialism in the Western world.'

'Suvlov had no surveillance on these people?'

'There was no cause. No reason. Neither of *us* would have wired them up . . . ' Menichev stopped in mid-flow, as an aide tapped at the door. He carried a small file of computer printouts, the complete dossiers of the three names just mentioned. 'You can forget about the Middleton girl.' Menichev put the two other dossiers in front of Lupaiyev. 'She was killed in a road accident. I wonder if we should look up the Athay woman and Graves.'

'Just to be on the safe side.' The Marshal had already been seduced by the idea of Menichev's direct lies – to tell the terrible 'Lead' Leonid Vereshenko, and Premier Alymnov – The Steel Man – that Fadden was destroyed. His mind had even gone as far as detail: Fadden mutilated, so that there could be no identification; but some of his own trustworthy people giving positive proof that it had been the man, Fadden. There was absolutely no evidence that the Americans had seeded Britain with nuclear devices; so where was the harm?

Menichev said he would see to it. A team to Mrs Athay's Kensington flat, and a team from the Oxfordshire Constabulary to visit Rupert Graves. 'You would like your Service represented?' he was just asking, when the aide returned. There was a nasty anxious look in his eyes.

'Comrade Marshal; Comrade Menichev . . . ' He was a young man, British, eager to please and very subservient. 'The woman Athay.'

Menichev stood like a stone statue, urging the aide to continue.

'I thought you would like me to run the names through the recent-sightings computers.'

Lupaiyev cursed him to go on.

He told them. Mrs Mary Athay had been seen going into the American Embassy that morning. She had left carrying a small holdall. It was a routine report, accidental even; a man who knew her face made the report and it automatically went on file. But she had left by a little-used side entrance.

Lupaiyev was on his feet in a second, giving orders for Menichev to put the Oxford people into action. He would see to raiding the flat in Kensington. Fadden, he voiced loudly, might even be hiding there.

*   *   *

Mary Athay almost nodded off as they took the road out of Oxford, heading on the old A338 which would, eventually, take them on to the A4 which skirted Savernake Forest. Fadden urged her to stay awake. 'If you drop off and we hit a road block, you might not remember that you're Carol Hunter – surveyor extraordinary.' He grinned, adding that she must not worry if he was uncommunicative. His mind was on other things.

Indeed his mind *was* on other things. He reflected that his mind was almost someone else's mind. The most terrible thought was that he really knew more than the President of the United States. Nobody, not even the President, knew the exact location of the Last Trump. Those who had built it, and serviced it, were either dead, or had automatically done their jobs under hypnosis. Those few who did have an inkling knew only in their subconscious minds, for the system of deep-hypnotic cut-outs and secrecy was truly a maze of great complexity.

When Rupert Graves had triggered Fadden, the things he knew – implanted under hypnosis by the President – had leaped to the surface. Now he remembered the 'check-up' with the doctor in Washington. He had suspected hypnosis then. In the whole world he, Fadden, was now the only human being who had all the available facts about Golgotha.

What puzzled him was the strategic use: but that was political, and up to the President himself. It was not worth the effort of trying to unravel the complexities of how the First Executive of the United States would put Golgotha to its test. He hoped and prayed the President's way would not call upon him to blow the whole of the Last Trump.

He thought about the ingenious structure of the operation.

Sometime, years before, men, under drugs and hypnosis, had built the structure – the Last Trump, a control unit which could be linked to a satellite. This control unit was the key to other secret installations – thirty-four in all – built openly, though under some kind of maintenance cover, on United States NATO bases and restricted locations in Britain.

These installations were Golgotha's sting: thirty-four Ballistic Missile Silos, all but one containing six missiles. Mainly, Fadden reasoned, the old Mavericks or Titans; though there would be a good sprinkling of Scram-type rockets, each capable of launching nine or more nuclear warheads. In all, he figured, a minimum of two hundred and fifty weapons, placed so far under the ground, and so well-shielded, that not even enemy satellite scanners could detect them. Number twenty-nine contained only one missile.

The same hypnotic techniques had been used to maintain these silos – a massive stay-behind nuclear threat, if American Forces were ever forced to leave their British bases.

The missiles had been regularly programmed for maximum effect, automatically targeted on the known major military sites within the Soviet borders; he imagined they would cover possible threatening nuclear and neutron silos, the major control and command posts, and airfields. He knew for certain that a whole bank were destined for non-military targets – Leningrad, Moscow itself, ports and docks. The Scram-type rockets would certainly be programmed to move fast, and seek out, by self-finding mechanisms, the major and threatening nuclear submarines of the Soviet Navy.

As he drove, Fadden worked out the possible sequence of events. There had to be a Golgotha satellite in orbit shortly before the President required the Last Trump.

The President himself could carry an activator, no larger than a matchbox, which would pass Go-and-Stop signals to some radio installation – possibly within the American Embassy in Dublin. Those signals would be bounced from the Golgotha satellite to the control board where Fadden would be sitting – the Last Trump. As he pressed the required buttons, the satellite would again receive, and bounce them back. In his mind, he saw huge blocks of masonry and metal, gouts of earth, explode to reveal the silos. Then the missiles would rise at breathtaking speed from their tombs, homing in, and hitting within a matter of minutes.

The Soviet scanners would be in readiness for attack from the West – from America itself – but not from what it now regarded as its own territory. He wondered if there were other men, like himself, working their way towards similar Last Trumps in the countries which used to form the basis of the NATO powers. He concluded there must be. This could be the complete destruction of the totalitarian Communist dream in Europe. Maybe, he added soberly to himself, the end of Europe. There would be considerable nuclear fall-out over the continent. America would be safe though, and there would be a chance for a new start in the, now, Communist-occupied countries.

The satellite bothered him a little. At the time of the Soviet take-over, the American communications satellites had all been put off the air quickly. In Washington, he thought Tim McPherson had said something about more advanced communications and intelligence satellites being ready to go. If that was true, Golgotha would be launched with them.

Paul Fadden began to ponder on the first, lone, firing. Button number twenty-nine. A warning shot? He smiled to himself; in the far distant past the British were said to use gunboat diplomacy. Perhaps now the Americans were about to use its modern counterpart. A shot across the bows of Communist Colonialism.

They were making good progress – now on the outskirts of Hungerford. Within less than an hour they would be turning off the main roads, hiding the car – for that was his plan – and going on foot to the Last Trump, deep within the Savernake Forest, one of the great legendary forests of England.

Paul Fadden was oblivious of the fact that, in London, Lupaiyev and his men had found his traces in Mary Athay's flat; while, from Oxford, with a shaken Rupert Graves in custody, the description, and licence number of the car, had been circulated.

*　　*　　*

Constantin Mikhilov Lupaiyev was having second thoughts about lying to his boss – 'Lead' Leo – and the Premier. Something was up; he could smell it; feel it in his bones. So could Menichev. Menichev said it out loud.

'The scanners show nothing, but Fadden has some plan – some instructions.'

Gloomily, Lupaiyev voiced the opinion that, perhaps, it was a case of raising subversive groups in Britain. Nothing as large and complex as they had imagined. While he gave orders for the old Rover 2200 to be picked up – preferably with the occupants alive and intact – he kept asking Menichev if he should still tell the Head of the KGB, and the Soviet Premier, that the hunt was over? That there was no danger?

'What have you to lose now?' Menichev replied every time.

They both knew what could be lost.

*　　*　　*

Fadden felt relaxed at the wheel. Another fifteen minutes, he told Mary Athay. A quarter of an hour, and they would be able to dump the car. He even increased speed as they cleared the village of Froxfield. The roads had been virtually empty: only the occasional commercial vehicle, or military car.

They rounded a bend and he saw, directly ahead, three police cars, an armoured vehicle and a personnel carrier pulled up, about to set their transports into the familiar zig-zag checkpoint position.

★ 30 ★

Instinctively, Fadden reached for the gun – the automatic he had swept up after disposing of Ashworth – and slammed the brakes on, spinning the wheel as he did so.

He had the Rover in reverse, and was backing at speed before the police and troops ahead had time to realise what was happening. It was impossible, but he thought he could hear orders being shouted. He was certain that, in the last instant, as his car disappeared backwards up the road, he spotted men dashing for the personnel carrier.

Three hundred yards back there was a turn-off – a narrow lane. Accelerating smartly, Fadden charged the car into the lane, shouting at Mary to grab hold of the map.

'We're going to dump the car as soon as possible. It'll mean going ahead on foot. Probably dodging patrols. But if we move carefully, once it's dark, we'll make it.'

He drove the car flat out, knowing that if the personnel carrier was chasing them, it would find the lane difficult to negotiate at speed. After about two kilometres, they came to a track leading to the right. Fadden calculated the track ran almost parallel to the main road they had been following. They bounced over the rough earth, and he could see trees ahead, and a clutch of ruined buildings, like a decayed farm.

They leaped and rolled over the rutted and hard ground, Fadden with his foot down on the accelerator, whipping the car's engine into whining protest; then slewed into the deserted farmyard, and, with a shout of 'Hold on, for Christ's sake,' Fadden aimed the vehicle at a pair of large rotting barn doors.

As they smashed through, Fadden stood on the brakes, wood splintering and tearing, the doors pulling their supports with them. Behind the car came the rumbling crash as the whole front of the barn collapsed.

Mary sat white, shaken but unhurt. Fadden was panting, his stomach churning from the sudden action. Gently he climbed from the driver's seat, gesturing at Mary to follow.

Dust settled all around them, and the roof sagged, ominously, above: a sieve of broken tiles and decaying beams. Even if the chase vehicles could see the ruined farm from the narrow lane, they could only be alerted by the dust and earth which still hung in the air. The battered car would be hidden from them by a wall of rubble.

Fadden motioned Mary Athay to get out carefully. He found himself whispering, 'Bring the map.' They had been using an ordnance survey map to follow the route. 'And I noticed a torch in the glove compartment.' Leaning back, he opened the rear door to drag out the suitcase, constantly looking up at the sagging barn roof. There was no exit except over the rubble, and Fadden, still whispering – as though undue noise might bring the slates, beams and tiles down on them – instructed Mary, pointing out the best way for her to climb over the wrecked front of the building.

She gave him a nervous look, then began the journey, scrabbling over the pile of masonry and brickwork which still steamed with dust. She crawled, as directed, over the rubble to the far right behind the car. If the roof went, that was the place where there would be least danger. As she reached the top of the pile, so the beams directly over Fadden's head, gave another angry creak, slipping to one side, sending a scattering of tiles splattering out on to what had once been the farmyard.

He hissed at her to go right, and lie down flat once she was clear. At the same time, Fadden edged around the car, walking gently to the point where she had crossed. 'Nearly over,' she called back, and he spat at her to keep her voice down. The main beams of the roof began to set up a spasmodic cracking sound, an anguished cry from the weight of wood and lead, stone and tile.

The case seemed heavy in his hand as Fadden began to pick his way over the rubble, trying to find strong footholds. He missed one, a brick dislodging, causing him to clutch out to prevent himself from falling – the pistol slipping from his grasp, bouncing down among the debris.

Mary was out of sight now – well clear; so Fadden put the case down, balancing it, swaying, on the bricks, while he shifted to reach for the pistol. He had just taken the weapon firmly in his right hand and grasped the handle of the case, when the roof above him gave its last screeching crack. He felt, and heard, the first tiles begin to go, and the creak which seemed to envelop him.

Move fast, his brain signalled. Automatically, Paul Fadden leaped up the rubble, slipping, but not caring where his feet landed, forging on, pushing himself over the hillock of brick. He half-slid, half-fell down the further side, the crash of the roof, and other walls, blotting anything else from his consciousness.

A tile struck his shoulder, and some small pieces of stone spattered over his head. The roar made him feel as though he was being sucked back into the vortex of a whirlpool. Then, like someone bursting into sunlight, he was clear, the noise behind him, the dust still clawing at him, as though to drag him back into the collapsing barn.

He was running, well clear, pulling up as he almost fell on top of Mary, crouched in the safety of a crumbling wall that had once been part of a cowshed.

He turned to see the death throes of the barn; the last fragments going down, in a strange twisting movement, as if in slow motion.

'At least it'll hide the car,' Mary said.

He told her he wanted to get to as high a point in the old farm buildings as possible. The noise of the collapsing barn had died, and the pall of dust around it sank, all too slowly, to the earth. Fadden was worried that the noise, or the dust cloud, would bring the troops and police in their direction.

He surveyed the remains of the buildings. The wall against which they sheltered was half down. To the right there was another completely ruined building. On the other side of the barn stood what was left of the original farmhouse – in a state of decay, but with the roof and walls intact – the broken windows and swinging doors making it look uninviting, even menacing. The wall in front of them, and adjoining it, at right-angles with the farmhouse, was serrated and breached in several places. There was a clear view across its remains to the track down which they had come – about a kilometre from the lane.

Nothing moved.

Leaving the case with Mary, Fadden went out through the breach in the walls, which had marked their entrance in the car. Any fool could spot the tyre tracks, and see where he had slewed the Rover into the barn door. Constantly glancing towards the lane, Fadden did his best to cover the tracks, then went forward, around the outside of the ruins.

At the rear, the ground swept away below him – open and with no cover – towards the forest: Savernake Forest, in which lay the Last Trump. He looked at his watch, and then at the sun. There would only be about another half-hour of daylight. As soon as dusk fell, they could take their chance on the Forest.

During the last half-hour or so, Mary had shown little sign of fear. Now Fadden wondered if he detected glimmers of shock in her eyes. He kissed her lightly, told her what they were going to do, and led her to the decaying farmhouse.

It smelled damp, musty, full of decaying memories. Fadden always wondered about the people who had once lived in ruined houses. He wondered now; the image of some fat jolly farmer's wife baking in the cobwebbed kitchen.

The stairs looked safe enough, but he asked Mary to stay at the bottom, with the case, until he had tested them.

The house had only two storeys, and, while there were holes and rotten areas in the floorboards, the second storey seemed safe enough. It crossed his mind that they should not stay up there until it was fully dark, in case of treading on rotten wood.

'Leave the case there,' he called down quietly. 'Watch your step; I'm going to what they might call the master bedroom – at the front.'

He heard her giggle and start mounting the stairs as he crossed the room. Paper hung from the walls – an old floral pattern – like posters unhinged from street walls by rain.

The window gave him a clear view right across the track down which they had come. He could see the narrow lane running at right angles to it. Then he stopped. The personnel carrier was in the lane. There were police cars drawn up also, as if they expected the Rover to back-track down it.

But they obviously did not think that would happen. The troops from the personnel carrier had formed up between the vehicles in the lane, and the armoured car, hatches down and turret swinging, was edging its way on to the track. The troops began to follow, fanning out as they did so, beginning a wide slow sweep which would take in the farm. As he moved away from the window, Mary came into the room smiling, her mouth changing as she saw the look in his eyes.

He calculated that the armoured car and troops would be fanned around the ruins in a matter of less than ten minutes.

Fadden almost pushed her back along the short landing, holding her arm tightly as they negotiated the stairs. As they went, he gave her instructions.

'They'll be here in less than ten minutes. We'll work our way round to the back; then it'll be a long downhill run in the open. About half a kilometre. Hope you can run. If we make the edge of the forest before dark, I can have a quick look at the survey map. With luck – and my boyhood memories – we could make safety in an hour or so.'

In his head, he tried to work out the direction he would have to take through the forest – if they got to its shelter in time.

At the foot of the stairs, Fadden grabbed at the suitcase, his right hand clutching the pistol, instinct telling him that

204

there must be a back door to the farmhouse.

Mary was beside him, asking if she could carry the case. 'I'm as strong as an ox, Paul; and I used to be a runner.'

'If I can't manage it, I'll chuck it to you.' He paused for a second in the kitchen, to kiss her lightly. 'Come on fleet-foot.'

There was a door, locked and bolted, from the kitchen scullery to the rear of the farmhouse. Fadden slid the bolts, and took his foot to the lock. The splintering sound echoed like a pistol shot.

Outside, the light was going fast. He tried to think, calculating the position of the troops in relation to where they were standing. The ground was now a darkish brown where – when he had last looked – it had been greeny-gold. The dark shelter of the Forest lay below: a black wall in which they could lose themselves. He whispered to Mary, trying to fix her eyes on the point that would give them most cover during the dash, so that the farm buildings would shield them for the longest possible time.

He heard her take a deep breath, and, gulping air into his own lungs, Fadden began the downhill run. Mary panted beside him, going flat out, her long legs moving in a loping rhythm. Fadden knew the first shots might come at any moment. The nearer the forest came, the safer they were, for they would begin to merge with the trees and become invisible.

The slope of the ground pushed up their speed, the momentum of their legs increasing as the angle of the slope grew sharper. Fadden heard Mary Athay's breathing start to go out of control, panting and gasping. He was also beginning to flag. Too old for this kind of lark. No, that was stupid. But the roaring blood in his ears, the pain building in his chest, the way he had to strain to get air into his lungs, told him he could not hold out for much longer.

They were almost at the very edge of the trees when the first shots cracked over their heads. Fadden had relied on the merging of their shapes with the trees to save them. It must be Mary's lighter clothes – probably a flash against the darkness – which allowed them to be spotted.

As they reached the shelter of the forest, so a whole fusillade of shots clipped and cracked around them. Over the roaring in his ears, Fadden heard the sound of the armoured car, and then the rattle of its machine-gun.

He yelled at Mary to get down, and they flung themselves into the first thickets, panting and gasping. Through his gasps, Fadden told her they had to go in, bury themselves in the forest. A searchlight – from the armoured car, he thought – was probing through the gathering darkness, and they could hear the orders, drifting down the hill.

Taking a last breath, Fadden hauled Mary up and they plunged into the trees, blundering against branches, bumping into the thick trunks, their feet crackling among the twigs and fallen logs, cheeks and faces scarred by flicking briar and bough.

Cut, bruised and scratched, they must have gone on for the best part of twenty minutes, their eyes slowly becoming accustomed to the night, before reaching an open space which seemed to be the meeting point of two small bridle tracks.

They stood, listening. There was no sound; then, from ahead, a long way off, the noise of an engine: something moving rapidly. Roads, Fadden knew, criss-crossed the forest. He tried to think himself into the shoes of whoever was in command of the small detachment of troops, and police, that had followed them to the edge of the trees.

It was unlikely he would order them into the depths of Savernake Forest in the dark. The better strategy would be to call up other troops; patrol the roads, which cut across and through the Forest, segmenting it; then, at dawn, with the whole forest encircled, move slowly in, trapping them within the trees, like animals cut off from all help.

*　　*　　*

These were the exact orders, being discussed at this moment, between Lupaiyev and the military commander of the Wiltshire area. Lupaiyev listened carefully to what the commander – a young colonel – had to say. The hunted pair had got into the forest, and the colonel was sending as many troops and vehicles to the site as quickly as he could. 'There are over four thousand English acres to cover,' the colonel said. 'I can have the few proper roads blocked through the night, and the whole place surrounded by armed men within the hour. It will be impossible to get out.'

'You mean we have them?'

'Unless some angel descends from the skies to whisk them away.'

Lupaiyev wanted to know why the colonel would not send men in now, to comb the forest; and the colonel told him that would be the quickest way to lose the quarry.

'My resources are limited,' he said. 'If my men miss them in the dark, so the fugitives put themselves outside the cordon, we could lose them for good. Marshal, we must wait until first light.'

Lupaiyev gave a direction that there must be strict security on the matter; that it might be best if the hunted pair were disposed of as soon as they were captured. All reports must come directly to him.

Marshal Lupaiyev had completely made up his mind. The threat Fadden had posed was minimal, he argued. He would lie to the Premier, and his tough old boss, 'Lead' Leo.

Menichev was by his elbow as the Marshal put down the telephone. 'They are caught?' he asked.

'Trapped. As good as in the bag. You heard my instructions. As far as we're concerned, Menichev, my old friend Fadden and this Athay woman are dead. That is our story.'

*   *   *

Huddled together among a clump of bushes, well away from the track they had stumbled across, Paul Fadden and Mary Athay examined the ordnance survey map by the light of the torch.

Knowing the area as he did, Fadden found it reasonably easy to pinpoint their exact position. Even during their run to the forest, he had experienced flashes of memory from his youth. The old farm had been known to him in its better days, but he had usually only seen it from the distance, from the forest edge.

It did not take him long to orientate himself. Already, from the special map, still hidden in the spine of Graham Greene's *Journey Without Maps*, he had plotted the thirty-fifth co-ordinate, so knew exactly where he was heading. Now that he had their own position, he was aware they would have to travel nearly two miles through the dense forest, along the small bridle paths and tracks, in order to reach their final destination, and the Last Trump.

They also had to cross a minor road.

It was only the road that made him uneasy. The Soviet forces would take a few hours to surround the forest; but they would almost certainly be patrolling the small minor roads – either in armoured vehicles, or using the local constabulary. The sooner he covered the distance to that road with Mary, the more chance they stood. He pointed out the route, turning the map to show Mary exactly where they were, in relation to the terrain, both within and without the great forest. She nodded quick understanding, taking in the tactical difficulties of the situation straight away, whispering that they had better move now.

Her professional grasp of the situation exhilarated Fadden. Mary did not know what lay at the end of their journey; she could not even comprehend that comparative safety waited for them; yet she was willing to start the difficult trek through the thick darkness of the forest.

Progress was slower than expected with Fadden constantly stopping to look at the map, using the torch, shaded by his handkerchief. They spoke little, except for the occasional whisper.

He thought of the irony. They were in the middle of one of the greatest of England's old royal forests, reeking with history. Henry VIII had ridden through it many times; it had been the scene of important acts in history. Even more, they were heading for a place that would take them further into the legends and truths of England's past. The thirty-fifth map co-ordinate, provided within the Golgotha labyrinth, was the site of what had once been a great English house – Wolf Hall: a legendary building which, when Fadden knew it as a boy, had been in a state of great decay. It was even possible that, when he had known it then, Wolf Hall had very little of its original fabric left – so many people had added to it; patched up the decay; moved sections of the house.

Wolf Hall was, long ago, the country seat – well-protected within the Savernake Forest – of the famous Seymour family. Henry VIII had come to the original Tudor mansion to court Jane Seymour: the lady who, after Anne Boleyn's execution, eventually became his queen, and bore his son, Prince Edward. So the historic links were cable strong.

The Seymour family had owned the Hall, and been wardens of Savernake Forest, for a large part of English history – their lineage going back to the time of the Norman conquest.

On Henry VIII's death, the young Prince Edward – who was to die before he was sixteen – began his short reign. But the man who held the power, and had England in his grasp, was Jane Seymour's brother: The Lord Protector of England – Edward Seymour, Earl of Hertford and Duke of Somerset.

Fadden thought it a magnificent irony that Britain was now to be defended, through the Last Trump, from the home of that ruthless and powerful Duke of Somerset, who, so many centuries ago, had engineered intrigues and power struggles from this very Wolf Hall, brooding in the midst of the forest.

In all, it took them nearly two hours to reach the minor road. Fadden thought, if his reckoning was correct, they were now within easy walking distance of the ruined Hall.

They kept to the forest, not straying on to the road: for twice, in a matter of ten minutes, they were forced to flatten themselves among the branches and bushes, which lay between the verge and the deeper clutches of trees. Police cars moved slowly back and forth along the narrow road, two of them, like sentries, cruising to and fro, passing one another constantly, as they covered this particular stretch of ground. Both of the cars had spotlights which they played upon the bushes, trees and roadside as they went by.

Fadden and Mary Athay used the short periods while the road was clear, to run, in bursts, towards their goal. If his memory was correct, Fadden judged that Wolf Hall lay at a junction of minor forest roads, the ruin standing back among the trees. He was also certain that it lay on the other side of the road up which they moved. It could only be a few metres from them now, and he silently thanked God that, as yet, there were only police cars in the vicinity. He was certain that personnel carriers must be on the way.

If the Soviets were going to surround the forest, to keep the minor roads under observation, very soon armed troops would be stationed along this stretch. Continuing to make the short runs among the bushes – avoiding too much movement, and the searching spotlights – they finally reached the point which Fadden calculated to be almost opposite Wolf Hall.

They waited, to time the police cars; discovering there appeared to be a five-minute period when the crossing point was virtually free of surveillance.

'It'll take us all of five minutes to find the place, once we've crossed,' Fadden whispered. 'Possibly another five minutes to reach the entrance.' He explained they were searching for a ruined house.

During the next clear period, they crossed the road, once more finding themselves blundering into thick undergrowth, and a close wall of trees. Again they had to lie flat, as the cars prowled up the road. In the distance, getting edgily close, Fadden thought he could detect the sound of heavier vehicles; but, as he lay flat, trying to avoid any particle of light from the police spots, he at last saw the shape of a structure ahead, among the trees. They were almost at the entrance of Wolf Hall.

The west wing, Rupert Graves' clue had told him. That would be on the side furthest away from them. He waited until the next clear period from the cars before touching Mary's arm, pointing towards the shape looming from among the trees. Almost as he did so, Fadden was conscious of more lights on the road. Military vehicles moving at speed. Stopping. Orders shouted. He pulled at Mary's arm and they set off towards the Hall.

A flare rose high above them. Then another, turning the darkness into brilliant relief. Once behind the building they would be screened from the road; but the going was difficult, and the place now seemed alive with sound – shouts, the clatter of equipment, and roar of engines.

The old house had given up most of its ghosts; collapsing here and there in fragments. The light from the two original flares was just dying, when searchlights swept through the trees from the road, and another cluster of flares rose, almost languidly, into the night sky. By the light, which was a threat to them, Fadden and Mary picked their way over masonry, piles of bricks, large chunks of stone and rubble.

The shouts and orders appeared to be coming from all around them now, as though they were being encircled, the troops making no attempt to disguise their presence. At least that gave Fadden heart, as they reached an area of wall that seemed intact – the beginning of the west wing – for it meant the troops had not actually pinpointed them.

Mary took the case from him as, together, they made their way along the wall, past boarded windows and long beams of timber, set at intervals to prop up the bulging stone. They both felt naked and tense in the unnatural light, expecting a cry or a shot at any moment.

Fadden prayed for the door, but they reached the corner of the wall without finding it. Ahead of them, at right angles, was the furthest wall – shorter, but, like the other, propped at intervals by wooden stanchions. There was one large, boarded window, then, at last, the doorway – strong and sturdy; reinforced, Fadden considered, from the inside. He felt for the keys attached to the chain around his belt, whispering for Mary to put down the suitcase and stand by with the torch. The searchlights still probed on the far side of the building, but the flares were dropping, like miniature setting suns, throwing everything into a ghastly, shadowy grey relief.

His mind concentrated back on to the final instructions, dredged from Rupert Graves' subconscious.

In the dim light he saw the letter A on the key. It slid home easily. Three times clockwise. Once anti-clockwise. The mechanism was obviously intricate, for the noise which followed was that of a series of clicking thuds, as though numerous bolts were being withdrawn in sequence. A memory stirred, from somewhere in Fadden's past – a visit to Woodstock and Blenheim Palace, where the lock on the massive door was a complex, and exact, copy of the original locking mechanism for the gates of Warsaw: the only existing replica in the world, following the destruction of the Polish capital in the nineteen-forties: all polished brass arms and hinges, with a cunningly hidden keyhole.

As the door swung open a blinding beam scythed through the trees and darkness directly behind them. For a second, it hovered to their left, catching them only in the periphery of its bright pool. Then it swung, with uncanny precision, on to the pair framed in the doorway.

There were shouts. *Stop. Halt. Stay. Stand still.* Fadden pushed Mary in front of him, almost falling through the door after her, as the first long raking burst of fire opened up from the trees, hitting the stone to their right. By the time the search troops found their aim, the door was closed, shaking as the heavy bullets found their mark.

'The kitchen,' Fadden whispered. 'Quickly.' He pressed himself against the wall to the side of the door as it slammed closed. As he had imagined, the rear of the door – and, indeed of the walls themselves – was reinforced with thick hard steel. He could hear the thumping clang as bullets flattened themselves on this protecting layer. As the door closed, so the bolts whirred back into place, as if enclosing them in a tomb. It would not be long, Fadden considered,

212

before the search troops would bring up heavy armament to blast their way through.

In the few seconds they stood there, it was apparent, by torch light, that this whole hallway area had been screened off by metal, even under the crumbling floorboards.

Because some of the old woodwork was still intact, the place smelled of decay; almost the stench of death. Through the walls they could hear shouted orders. The rattle of weaponry seemed to have ceased for the time being, but the walls and, in particular, the door, now shook to heavy blows, as though the search force was trying to break in with axes.

Lugging the case, Fadden led the way through the main passage, keeping the torch down, noting that the old staircase had been blocked off with a steel wall which cut through it at about the fourth stair. There was only one way for them to go, straight on through a narrow metal-walled passage to the left of the stairs, then down six stone steps into what had once been the kitchen, complete with flagstones which seemed tightly embedded, even cemented, into place.

He called Mary closer with the torch, and saw a small area where part of the stone rocked slightly under the pressure of his hand. As he found it, so came the first shattering crump of a shell, or some armour-piercing projectile, aimed at the door. Mary's hands went to her ears, the torch spinning over the floor, the hallway behind them filling with dust and the reek of explosive.

Fadden scrabbled for the torch, his own eardrums singing from the pressure of the explosion. He reached for the flagging, but his fingers were too large to insert between the cracks, trying to prise the piece of stone upwards.

There were two more explosions; they seemed to be aimed around the door – heavy crumps – mortars, Fadden thought. Mary looked white, frightened and trembling in the meagre light. Give her something to take her mind off the Soviet troops, Fadden reasoned.

Between curses he explained things, in quick rattled sentences, and Mary gently pushed the torch back into his hand, drawing him out of the way. Her smaller fingers easily worked the stone loose. Fadden stretched down to help with the last pull. As the stone came away, so there was a whole barrage of explosions – some seemed to come from above, others from the door section. Dust was clouding in around them now, so that they coughed and spluttered, peering into the small space under the stone.

The top of the box, beneath, was of metal, the keyhole sunk into the centre. Key B was in Fadden's hand. Another barrage, the ground shaking, their ears deafened by the blast; more dust and smoke, a smell of burning. It crossed Fadden's mind that they could well be caught by flames inside the metal protection, roasted like a pair of chickens.

He turned the key. Three times anti-clockwise; one clock-wise. The metal lifted easily, on oiled hinges, revealing the combination lock beneath.

Mary had the torch again. Motioning her to come closer so that he could see more clearly to read the numbers on the dial, Fadden set it to zero and, remembering to turn the dial alternately clockwise and anti-clockwise, he began to go through the sequence.

There was another series of explosions which made the ground under them tremble and must have been doing severe damage to the front of the west wing.

Fadden bent to his work with speed and concentration. The combination was easy enough to remember: seven – fifteen – twelve – seven – fifteen – twenty – eight – one – child's play to even a schoolboy with the rudiments of ciphers. It was almost too simple – each figure correspond-ing to the letters in the alphabet spelling *Golgotha*. As the dial reached *one*, he heard the distinctive click, even above the rumble of the explosions, which seemed to be more intense. Fadden tugged to the right. A section of the flagging, heavy with a good six inches of steel beneath the stone, slid smoothly to one side.

Before letting the section run its full course, Fadden re-locked the metal box, pushing the loose stone back into place. Together they slid the section of stone and steel to one side. The torch showed a wide metal stairway running deeply down into the earth.

Below them must lie the heart of Golgotha – the Last Trump.

He motioned Mary into the cavity, and as he did so, there came the largest explosion of all, from the door area. Metal began to fly, and smoke now filled the kitchen, clawing at Fadden's eyes. Mary, already well into the stairway, cried out. Fadden needed no further warning. He leaped down, following her into the earth below Wolf Hall.

★ 31 ★

Air Force One touched down only five minutes off schedule at Rome's Leonardo da Vinci airport. The few people who lined the streets, as the United States' President's motorcade went past, on its way to the Vatican, stood in silence. There was immense security. None of the officials showed any sign of friendliness, or pleasure, towards the President. During the night there had been more terrorist acts – all of them against Soviet military installations, both in Europe and within the confines of the Russian border.

Accusations had been made, threats to call off the summit. But, after hearing both the news and reaction – on board Air Force One – the President had issued a firm and positive statement: America had no terrorist agents in Europe. Their affairs could be looked into, with close scrutiny, by the Soviet's powerful ally, the People's Republic of China, if they so wished. The message read:

I come to meet the Soviet leaders in peace. I am determined to get reassurance from the Soviet powers that peace will be regained, and that the peoples of Europe will have their own freedom and authority returned to them. Peace is my pledge to the rest of the world. Freedom is my pledge to Europe.

The statement was ambiguous.

Inside the Vatican, the old President met with the middle-aged Pope John Paul IV – elected only a few years previously, and known to be a man dedicated to the cause of

216

reconciliation between the peoples of the world.

The Pope was a tall man, leather-faced, with soft blue eyes which seemed to shine into the very souls of those to whom he spoke. After the normal religious courtesies, his chaplain and other advisers were asked to withdraw. The bodyguards and aides, who had come with the President also withdrew.

'Your mission is truly peace, my son?' The Pope sat opposite, but close, to the President.

'My mission is for both peace and freedom, Holiness.'

His Holiness moved his head gravely, the merest gesture of a nod. 'I cannot see, Mr President, how you can possibly attain both. The political ideology of Communism is near to the religious ideology of Christianity; but it binds men's wills – their minds and souls – so it has a basic repugnance to us. How can I be of help?'

'Holy Father, I come to ask you to hear my confession.'

'Any priest could have done that, Mr President. Does your lofty position require me to give you absolution before you undertake your task?'

'No. I also realise that you are bound by the seal of the confessional. However, in matters of such great importance, the very hearing of my confession may allow you some freedom to speak your mind truly. I am humbly asking you to make a statement to the world before the Dublin Conference begins.'

Pope John Paul IV thought for several minutes before nodding agreement. He went to his desk, took out the purple stole he had to wear to dispense absolution, kissed it, and placed it around his neck.

The President of the United States knelt beside the Pontiff and began, 'Bless me Holy Father, for I have sinned . . . '

When the President finally left the Vatican, Pope John Paul IV sat down, gravely troubled in mind and spirit, to write his message to the world, on the eve of the Dublin Conference.

The President would stay within the walls of the Vatican during the night before flying to Dublin for the start of the

217

conference. Already the Secretary of State was in Ireland, together with military aides, and many advisers.

The leaders of the People's Republic of China were also en route to Dublin – Tai Yen-Sen, leader of the Chinese Communist Party, and the Premier, Shih P'eng Te.

The Soviet Premier, Mr Alymnov, was in London, as was the head of Russia's intelligence service, the KGB – the terrible 'Lead' Leo. The Premier had taken part in talks with the British Prime Minister, who was also travelling to Dublin. He would go accompanied by both British and Soviet security agents. Anyone who had seen the Prime Minister since his historic request for Soviet help would have noticed his rapid decline in health – the haggard expression and sunken eyes, the signs of grave strain deeply etched into his face.

The Presidents of France, Italy, the former leader of the German Federal Republic, and other political chiefs of the new Soviet Bloc countries were also on their way.

Back at the CIA complex near Washington, the Director, Don Marks, waited. With him was the go-between Chinese Minister K'e Hu-We.

At the Pentagon, and in the deep underground operations centres, the military, air and naval strategic specialists, were at their posts, resting turn and turn about. Military and airborne units were all on standby, and America's main airbases seemed oddly silent, though thousands of aircraft were ready to roll at two minutes' notice.

Out on the refurbished launch pads at Cape Kennedy, eight massive rockets sat, ready for launching, their countdowns already started. On top of seven of the rockets were the most technically-advanced communications satellites. The eighth rocket carried the most complicated and sensitive satellite of all. It was merely spoken of as the GA-One, and had been in storage – handled by only a few specialists – since the mid-nineteen seventies. In the time since then, the GA-One had undergone many modifications. Only the President, and a couple of other people, would ever speak, or think, of it as the Golgotha satellite.

Five other rockets awaited positioning on the launch pads, once the communications satellites were fired. These were, again, more sophisticated than anything yet put into orbit – the new intelligence-gathering satellites.

That night, Pope John Paul IV issued his message of blessing, and advice, to the world leaders who were to gather in Dublin. The text would not be made public until the President of the United States had landed in Ireland, but the news services passed it on to political counterparts without any question of conscience. It read:

Brothers in Christ I am aware that, in speaking to the world's political leaders, meeting together in Ireland, I am speaking to many who do not, and cannot, share the Christian faith. I feel, however, that I would be lacking in my pastoral and spiritual responsibility, if I remained silent.

In the past weeks we have seen something happen in the world which should be repugnant to all Christians. We have seen a strong nation take, by threat and force, the land and resources of weaker nations. A great predecessor of mine was strongly criticised long ago in this present century, for not opposing the totalitarian methods of the Nazi regime, which sought to subdue the peoples of Europe and force their particular political ideology upon them.

I shall not make the same error. I have to speak out. What we face amounts to slavery – of the mind, spirit, heart and soul. It is not freedom; and man must have freedom, both within himself and within his country. Man's personal freedom can only be curtailed when he has broken the natural laws of mankind – when he has stolen from his brother; murdered his brother; defrauded his brother.

The largest number of European people now live under a law, and political system, which they have not chosen of their own free will. It has been forced upon them. They are, under this force, not free to think or do as their natural consciences dictate. This is neither consistent with the law of God nor that of Man.

Among you in Dublin, will be a man of great integrity, the President of the United States of America, who has spoken to me of his own personal problems regarding the present state of the world. I ask you, the other world leaders, to listen to him with care, and I, as the anointed leader of Christ's Catholic Church on earth, plead with you to take heed of what the President has to say to you. To listen to his voice, and not let it be a voice crying in a wilderness of people who are deaf to everything except their own power.

Be assured from me that the American President also holds power. He is a man of peace, who will fight for peace. I pray and urge you, my brethren, whatever your politics, whatever your creed; listen to him. Let him be weighed in the balance.

May the blessing of God the Father, Son and Holy Ghost, be upon you in your deliberations; and upon the world at their outcome.

The Soviet leaders wondered, and worried, over the wording of the text. Mr Alymnov seemed particularly disturbed. 'It reads like a warning of doom,' he said to his Foreign Minister.

Marshal Lupaiyev had personally seen the Soviet Premier. He had also spent a couple of uncomfortable hours with the Head of the KGB. Both he and the detective, Menichev, assured the powerful Soviet leaders that, as far as Britain was concerned, there were no dangers. The man, Fadden, was dead; and their first analysis of the situation had proved to be drastically unimaginative.

When the American President's aircraft finally touched down at Dublin airport, the first person to go on board was

Tim McPherson from the Embassy. He brought two code words. They meant that the German – who they had sent into the Golgotha labyrinth in Europe – and Paul Fadden, in Britain, both appeared to be in place.

The President sent an urgent message to the Soviet Premier, who had reached Dublin an hour or so earlier, that he would like to see him in order to get guarantees, before the conference, that the Soviet Bloc would take no action against the launching of new communications satellites. His argument was that it would make matters easier, and the conduct of business smoother, if these communications were restored. If the Soviets detected anything other than normal communications satellites, they were at liberty to take action.

Mr Alymnov took advice from his military and specialist personnel. In his message, the President had indicated that his request, and the Soviet reply, would be a guide to the measure of trust he presumed still existed between the two countries. It would set the tone for a fruitful conference.

Alymnov was against allowing the launching, but his advisers were not so certain. During the night they had captured two of the so-called terrorists. They had turned out to be senior army officers of the country concerned. Both made statements saying that they acted on military contingency plans, made long ago within their commands. They claimed there was no help, or advice, given by the United States. China was not mentioned during the interrogations. The two men had gone to their graves with their secret safe.

Exactly an hour after receiving the President's request, the Soviet Premier gave permission for the launchings. After all, his military and space advisers told him, we have the means to jam the satellites if necessary. They did not know the new satellites contained advanced anti-jamming equipment which, while still in its testing stage, was highly efficient against the, already known, devices used by the Soviets during their previous attack.

The countdown went to its final stage, and the eight

rockets blasted off from Kennedy, one after another, each placing its complicated parcel of electronics into precise orbit.

The first rocket to go was the one that carried GA-One – the Golgotha Satellite.

★ 32 ★

Deep under the west wing of crumbling Wolf Hall, in Savernake Forest, lay four solid chambers. One was a bathroom and lavatory; the second a small kitchen, with supplies and cooking equipment; the third a bedroom, containing a cot, table and books. In the fourth chamber stood the control panel that was the Last Trump.

A small box was set into a wall in each of the chambers, with lights and a tiny loudspeaker, so that whoever was to blow the Last Trump would be in constant contact with the main panel.

The four-chambered complex had its own generator, providing both light and air, recycled through an ingenious device already perfected as early as the nineteen-seventies.

Above them, the ground sent down tremors, as though the old Wolf Hall – plus its reinforced chamber in the west wing – was being demolished piece by piece. By the shaking and regularity of the explosions and thuds, Fadden guessed that troops had entered the house above them, and were now clearing the upper structure with planted charges. If they were lucky, the search troops might still imagine their quarry to be hidden in some sealed area above ground.

Fadden had been able to slide the stone and steel entrance back into place before the first troops arrived inside the house. It was now a question of time before the Soviet forces realised they were probably in this underground bunker, and then time before they blasted their way down into it. Fadden reckoned on a minimum of twenty-four hours, and a maximum of forty-eight.

In spite of the proximity of the troops, and the noises from above, Mary Athay almost squealed with delight at the relative luxury of this otherwise austere hideout – 'The air-conditioning keeps us at a constant temperature of sixty-five. We can have baths and everything.'

Fadden said that was good (wondering if the temperature would, indeed, keep that low once the search troops got to work with lasers and other cutting gear). He left her to sort out the domestic arrangements. Personally, he would be engaged in work of a different nature, and of greater importance. It crossed his mind that it was as well she had made the escape with him, for her presence allowed him greater freedom of action with the Last Trump.

The control panel was smaller than he had imagined, yet exactly as described – a grey metal unit with a padded swivel chair for the operator. Everything was in its place: the two banks of seventeen neat buttons, like those of an old IBM typewriter, though spaced apart, and each numbered, one to thirty-four: the small round lights above each button like dead eyes, unlit.

In the top left-hand corner was the activating switch, with two circular lights, also dead, to its right. The only thing missing from the original description was a small loud-speaker which Fadden now saw, countersunk below the master switch.

For some strange reason, he had not been prepared for the masses of wiring, and the computer cabinets, their doors locked, which took up almost the whole of the remaining space in the chamber.

Fadden obeyed orders immediately by throwing the main switch. The red light nearest the switch came on with a strong glow, and there was a low, almost inaudible, buzzing.

A second or two later, the other lights, along the rows of buttons, lit up, one after the other – a ripple effect of red lights shining clearly. The control panel, which was the Last Trump, seemed now to be a living thing: a being designed to do a job; something with a mind of its own. Fadden was there only to guard it, carry out orders, be the finger on its devastating trigger.

224

He reflected that they should have given him the cryptonym Gabriel, if he was to be the one to blow the Last Trump. In his heart he hoped that the President's skills and political tactics would prevent this. With the knowledge learned in Washington and during the hazardous journey through the labyrinth of clues, and from the facts planted in his subconscious – brought to light by Rupert Graves' trigger sentence – Fadden was well aware that to blow the Last Trump might truly mean the world ending in a confusion of destruction.

He looked at the machine, pulsing steadily, then turned and went back into the bedroom chamber. Vaguely he realised that the rumbles and explosions from above had ceased.

Mary had already unpacked the few belongings from the case, saying she was going to clean herself up and shower. Fadden thought he probably had time to do the same. If his calculations were correct, the President would just about be leaving Rome en route for Dublin.

It was just as Mary left for the bathroom chamber that Fadden caught sight of the one piece of decoration added by the designers of this secret place. On the wall hung another reproduction of the painting which seemed to have haunted his journey: the gravestones with the mist bubbling around them.

He stood and looked at it for a long time, knowing the painting had been a kind of motif, a recognition of the path down which he had travelled. Was it, then, meant to remind him of the finality of the Golgotha scheme? – or signify some new hope that mankind would, in reality, be joined afresh in a resurrection?

In his mind, he could hear the elderly chaplain at school, reading the lesson on a drowsy Sunday morning – *Behold, I show you a mystery; we shall not all sleep, but we shall all be changed; In a moment; In the twinkling of an eye, at the last trump.*

It was a message – that the weapons, dead in Britain's earth, may have to rise up to save mankind, who, in the end, would rise, at the Day of Judgement, to life everlasting. That, the fact of their deadly presence in the earth, was a symbol of hope. If the weapons were not used now, mankind had a chance of conquering obliteration. If they were used, mankind was still not lost; for that Day of Wrath and Doom, which was the promise of the Christian Faith, would eventually bring forth a new kind of life.

Maybe, Fadden thought, he was muddled; perhaps he was reading too much into the painting's symbolism. Or too little. It did not matter, for the end of this era could only lead to a new beginning. Hilary Keville's message had said that – *the keys you hold are the keys to either the Alpha or the Omega.* The Alpha and the Omega. Greek. The Beginning and the End.

As he gazed at the picture, so the painted mists around the gravestones seemed to swirl and move. Paul Fadden hoped with all his heart that this was the Alpha – the Beginning.

Then all hope seemed to go as, from deep in the earth, came a series of quaking rumbles: four distinct explosions, sending their shock-waves right into the bunker, almost at its four corners. The Soviet search force had moved faster than Fadden had imagined. He had no doubt they were now systematically placing charges deep in the earth – blowing themselves into the old foundations of Wolf Hall, starting at its outer edges. It would take time for them to get close and do damage: but Fadden was probably running out of time. There was no way of knowing when the signals would come into the Last Trump. Mary stood in the doorway, dripping from her shower, face drained, mouth opening and closing as if she wanted to ask what the latest explosions meant.

*   *   *

In the round, cake-like building that is the American Embassy in the Ballsbridge district of Dublin, the President carried out his final briefing with aides, Secret Service men, security officers – under Tim McPherson – the military advisers, and his Secretary of State.

The room they used was a special conference room, far under the building, screened by layers of anti-electronic surveillance equipment. The President spoke first; then Tim McPherson gave his special orders, the President adding a few words at the completion.

What was said came as a shock and surprise, a mind-boggling, almost incredible secret laid bare to most of those in the screened room. Even the Secretary of State showed visible signs of agitation and disbelief, voicing the opinion that they were going to be engaged in undemocratic actions. 'We are going to force an issue at gunpoint, Mr President. That's not the way America does things.'

'It's the only way it can be done, Mr Secretary. I'm not interested in the finer points of political morality now. This is a life-or-destruction battle over the table. The result will be either the end of freedom and life, as we know it on this planet; or a new start, with great work ahead for every-one – a time for yet another struggle to bring peace and order from chaos and political thuggery.'

As he spoke, other world leaders were leaving their Embassies and Consulates for the Mansion House where the famous Round Room had been converted, and secured, as the Summit Conference meeting place.

Dublin had risen – as she always does – to the sense of occasion. It was the first time that such a gathering of the world leaders had been held in the city. Despite the sombre underlying seriousness of the occasion, Dubliners looked upon the day as one of spectacle and holiday. Crowds lined the broad imposing O'Connell Street, up which some of the leaders would arrive. Narrow and smart Grafton Street was closed to all but official traffic, as was Dawson Street – now packed with people – waiting to glimpse the world's greatest politicians: for the newly-painted white Mansion House lay half-way up this pleasant road.

Above Dawson Street, people surrounded St Stephen's Green, the trees, shrubs and flowers, behind the park railings almost obliterated from sight by the throng.

Every street was decorated with the flags of all nations involved; bunting hung from windows; the beer flowed in the lounges and bars, ice-cream sellers did a roaring trade, and the police – the Gardai – were hard-pressed to keep matters under control.

Irish troops lined the streets, and armed security men, from both the Gardai and Army, surrounded the Mansion House.

On the Papal instruction, every church in the city – indeed in the whole country – had a special Mass said for the outcome of this historic Summit.

The Department of Posts and Telegraphs had worked for a week on the installation of special lines within the Mansion House, for the world's press, who were given one room, and the security people who had another at their disposal.

In the Round Room – once the scene of famous balls and parties, later the place where the Declaration of Independence was signed, in 1919, and the Treaty of 1921 with Britain two years later – there were to be only two telephones, both red, and placed equidistant on the great oblong table. They were linked to a switchboard which, in turn, was manned by four operators. Anywhere in the world could, in theory, be linked with the Round Conference Room, within minutes.

Tim McPherson, in charge of the Presidential security, left Ballsbridge almost before the President had completed the briefing. He travelled with four other security officers, and went straight to the Mansion House. It had taken much bargaining with the Soviets, but agreement had been reached, late on the previous evening, that security within the Mansion House could be handled on a joint basis. Two Soviet Special Guards, in their grey and olive uniforms, and two United States Marines, would bar the doors to the Round Room. The Soviets armed with Kalashnikovs, the Marines with the latest mark of the M.16 carbine.

The Irish, punctilious in these matters, were insistent about controlling the exterior security; although there had been concessions which allowed both American, Soviet and Chinese officers to mingle with the crowds, and accompany armed Irish police in high-point surveillance.

Other major posts within the building, such as the doors to the press room, and the switchboard, were overlooked by trios of Soviet, American and Chinese plainclothes agents.

The personal bodyguards of each head of state were allowed to accompany their charges as far as the conference room. Following that, they were banished from the building, and would be called back when the conference broke for lunch. One officer, from each of the three represented major powers, would be allowed near the main doors of the Round Room, and there were three special teams with roving powers within the building. Tim McPherson's team was one of these.

In the street outside the Mansion House, the crowds cheered everyone, irrespective of country or politics. The French and British contingents arrived first: Britain's Prime Minister looking bent and haggard – an old man at less than sixty – as he mounted the steps to be greeted by the Irish President.

The President of the United Republic of Ireland had agreed, as leader of one of the few neutral states, not to be present at any of the deliberations. His job, as head of the host country, was to greet the other politicians individually, and give an address of welcome. After that, he would leave, returning only for any other official function – such as the dinner that was to be held at the Mansion House that evening (though, in truth, many of the Irish President's political advisers had told him not to be too quick in getting dressed up for it. Behind the scenes, there was a distinct air of pessimism, and the bookies were taking odds on the whole Summit Conference being over before the day was out – the Americans and Russians at each other's throats).

People started arriving quickly after ten o'clock – the Italians, Spanish, and representatives from the other vanquished countries. They looked like the solemn puppets they were, showing no real hunger for the affair.

Then the Germans and heads of the Low Countries were followed by an impressive cavalcade bringing the Chinese leaders, Tai Yen-Sen, and Shih P'eng Te.

As the Chinese arrived at the Mansion House, so the President, with the Secretary of State, left the American Embassy in Ballsbridge. The President seemed too relaxed for the Secretary's liking, even remarking on what a bright and clear morning it was and reminiscing about a holiday visit he had made to Ireland several years before. Occasionally, the President slipped his hand into his right jacket pocket, in which lay an oblong object, no bigger than an old box of matches. The object was black, and enclosed in a small screening case of clear treated plastic, of a kind designed to escape detection by scanners.

Just before they left the Embassy, the President had been assured that all the communications satellites were in orbit and functioning. '*All* of them,' the aide stressed on giving him the news.

The President tried to clear his mind. The things he had to do now needed a certain confidence and peace of mind. They were not acts with which he would normally associate himself. In truth they were almost the acts of a clandestine operative.

* * *

The shattering earthquakes came at roughly one hour intervals. Fadden tried to check them with his watch: waiting for each new burst of explosions, trying to pinpoint their direction – an almost impossible task.

Of one thing he was certain – the Soviets had ringed what had once been Wolf Hall, destroyed its upper limits, and were now working under it by blasting down many metres below the surface.

In the silences between the explosions, the earth occasionally seemed to quiver. Drills, Fadden thought, drills going deep, gouging out the earth ready for another explosive charge.

Mary Athay kept asking what would happen. He lied.

Nothing, he said. Nothing, for the explosives would not get through the vast thickness of steel which protected them from outside forces.

Inside, he knew well enough what would happen. They would either be burned, blasted or crushed inside the tomb of Golgotha. Unless some order was transmitted through the Last Trump, before the fast-closing explosive dredges reached them.

* * *

The Soviet Premier, together with bodyguards and aides, timed their departure so that they would be the last to arrive at the Mansion House. Mr Alymnov put on his grave face – the impassive look he preferred to present to the crowd. Alymnov was an almost unfathomable figure: a man who spoke a great deal, but seldom appeared in public. Few doubted that, as far as the Soviet Bloc was concerned, he had taken Communist policies and politics back decades, to the age of Stalin himself. For Alymnov was not just a figurehead – like those who, supposedly, ran his satellite countries. In every way he was a supremo of the old-fashioned variety. A dictator of dictators, with an almost psychopathic desire to rule the whole world according to his brand of Communism.

Today he would challenge his biggest adversary, the President of the United States. He reasoned that he may well have put the man off his guard by allowing the communications satellites to be placed in orbit. His experts had informed him early that morning that the satellites were in place, and appeared to be nothing more sinister than communications links.

He was not to know that, as his car entered St Stephen's Green, men in the basement of the American Embassy were tracking one of those satellites in particular: sitting with headphones in place and eyes glued to the scanners. GA-One had settled nicely into its place, high over Europe.

Alymnov, his Foreign Secretary, and Marshal Fadenovich,

231

the chief military adviser, entered the Mansion House exactly four minutes after the arrival of the Presidential party.

Everyone waited for him in the Round Room, each member of the great summit conference standing at his or her place around the long polished table, with its blotters, water carafes, pen-holders and agenda lists.

There was complete silence as the Soviet party entered. Alymnov looked neither left nor right, acknowledging nobody, going straight to his appointed place, and standing with a bored expression while the Irish President made his short speech of welcome.

There was polite applause, and the Irish President slowly left the room with his retinue. The doors were closed; the Soviet uniformed guards, and the U.S. Marine Corps men, took up their posts. Nearby, the three-man – American, Chinese and Soviet – security guards relaxed into chairs.

The Summit had begun. Soviet Premier Alymnov rose slowly and pointed an accusing finger at the President of the United States.

* * *

In another part of the building, Tim McPherson and his team looked at their watches. McPherson nodded. 'Give the Mick President time to get clear,' he said. 'About three minutes. If the Chinese keep to their part of the bargain, all hell will be breaking loose in the Round Room within five minutes or so. O.K., be nimble.'

McPherson himself left the others, heading towards the doors of the Round Room. The uniformed guards stirred as he reached them, but McPherson grinned and flashed his ID.

'I don't want to come in, just speak to my buddy with the detail over there.' He nodded towards the three security men. 'Can I have a word, Joe?'

The American plainclothes agent nodded at the Chinese and Soviet officers, slowly walking to where McPherson stood, near to the Round Room door, placing himself close to the pair of Soviet armed guards.

Out of sight, but nearby, waited another pair of McPherson's team.

As the agent called Joe got within a couple of paces of McPherson, so the Chinese agent moved towards his Soviet counterpart. The big Russian smiled, for the Chinese was offering him a cigarette. He took one, thanking the bowing Chinese agent in Russian. The Chinese lit the cigarette for him.

It took two long drags on the smoke before the Russian realised something was wrong – but it had required the first drag to hit the cyanide pellet. The Russian clutched at his throat, going down without another sound – the Chinese holding his breath and stamping hard on the cigarette butt, then stepping out of the way, waving his hands to disperse any stray fumes which might have escaped.

It all happened very quickly. There were a few seconds' delay before the pair of Russian guards realised their security colleague had collapsed. Their hesitation became their undoing. As they moved, raising their Kalashnikovs, so Tim McPherson, and the agent called Joe, stepped close to each of the men, with the speed of long practice, applied pen guns to the Russians' throats, the guns making hardly any noise as they injected deadly pellets into the men's windpipes. The Russian guards went down as if pole-axed.

The two Marine guards, briefed just before taking up duty, caught the Kalashnikov rifles, as the other two members of McPherson's team appeared from around the corner.

The whole thing took only around three minutes from start to finish. At the end of that time, the Soviet guards had been replaced by the two men from McPherson's team – looking quite the part in the uniforms. The real guards were dragged away and locked in a cupboard, together with the body of the Soviet security man, whose place was now taken by the third agent on McPherson's team.

Elsewhere in the building, the Chinese roving team of agents had taken out the Soviet team, using the skills of

233

silent killing which McPherson and Joe had so admirably demonstrated.

Together, the Americans and Chinese had secured the area immediately outside the Round Room. Inside, nobody heard a sound.

McPherson collected his fourth agent, and together they made for the small room which housed the switchboard. By the time they arrived, the work had already been done, the American and Chinese security men on duty having neatly disposed of their Soviet colleague by the simple device of using a hard object on the back of his neck. If done perfectly, the spinal cord breaks. Death is instantaneous. It had been done correctly.

McPherson's fourth agent – all were Russian speakers – quickly took the place of the Soviet. 'Give it a few minutes,' McPherson told them, 'then take over the switchboard. I'll be around in case we get any flack.' He headed back towards the Round Room.

All strategic points had been secured in a minimum amount of time.

*   *   *

There had been six underground explosions on the last occasion. They had also been closer, as though the search force were using larger charges, or skipping inwards at a faster rate.

It was an illusion, Fadden knew, but the whole underground set of chambers seemed to tilt as the charges fired. It reminded him of old movies about submarine warfare, when the sub was being depthcharged.

Mary appeared to be suffering from a mild claustrophobia now; nervously strung-out, and restless, on the verge of hysteria.

Fadden spent most of his time making sure she was as calm as possible, and checking out the Last Trump console which still buzzed and showed all lights glowing. He looked at the pulsing machine, trying to will it to give him some instruction. He had an hour – two at the most – he thought.

* * *

The Soviet Premier began with a tirade of accusations against the United States in general, and their President in particular. He accused them of interfering with the policies of other nations, threatening the peace of what he called 'New Europe', and being behind 'acts of aggressive terrorism against the forces, and peoples, of the Soviet Republics'.

The President sat, impassive, during the first few moments, then he looked up and caught the eye of Shih P'eng Te, the Chinese Premier. There was a ghost of a smile on the usually calm, unreadable face. Shih P'eng nodded, slowly getting to his feet.

The Soviet Premier had been speaking in good English. Shih P'eng Te matched the language, his voice rising above Alymnov's diatribe. 'You should have evidence, Mr Premier, before you accuse the Americans. Your own aggression and war of colonisation has perturbed my own people. What evidence can you offer?'

Premier Alymnov opened his mouth, then banged a fist on the table. 'What evidence do I need? Who but the Americans would carry out such acts: attacks on women and children . . . '

'Oil wells, military installations, fuel dumps . . . ' The American President spoke firmly.

'Yes. All military targets, Mr Premier.' The Chinese Communist Party Leader, Tai Yen-Sen, was on his feet now. 'We know, Mr Alymnov. We know, because we, the People's Republic of China, were responsible for these acts. I fear that I bring bad news to you at this conference. I am instructed to inform you that the Chinese People's Republic no longer supports you and your colonial war.'

For a second, the Soviet Leader appeared stunned. 'Then you face the whole might of the Soviet Bloc. We shall blast you from the face of the earth.'

'America also?' The President of the United States did not rise. Only his hand moved, under the table, fingers closing around the small oblong box, which he had quietly removed from his pocket, flicking away the protective casing.

'With your forces spread so wide, your supply lines disrupted, your fuel situation in trouble?' The President hardly moved in his chair. 'Mr Alymnov, I have a proposition to make.'

'So have I; and *my* proposition will not surprise you, Mr President. It concerns an all-out nuclear war.'

'We have weapons also, but my proposals are, I think, better; safer; more secure for mankind.'

'Mine are for my people and my country – its policies, growth and future. If you wish for confrontation, President, you have it.'

'May I state my case, and ask certain questions, from those here who are the Heads of State in countries you have overrun?'

Alymnov said he could ask what questions he wished. He, as Premier of the Soviet, had no doubt that the whole of Soviet Europe was behind him.

'Including my own former ally, Britain?' The American President stared hard at the British Prime Minister as he spoke.

Alymnov made a gesture with his right hand: a movement of both arrogance and dismissal – as though Britain was nothing to him.

As he spoke, the President continued to look at the British Prime Minister. 'Prime Minister, we have known each other for a long time, both in and out of political office. I solemnly assure you that this is the moment of truth – for you, and the rest of mankind. The world has been told that you, of your own volition, requested Soviet troops to occupy your country – Britain. You asked for Soviet troops; invited them into that small gutsy island which has such a history, and has been such an inspiration to free people the world over. Knowing you as I do, it is hard for me to believe that story. Please, for the good of all – whatever the outcome

– we need to know if you did this thing. Mr Prime Minister, did you invite the Soviets into Britain, and urge your countrymen to co-operate with them? Did you do this thing of your own free will?'

The Prime Minister shifted his eyes away from those of the President, giving Premier Alymnov a quick, almost frightened, look. He was, the President thought, a man whose whole political life appeared to be crumbling at this very table. You could see it in the sagging features, in the eyes, and the whole slump of his body.

'For the sake of humanity and mankind, you must answer to the world.' The President spoke evenly, quietly, making each word count, forcing his message into the mind of the British politician.

'For the sake of humanity,' Alymnov muttered caustically.

The President turned on him, like a tiger – 'Yes, Premier Alymnov, for the sake of humanity.'

He turned his gaze back to the British Prime Minister, who had straightened in his chair, as though his mind was suddenly made up, and a new resurgence of power had been given to him; like a dying man rallying and fighting for life.

When the Prime Minister spoke, it was with a strong voice. 'I have to declare the truth. That is obvious. To be Prime Minister of Britain has always been a great honour; a position of trust. Through fear and pressure, I have dishonoured that trust.'

Alymnov half rose; his military adviser, Marshal Fadenovich, grasped his arm, whispering in quick Russian.

The Prime Minister took no notice, but simply went on: 'My Government, Parliament – the Mother of all democratic Parliaments – my Cabinet, were all riddled with people who had sympathy for the Soviet conception of politics. I was placed under great pressure by these people.' He paused, his voice dropping, then rising again, as in a new lease of life. 'It was obvious to me that the Soviets wished to save Britain from the destruction and chaos of active warfare. They wanted this for many reasons: because of the strategic position of our island; because of its wealth of history, from which they could make capital; for our bases, and their tactical importance in Europe.'

Alymnov grunted, moving in his chair, Marshal Fadenovich still holding him in check. The grunting became intelligible words – 'Lies. Lies.'

Still not acknowledging the Soviet Premier, the Prime Minister continued. 'It will probably be hard for you to believe this; but I fought, as best as I could, against the traitors within – though you should know that even some of these have been disillusioned by what happened following the arrival of Soviet forces in Britain. As for the plea for Soviet assistance; well, those members of my Cabinet, my government, whose sympathies lay with the Soviets, engineered the introduction of armed members of the Soviet security forces into my offices – into number ten Downing Street – at the most crucial moment of the crisis – at the time when I was preparing orders for Britain to stand firm.' He stopped, as though overcome by guilt and emotion.

The rest of the delegates shifted uneasily, and there was a muttering from some of the committed Communist leaders, placed in power within their own countries after the takeover.

The President of France shouted for silence. 'You are hearing the truth now,' his voice carried and filled the room. 'See the way your beloved masters really work. Listen.'

'I collapsed through my own weakness.' The Prime Minister's voice broke. 'I capitulated because of fear. Of course I wished to avoid destruction, and bloodshed; but I cannot claim that as a mitigating circumstance. It was my own fear of what they would do to me – possibly to the whole country – I don't know. Yes, I made a statement, on radio and television, asking for Soviet assistance. I lied about the confusion in my country, and I did it all under duress.' His voice rose to a shout. 'As some of the leaders of the so-called "New Europe" are acting under duress now. They held me at gun point.'

Alymnov rose, turning towards the President of the United States. 'We've heard enough of this rubbish. I understood we were here to discuss co-operation, and co-habitation in the world.'

'And it's turning into a vulgar brawl?' the President asked calmly. 'Then, Premier, what do you suggest? Your forces are, as I have already said, stretched to the limit. The balance of power has shifted. You are up against the combined might of America and China.'

Alymnov laughed. 'America and China can be devastated in a matter of seconds. See . . . ' He reached towards one of the telephones.

It was at that moment that the President of the United States grasped the small black transmitter in his hand, depressed the activating switch, and then, firmly, pressed what was known to him as the *Go* button.

The Soviet Premier jiggled the telephone rest, muttering that it appeared to be disconnected.

'Put it back for a moment.' The President remained icy cold. 'I think you'll find that it will ring in a matter of minutes; and that the call will be for you.'

For the first time, there was a glint of surprise – almost fear – in Alymnov's eyes.

* * *

Things were most friendly at the main switchboard within Dublin's Mansion House. Tim McPherson had been there when the two Americans – one having taken the place of the Soviet agent – and the Chinese security man, had walked in, automatic pistols held in their hands, loosely and not in any menacing attitude.

McPherson himself explained the situation to the four switchboard operators, stressing that this was necessary because the entire western world was at risk. It would be for a short time only. What they were doing was an attempt to avoid a devastating nuclear holocaust. With the operators' assistance this might be managed.

They were to disconnect the telephones in the Round Room; reconnecting them when an urgent call came through, from the Russian Embassy – personal, for their Premier. It would come, McPherson said, in a very short time.

* * *

The last set of explosions seemed to come almost on top of them. Mary had screamed and shrieked that the walls were moving with the blast; though Fadden thought this was simple panic.

He soothed her, his ears singing, and straining for the noise of drilling, or, more welcome, a signal from the Last Trump. He wandered into the control chamber, and so was actually there, looking at the panel, when the President pressed the *Go* button.

The tiny transmitter in the President's hand relayed an urgent, easily detectable, tone to the men sitting in the basement of the American Embassy in Dublin's Ballsbridge.

The operator – upon whom the rest of Golgotha depended – went through a series of checks, then unlocked a small panel, pressing one of the two buttons which, up to that point, had been shielded. The buttons were marked in red and green, also in lettering – the red for *Go* and the green for *Stop*. He depressed the red button.

High in space, the GA-One satellite received the signal, bouncing it down to earth, where it overrode electronic locks and cut-outs, sending the signal into the heart of the Golgotha computer, deep in the earth below Savernake Forest. It also sent a signal to a similar system within western Germany's Schwarzwald – the famous Black Forest.

The second red light now began to bleep its warning on Fadden's panel. He shouted to Mary that things were happening, realising that she would not comprehend the full impact. He had kept his faith, telling her nothing.

After a few seconds, the bleeping tone stopped, and a taped voice came clearly from the small speaker. 'Fire twenty-nine.'

Without hesitation, Fadden pressed the button, knowing that he was starting to blow the first blast on the Last

Trump. There was a second's delay, then the red light above button twenty-nine flicked to green.

It was done.

During the final hours, Fadden had retrieved the special original map, from the spine of Greene's *Journey Without Maps*. He knew the reference point of number twenty-nine – a remote clearing, miles from human habitation in the highlands of Scotland. At that place, at that very moment, there was a dramatic sight, not witnessed by man – though the noise and shock waves were carried over many miles, shaking cottages and houses occupied by people who lived in this secluded part of the world.

At reference-point twenty-nine, there was a rumbling from under the earth, followed by a series of deep, heavy, explosions. Turf, soil, roots, and hunks of metal began to geyser from the ground; then, with a final explosion, tons of these substances shot upwards in a great burst. A watcher would have thought some extinct volcano had come to life.

The metal, earth, stones, and other matter, rose high, exploding outwards, dropping in a great circular cloud, leaving a gaping hole from which, a few seconds later, came a billow of what appeared to be smoke: a cloud which rushed upwards with speed, like steam jetting from a million boiling kettles.

The roar became louder. Then, almost slowly, the nose cone, and long cylindrical body of a huge Titan missile began its upward climb from the silo in which it had been buried for years. It appeared to hesitate as the whole weapon cleared the ground. Then, with a roar that would have damaged the eardrums of anyone nearby, the mighty harbinger of destruction, obeying its gyroscopes and targeting computers, streaked away into the heavens, leaving only a small trail of smoke hanging in the air; its rocket motors pulsing their power; the flame diminishing to a spot in the clear sky, then out of sight in a fraction of seconds.

A similar series of events was happening in the western part of Germany – relatively closer to the panel in the

16

Black Forest, where the German agent had been waiting for the past two days.

Both rockets settled into their trajectories. The Soviet scanners picked them up only at the last moment, even then not knowing what to make of them.

The Titans were fitted with high-explosive warheads, but they were big enough to send shock waves over hundreds of miles, to sensitive seismological instruments in the main Russian cities.

Both Titan missiles landed, within half-a-kilometre of each other, aimed and targeted in on one of the large, uninhabited, areas of Siberia. In the Soviet Union itself, there was no doubt – within minutes – in the minds of military commanders, that the recorded explosions came from ballistic missiles. These had arrived with unexpected speed, and with less than thirty seconds' warning.

The Premier, in his chosen role as Supreme Commander of the forces, was the only person who could give a positive order. The military commanders worked on information available, to track and pinpoint the source and launching points of the two projectiles. A Red Alert went out to all Soviet units in Russia and throughout the new European Soviet Bloc. At the same time, a priority call was made to the Summit Conference in Dublin.

Fadden waited, his eyes on the glowing lights, ears ready for the next order. The tiny loudspeaker emitted simply the low bleep which meant he should hold in readiness.

Mary tried to say something, ask a question, but Fadden told her, quietly, to stay silent. They would not have long to wait, he said.

*   *   *

In London, Marshal Constantin Mikhilov Lupaiyev was in his office, going through files and making out his doctored report on Fadden's supposed death. The detective, Menichev, was with him. Both waited anxiously for any positive news from Savernake Forest. They were arguing over a small point in the wording, when an aide came in to say there was an unconfirmed report that at least two ballistic missiles had landed in the Siberian wastes. At that time, the rumour was that the missiles were nuclear. Both men looked at each other, each trying to read the thoughts in the other's eyes. For a few seconds, the truth passed silently between them.

'There has been no news from the Savernake Forest?' Menichev asked, his voice a whisper.

'You know as I do. They have gone to ground. They cannot escape capture or death.'

'Unless . . . ?' Menichev did not complete the sentence.

Marshal Lupaiyev tried to pass it off. 'In the Siberian wastes? No harm is done.'

'What if there are others?' Menichev came closer. Lupaiyev could smell the cologne mixed with last night's vodka.

They both knew there had to be more.

At that moment, the switchboard operators at the Mansion House in Dublin were accepting a personal urgent call for the Soviet Premier. Getting the nod from the three agents watching them, the operators reconnected the two telephones inside the Round Room.

The red instruments began to ring.

★ 33 ★

'It will be for you, Premier Alymnov.' As he said the words, so the President of the United States indicated to his Secretary of State, that he should listen in on the other phone. The Secretary was a fluent Russian speaker.

Alymnov looked puzzled, and, as he reached out for the instrument, the President spoke again. 'If you value your country's future, I would advise you to give no orders until we have spoken further. What you will hear should convince you; but I must add that time is running out.' He glanced at his watch, to give underlining weight to his words.

The Soviet Premier picked up the telephone and listened to the rapid voice at the other end. His face glowered with anger.

'They want orders,' the Secretary of State muttered to the President. 'They say they had less than a minute's warning.'

Loudly, the President called across to Alymnov. 'Tell him to wait for orders, until you have spoken to the Conference. Otherwise your whole country is finished.'

Alymnov spoke a few quick sentences.

'He's told them to wait. He'll give orders soon,' the Secretary of State whispered.

Alymnov replaced the telephone and, slowly, looked around the room. 'A few minutes ago,' his voice sounded hollow and full of fury, 'two ballistic missiles, with high-explosive warheads, landed on an uninhabited piece of wasteland, within the borders of my country. The information available tells me that these missiles did not come from either America or China: but they came, I am certain, with the blessings of the Americans . . . '

'And of the Chinese People's Republic,' Tai Yen-Sen said loudly. He had been given no details of the operation which the President called Golgotha: only certain crucial timings.

'Then America and China will be wiped off the face of the map.' Alymnov's aides were on their feet with him now. 'What good are missiles if they land in unpopulated country? What good are they if they do not hit military targets? The Conference is at an end. I am returning to my Embassy. The equipment in my car will relay the necessary code. America and China are already obliterated.' He began to move towards the door.

The President shouted after him, 'Your own country will be gone, long before you can fire a single rocket. I told you to listen, Alymnov. Those missiles were shots across your bows. The rest happens automatically. It is timed and computerised. Only *I* can stop it; and I refuse to do that, until you have agreed to certain conditions.'

The Soviet Premier seemed to slow his step, but still made towards the doors. He took three more paces; then the doors opened to reveal Tim McPherson, flanked by two U.S. Marines, and what looked like a pair of Russian guards. McPherson held an automatic pistol in his hand; the Marines and Guards had their M16s and Kalashnikovs at the ready. All five weapons were pointing at Alymnov and his two advisers.

The Soviet Premier turned, spitting towards the table. 'What do you call this? Holding a Head of State to ransom. Democracy at pistol point?'

'And your assault on Europe? Your armed demands on Britain's Prime Minister? What were they, Mr Alymnov?'

There was a slight rustle around the conference table, as McPherson and his men closed the doors behind them. One of the Soviet Bloc delegates made a move to go to Alymnov's assistance, but was held back by a Scandinavian politician.

'I shall say this once, Mr Premier. After that, it is for you to decide.' The President rose, his old head cocked at an angle, his right hand clasped around the tiny transmitter which held the devastation of Europe in the balance. 'The two missiles which landed on your country without warning, are the first of many. The others, I *do* assure you, are not armed with high explosive. Your people will have no idea of the direction from which they will come; but it is very close. Do not rely on your nuclear submarines either, for they will also be targets; and, please, do not, for a second, imagine that I am bluffing.'

Alymnov looked steadily at the President, as though trying to detect some trickery; hoping that the American might be playing a dangerous brinkmanship poker game.

'Those two rockets, as I have said,' the President continued, 'are simply the beginning. In a matter of minutes, the greatest rain of hellfire the world has ever seen will start to fall on your country, on your military bases, and your ships. Very few places in Europe will be free from this. Yes, I activated this Last Judgement . . .'

'You play God,' Alymnov sneered.

'The Holy Father – the Pope – said something similar to me in Rome.' Not a flicker of a smile passed the President's lips. 'I answered by telling him that, if men were to be free, then that freedom might possibly be bought only through death and devastation. If I was playing God, it only meant I was following my conscience.' He glanced at his watch again. 'Time is running very short. Soon I shall not be able to stop the course of events.'

'There is a price on your stopping this . . . this . . . ?'

'Armageddon?'

The Soviet Premier shrugged. 'A word,' he said, as though words were meaningless now. He could see that this was no game of political poker after all. The American was in earnest.

'There is a price, of course.' The President cleared his throat. 'The price is that you order all your forces of occupation in Europe back to their original positions. That you immediately give that order, and hand back the true power to the leaders of the countries you have occupied. That you immediately remove your forces from Britain.' He turned to the whole body of men and women seated around the table. 'If this pledge is made by Mr Alymnov, I will also give a pledge. First, that I shall immediately – and I can do it now, in this room – prevent the storm of nuclear destruction and death throughout the USSR and Europe.'

With the help of the Chinese leaders he then made it clear that this first crippling attack would have been followed, immediately, by a secondary assault from the United States and Chinese mainlands: all within less than an hour.

The President continued, 'If you give this order, Premier, you will also give orders allowing neutral American troops to land and observe the dismantling of your bases, and withdrawal of your forces. I pledge to you all that these American observers will also withdraw as soon as things are returned to their status quo, when all countries have returned to the borders and states which existed before the Soviet take-over of Europe. Apart from whatever damage was inflicted during the fighting, those countries will be left intact and allowed their complete freedom. The Soviets will allow Europe to go in peace. The countries concerned will then choose their own destinies, in a democratic manner. They will be allowed a free vote, without pressure from your regime, Premier Alymnov. Some may even decide to come into your fold . . . '

'This would take several days . . . ' The Soviet Premier was still obviously trying to think, fast, on his feet.

'And during those several days, my threat still stands. My operation can be set in motion again at a second's notice. American observers can be in Europe within hours. Yes, it may take several days for your people to withdraw,' the President waved a hand around him – 'but we have comfortable surroundings here. I'm sure the Irish authorities will allow us food and bedding. Should we not stay here until this is done? Get to know one another? Perhaps make the real plans which could be the basis for future peaceful co-existence?'

Premier Alymnov looked about him, like an indecisive animal.

'Truly,' – once more the President looked at his watch – 'there is very little time left. How say you, Mr Alymnov? Desolation; your country in ruins? Europe in ruins? Or a chance for true peace?'

The Soviet Premier still appeared to hesitate.

'How says the rest of this delegation then?' roared the President. 'Destruction or Reconstruction? You have less than five minutes.'

The few seconds' pause stretched on into what seemed to be an eternity. Then a mighty shout echoed around the room: a shout in a dozen languages, but a shout which had only one meaning, urging the Soviet Leader to the only course of action. 'Reconstruction,' yelled the delegates.

Alymnov's shoulders slumped for a moment. Then he bowed his head, walking to the table and picking up the nearest telephone.

The American President nodded to McPherson, who slipped away to the switchboard to oversee the call and listen in to the orders given by Alymnov.

The Soviet leader spoke quickly. He was connected immediately with his military staff, who had been kept linked to the switchboard. Within seconds of Alymnov ceasing to speak, Tim McPherson came back quickly into the room, nodding to the President.

Only then did the President juggle the buttons on the small transmitter, pressing the *Stop Button* firmly three times – an act which had special significance.

The signal was picked up at the Embassy, in Ballsbridge, and relayed, instantly, to the GA-One – the Golgotha – satellite.

Then the President again looked at his wristwatch. There had been three minutes to run – exactly three minutes before the satellite would have automatically given both Fadden, and the German, hunched over their respective panels in

Savernake and the Black Forests, orders to release the incredible destructive power upon Europe and Russia.

Alymnov slumped into a chair, his Foreign Minister and military advisers hardly daring to look at him.

McPherson whispered into the President's ear that he was making arrangements for the Mansion House to be sealed off. The world's press were being told that, as part of a new understanding, Soviet Forces were about to move back to their own original borders; that the conquered countries would be vacated; that the 'Peace Keeping' Soviet presence in Britain would start to withdraw within a few hours; and that American troops, acting merely temporarily, as observers, would fly into the major European countries, their capitals and military bases, within hours.

The Irish, McPherson told him, were being approached with regard to food and accommodation. Some new formula was to be thrashed out, and the delegates of the Dublin Summit Conference requested that they stay within the Conference Room for as long as it took. Links with the outside world would be strictly monitored by McPherson's men.

The President reflected that he did not like this new-style of gunboat politics. In fact the whole thing offended him, but the desperate throw appeared to have had the desired effect.

*   *   *

There had been another set of underground explosions after Fadden pressed the twenty-nine button. This time he realised Mary was right: the whole chamber did move, trembling and shifting within the earth, disturbed by the charges. It passed through his mind that the Soviets must be using massive amounts of explosive, and when they got to the thick metal walls they would, most likely, bring up anti-metal charges which would melt away even the strongest protective armour.

He tried to turn his mind away from this revolting prospect just as all the lights – save the first red glimmer near

249

the main switch – went out on the control panel. Even the pinpoints of colour, above the buttons, glowed bright and then went off. For a second, Fadden thought the last explosions had disrupted the equipment, for the bleeping tone had stopped, its place taken by a long steady whine. Then the loudspeaker crackled.

'Golgotha is temporarily suspended,' the taped voice said. It was a voice which seemed, to Fadden, to be without soul. 'You will leave the panel switched on, and act on instructions, should Golgotha be resumed ...'

The earth near the chambers heaved in a very close blast, making Mary Athay stagger, and nearly throwing Fadden from his padded seat at the console. He braced himself for another explosion but it did not come. There was a strange silence, as though someone had interrupted the search force above them.

From the loudspeaker, the disembodied voice was repeating the orders. Fadden listened, knowing they had missed the ending.

' ... should Golgotha be resumed. This is a precaution which may last several days. It is unlikely that you will be required to blow the Last Trump.'

Fadden and Mary Athay looked at each other. Fadden told her to listen. The familiar drilling noises which came between explosions, had ceased.

'Do you think ... ?' Mary started.

Fadden nodded.

'Several days,' she said, her head cocked, listening to the silence. 'What on earth shall we find to do down here for several days?'

*   *   *

In the tall building near Westminster Bridge, they were burning confidential documents. Every few minutes Lupaiyev and Menichev could hear the whine of aircraft, either leaving, or arriving, at Heathrow. Soviet troops were moving out in great haste. The speed had been underlined from the Supreme Commander, Premier Alymnov, himself. The entrance to Heathrow – as with the roads to all other airfields and bases – was blocked by slow-moving men and machines. It was the same in all but the old Soviet Bloc countries.

The Americans had arrived, showing unexpected friendliness, which was more than could be said of the police forces up and down the country, who made it plain they were glad to see the back of their Soviet counterparts.

Suvlov had been released, early, from what was once again St Mary Abbotts Hospital. He sat, a blank look on his white face, in a corner of the office while the Marshal and his old detective friend worked.

That was how they were found by the six men, sent directly on Leonid – 'Lead' Leo – Vereshenko's orders. They were to return to Moscow for an investigation, the trio were told. Outside, in a busier street than of late, Lupaiyev, Suvlov, and Menichev, were assisted into a large black Volga, which pulled away from the building, taking them back to Mother Russia for the last time.

*　　*　　*

Paul Fadden and Mary Athay were kept in the control bunker for almost a week. After six days, the panel came alive again. This time it was a familiar voice coming through the loudspeaker. Tim McPherson had overridden the computer system.

'If you're alive, you can come up, Paul. We've shifted most of the rubble and I'm opening the door – they've given me the secret now. If you don't come up, I'll come down. You're going home.'

Paul, who had no way of communicating with the outside world, asked Mary where home was? Wherever you like, she told him, and he grumbled on about McPherson asking if they were alive. 'He should have just come down if things are as bad as that up there.'

Tim McPherson showed no surprise at seeing Mary Athay surface with Fadden. His only surprise was that they were alive at all. Fadden looked around and also wondered how the generator, and even the steel-walled underground area, had remained intact. Outside, it was like a battlefield: trees blasted, rubble in great piles, or scattered over a wide area. The search force had blasted to within metres of the control bunker, but the blasting pattern had obviously been haphazard. 'Whoever did it just wanted to show willing,' McPherson grinned. 'I doubt if he'll win any medals now. Enthusiastic bangs and stinks merchant.'

McPherson's car stood, parked among tree stumps and bricks, on what had been the road. Further back, among the charred trees, there were lorries and British troops – engineers, Fadden presumed, who had cleared the debris that had once been Wolf Hall, so that the CIA man could pinpoint the entrance to the chambers.

On the way back to London, McPherson explained the incredible and momentous changes that had been taking place in Europe, and the world, during the past few days.

The President, now back in Washington, had expressed a desire to see Fadden – 'I guess you'd better both come,' McPherson told them.

Mary was silent as they drove into London, now empty of Soviet uniforms. 'Nothing's really changed,' she said at last. 'The Soviet Bloc is where it always was. It may even have a few more adherents, after these elections Tim talks so glibly about. The means and the weapons are still with us. It can all happen again at any time. If a country as large, and dedicated, as the Soviet Union, wishes to show militance on behalf of its political way of life, nobody will stop them. The old ideas of rationality and democracy are finished. It's never going to be the same again.'

'The world's said that many times, Mary.' Fadden took her hand. 'In this century alone, it's been said so often I've almost stopped counting. You know your history. They said things could never be the same again after 1914. They said it after World War II; then after the H-Bomb; they said

252

it after Jack Kennedy; after Vietnam; after Nixon and Watergate; they've said it after every crisis since; and they're bound to say it now, after the biggest crisis of the century. Yet, somehow, people pick themselves up and go on. Setbacks? Yes. But Man goes on. It's like that old, old song – pick yourself up, brush yourself off, and start all over again.'

'I've never heard that,' she said. 'Sing it to me.'

'It's a banal old lyric, and my voice isn't up to it. Maybe, some day, in my bath. Look the sky's red in the sunset.'

Behind London's stretching, ancient and modern façade – dirty, scabbed and heavy with history – the sky flamed dark crimson, as though the city burned.

THRILLERS

Δ	0352397012	George Arnaud **WAGES OF FEAR**	70p*
		DICK BARTON SPECIAL AGENT Mike Dorrell	
Δ	0352303077	**No. 1: THE GREAT TOBACCO CONSPIRACY**	60p
Δ	0352303085	**No. 2: THE MYSTERY OF THE MISSING FORMULA**	60p
Δ	0352303093	Alan Radnor **No. 3: THE CASE OF THE VANISHING HOUSE**	60p
Δ	0352303107	Larry Pryce **No. 4: THE GOLD BULLION SWINDLE**	70p
Δ	0352303468	Murray Teigh Bloom **LAST EMBRACE**	90p*
	0352396474	Paul Bonnecarrere **ULTIMATUM**	95p
	0352302607	**THE GOLDEN TRIANGLE**	95p
	0352304502	**THE LOST VICTORY**	95p
	0352396059	Richard Butler **WHERE ALL THE GIRLS ARE SWEETER**	95p
	0352395354	**ITALIAN ASSETS**	95p
	0352396067	Henry Denker **THE PHYSICIANS**	95p*
	0352300523	**A PLACE FOR THE MIGHTY**	75p*
	0352302127	Robert Early **A TIME OF MADNESS**	75p
	0352304588	John Gardner **UNDERSTRIKE**	95p
	035230460X	**AMBER NINE**	95p
	0352304596	**MADRIGAL**	95p
	0352304618	**FOUNDER MEMBER**	95p
	0352398582	Burt Hirschfeld **'FATHER PIG'**	95p*
	0352395176	**SECRETS**	95p*
	0352398604	**BEHOLD ZION**	95p*
	0427004306	William Hughes **SPLIT ON RED**	95p
	0427004438	**COVER ZERO**	95p

† For sale in Britain and Ireland only.
* Not for sale in Canada. ● Reissues.
Δ Film & T.V. tie-ins.

THRILLERS

Δ	035230636X	Karji **CUBA**	95p*
	0352396253	Tony Kenrick **THE SEVEN DAY SOLDIERS**	75p*
	0352395559	**THE CHICAGO GIRL**	95p*
	0352301643	Dean R. Koontz **NIGHT CHILLS**	85p*
	0426186141	Malachy McCoy **KODIAK!**	75p
	0352305320	Michael McNamara **THE DANCING FOOR**	95p*
	0352304464	David Lippincott **THE BLOOD OF OCTOBER**	£1.25*
	0352395214	Richard Llewellyn **THE END OF THE RUG**	£1.50
	0352395052	**BUT WE DIDN'T GET THE FOX**	£1.50
	0352301716	**THE NIGHT IS A CHILD**	£1.50
	0352300078	Lawrence Sanders **THE FIRST DEADLY SIN**	95p*
Δ	0352397403	Robert Stone **DOG SOLDIERS**	95p*
	0352395435	Robert Vacha **THE OPEC PROJECT**	75p
	035230247X	**REQUIEM FOR A CROWN**	75p
	0352302585	**MOSCOW 1980**	95p
	0352303530	**THE BLACK ORCHESTRA**	95p
	0352305371	Donald Zec **THE COLONEL**	£1.25

CLINT EASTWOOD SERIES

Δ	0352302739	Paul J. Gillete **PLAY MISTY FOR ME**	75p*
Δ	0352302399	Wesley Morgan **THE ENFORCER**	75p†
Δ	035230099X	Phillip Rock **DIRTY HARRY**	60p*
Δ	0352301597	Dennis Shryack & Michael Butler **THE GAUNTLET**	75p*
Δ	0352302380	Mel Valley **MAGNUM FORCE**	60p†

† For sale in Britain and Ireland only.
* Not for sale in Canada. • Reissues.
Δ Film & T.V. tie-ins.

Wyndham Books are obtainable from many booksellers and newsagents. If you have any difficulty please send purchase price plus postage on the scale below to:

> **Wyndham Cash Sales**
> **P.O. Box 11**
> **Falmouth**
> **Cornwall**
> OR
> **Star Book Service,**
> **G.P.O. Box 29,**
> **Douglas,**
> **Isle of Man,**
> **British Isles.**

While every effort is made to keep prices low, it is sometimes necessary to increase prices at short notice. Wyndham Books reserve the right to show new retail prices on covers which may differ from those advertised in the text or elsewhere.

Postage and Packing Rate

UK: 30p for the first book, plus 15p per copy for each additional book ordered to a maximum charge of £1.29. **BFPO and Eire:** 30p for the first book, plus 15p per copy for the next 6 books and thereafter 6p per book. **Overseas:** 50p for the first book and 15p per copy for each additional book.

These charges are subject to Post Office charge fluctuations.